REA...
SCREAM,
REPEAT

First published in Great Britain in 2023 by Farshore
An imprint of HarperCollins*Publishers*
1 London Bridge Street, London SE1 9GF

farshore.co.uk

HarperCollins*Publishers,*
Macken House, 39/40 Mayor Street Upper, Dublin 1, D01 C9W8

Wolf Moon © Kirsty Applebaum 2023
Charlie's Twelfth © Sharna Jackson 2023
Game Over © Aisha Bushby 2023
The Light Bulb © Rachel Delahaye 2023
Talos Springs © Elle McNicoll 2023
The Pond © Jennifer Killick 2023
Underlay Underlings © Joseph Coelho 2023
Deep Water © Dan Smith 2023
The Green Ghost © Kat Ellis 2023
The Glass House © Polly Ho-Yen 2023
The Attic Room © Phil Smith 2023
Hide and Seek © J.T.Williams 2023
A Cry From the Graveyard © Jasbinder Bilan 2023

The moral rights of the authors have been asserted

ISBN 978 0 00 852780 8
Waterstones ISBN 978 0 00 866117 5

Printed and bound in the UK using 100% renewable electricity at
CPI Group (UK) Ltd

1

A CIP catalogue record for this title is available from the British Library.

Stay safe online. Any website addresses listed in this book are correct at the time of going to
print. However, Farshore is not responsible for content hosted by third parties. Please be aware
that online content can be subject to change and websites can contain content that is unsuitable
for children. We advise that all children are supervised when using the internet.

This book is produced from independently certified FSC™ paper
to ensure responsible forest management.

For more information visit: www.harpercollins.co.uk/green

THIRTEEN SPINE-TINGLING TALES

READ, SCREAM, REPEAT

CURATED BY

JENNIFER KILLICK

Farshore

CONTENTS

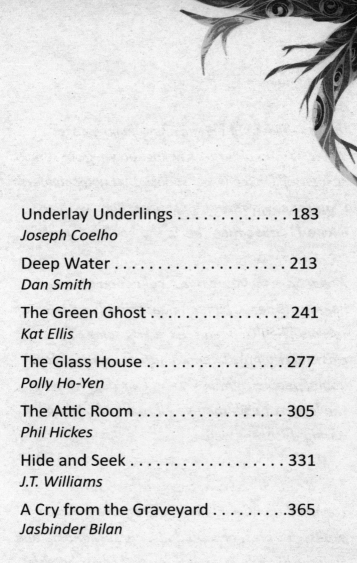

Dear Reader,

Do you enjoy a heart-lurching jump-scare? What about spiders-crawling-down-your-back suspense? Or scenes so spooky that you shudder? If you are answering these questions with an excited 'YES!', then this is the book for you!

Read, Scream, Repeat is a collection of short horror stories. Thirteen heart-thudding tales of terror. They've been created by some of the most terrifyingly talented authors writing for young people right now, and I am delighted by the levels of chill they've all reached in their darkly different ways.

The *Read, Scream, Repeat* authors have conjured up human-hungry creatures, missing skulls, zombies, creepy dolls, curses, ghosts and sinister birthday parties you will never be able to leave. Each story is frightening enough to leave you with a brain full of 'what ifs' and with goosebumps on your goosebumps.

And they're short, so they're perfect for sharing with your friends at breaktime, or sneaking in after lights out, or even reading around a campfire in the middle of a night-time forest if you're brave enough (make sure you keep an eye on those trees).

It has been a spine-shuddering joy to contribute to and compile this collection of stories. I hope that reading it makes your horror-loving heart sing, though you may want to steer clear of old nursery rhymes for a while. So please: read, scream, repeat in an infinite loop of doom if that's your thing. And make sure you tell your friends — it's much more fun to suffer with others than it is to wander the forest path alone . . .

Good luck!

JENNIFER KILLICK

WOLF
MOON

Kirsty Applebaum

WOLF MOON

Kirsty Applebaum

'Don't talk to any strangers!'

'Course I won't.' Toby shivered while Mum squeezed him goodbye. 'Stop fussing, I'll be OK.' Thank goodness she wouldn't be able to follow him on to the railway platform. She really was worrying way too much. Literally all he had to do was sit on the train until the very last stop and Gran would be waiting for him at the other end.

It was bitingly cold. Toby managed to put his ticket in the slot without taking his gloves off.

'Stay focused on getting to Gran's,' Mum called after him. 'Don't let that overactive imagination of yours run away with itself.'

Could she be any more embarrassing? Toby glanced around the platform to see if anyone had heard, but there were only about six people there and none of them seemed interested in him. They were rubbing their gloved hands and breathing steamy breath into the frosty air.

'If you sit by the window I might be able to give you a final wave,' shouted Mum.

Toby looked up at the sky. There'd be a full moon later. A *wolf moon* – that's what they called it in January, because someplace, somewhere, there were more wolves howling around the time of the January full moon. You didn't get too many wolves howling around here, though, no matter what time of year it was.

A deep rumbling started up from the track. Toby covered his ears as the train screamed into the station.

Toby stood in the aisle between the seats. Where should he sit? There were only two other people in his carriage: a lady in a denim jacket sitting in a window seat to the right, and a man a bit further back, out of sight except for the top of his head, which was bald and tattooed.

Oh – Mum had wanted to wave him off, hadn't

she? She'd been really annoying at the station, but now that he was on the train Toby had a horrible feeling he was missing her a little bit already.

I mean, here he was, in a tiny space with two complete strangers – and they were all about to zoom off into the middle of absolutely nowhere. They could be murderers for all he knew. Or kidnappers. Or master criminals. Or government assassins. Or –

Stay focused on getting to Gran's, Toby reminded himself.

He sat down next to the window on the left and tucked his rucksack between his knees. Sure enough, there was Mum, waving at him from behind the ticket gates. He gave her a thumbs up.

She got smaller and smaller as the train pulled away.

Toby stretched out his legs. His seat had extra foot space because it was one of those ones where the seats opposite face in towards you. The opposite seats were empty – well, almost empty. There was a bag on the one straight in front of him. It was oblong, like a small suitcase, and it had a flowery pattern all over it. Toby wondered if it belonged to denim-jacket lady.

He unwound his scarf and pushed it into the top of his rucksack. His mind wandered to tonight's full moon. He thought about werewolves. What would it be like, to transform for one night every month? To have thick hair sprout up all over your body? To feel blade-sharp teeth pushing through your gums? He pictured himself on the prowl through lamplit streets, searching for prey.

'Does that belong to you, kid?'

Toby jerked out of his daydream. 'Pardon?' he said.

'Does that belong to you?' It was denim-jacket lady. She was pointing at the flowery bag.

As if, thought Toby. He felt like saying he'd drop down dead of embarrassment if his mum made him carry a bag like that, but he'd promised he wouldn't talk to strangers so he just shook his head instead.

'Mmmm.' Denim-jacket lady frowned. There was a sticker on her top pocket. It said: *I give blood*. She turned to tattoo man. 'Excuse me?'

Tattoo man looked up. 'What?'

'There's some unaccompanied luggage here.'

She pointed at the bag again. 'Is it yours?'

Tattoo man stood up. He was right behind the seat with the bag on it. He reached his arm over and –

'Don't touch it!' said Toby. 'It might be a bomb!' Immediately, he realized he'd both spoken to a stranger *and* let his overactive imagination run away with itself. Double whammy. He squeezed his lips tight shut.

'Kid's right,' said denim-jacket lady. 'Maybe don't touch it.'

'It's certainly not mine, anyway,' said tattoo man.

'In that case, I'm going to find the guard.' Denim-jacket lady stood up. 'What is it they say these days? *See it, say it, sort it?*'

'Isn't it *See it, say it, sort-ED*?' said Toby. Oh no – he'd done it again! *Be quiet*, he told himself.

Denim-jacket lady gave another frown. 'Either way I think it works.' She disappeared through to the next carriage.

Toby stared at the bag. *Was* it a bomb? Almost certainly, he reckoned. If he unzipped it, he'd probably see a mass of coloured wires and some blocks of explosive, all fixed to a ticking timer with half an hour left on it. And half an hour would totally not be long enough for the bomb-disposal team to reach them, so Toby would have to try to deactivate it himself, following instructions from army experts over speakerphone. But, at the crucial moment, the train would go through a tunnel and connection would be lost and Toby would have to make his best guess because there'd only be seconds left now and of course he'd guess red because that's his favourite colour and the bomb would stop ticking and Toby would have single-handedly saved everyone on the train and –

The carriage door slid open. It was denim-jacket lady. 'Not a guard to be seen.' She rolled her eyes. 'Budget cuts.'

She stood in the aisle, stuck her hands on her hips and looked at the flowery bag. 'We should get rid of it,' she said. 'Chuck it off.'

Toby stared at her. So did tattoo man.

'Chuck it off?' said tattoo man. 'You mean, throw it off the train?'

'Yep. There's a good thirty-five minutes until the next stop and that bag is making me very nervous. We should just shove it through the window and be done with it.'

Toby had to admit it was making him nervous too. Maybe he'd text Mum and ask what she thought they should do. She was good at this kind of thing. He delved into his rucksack for his phone.

'But –' denim-jacket lady squinted at the top of the window – 'only that narrow part opens up, so I'm not sure it'll fit through.'

Toby found his phone. Completely dead. He'd forgotten to charge it.

Tattoo man leaned over the seat and checked out the flowery bag. His tattoos weren't only on his head. He had a curly-lettered word inked on to the back of each hand. They were sort of sideways and upside down to Toby, but he could still read them.

ANGEL and *DEMON*.

'It'll fit.' Tattoo man patted the window with his DEMON hand. 'I used to work on the railways. Seventeen years. There's a trick to getting these open wider than you think. But . . . I dunno. What if it's full of someone's most treasured possessions? Maybe we should take a look inside it first.'

'And risk getting blown up?' said denim-jacket lady. 'Better to just get rid of it. The longer it sits there, the more likely it is to explode.'

Toby shifted in his seat. Of all the places he

could have picked to sit in, he'd chosen the getting-blown-up place. He was starting to feel very hot and sweaty.

'You sure it doesn't belong to the boy?' said tattoo man. 'Come on, nipper –' he winked at Toby – 'own up – the bag's yours, isn't it?'

That disgusting flowery bag? Toby glanced at denim-jacket lady. She was staring at him too! They both thought it was his!

'It's not mine,' he blurted out. 'It's horrible! I'd never carry a bag like that!'

Tattoo man lifted his eyebrows.

'That's it, then,' said denim-jacket lady. 'We chuck it off. I'm not waiting any longer.'

Tattoo man pulled open the window and an icy *whoosh* swept into the carriage. The rhythmic clatter of the speeding train roared around them. Toby felt horribly close to the cold metal tracks and the tree branches clawing at the windows.

Tattoo man fiddled with the hinges and managed to open the window a bit wider.

'Right, then,' said denim-jacket lady. 'Easy does it.' Slowly, carefully, as if it was made of the most delicate glass, she lifted the bag up and rested it on the rim of the window.

'Stop!' Tattoo man put his ANGEL hand on top of the bag. 'I've got a bad feeling about this. I'm having second thoughts. I don't think we should do it.'

Toby held his breath. If the bag exploded, they'd be blown to smithereens.

'Look,' said denim-jacket lady. 'There's no guard and it's almost thirty minutes before we reach the next stop. If it doesn't have a bomb in it and we chuck it out, what's the worst that could happen? Someone has to go and buy a new pair of pyjamas? But if it *does* have a bomb in it and we *don't* chuck it out, it's goodbye and goodnight to all of us. We won't be worried about unaccompanied luggage after that; we'll all be riding that big train in the sky.'

She pushed at the bag but tattoo man held it firm.

Toby's chest tightened. The likelihood that he'd really be able to diffuse an actual real-life bomb, he realized, was pretty low. Even with instructions from army experts over speakerphone.

'We need to think about this a bit longer,' said tattoo man.

'We do not need to think about it!' said denim-jacket lady. 'We need to save this train and save ourselves! It's down to us!'

Branches knocked against the window and cold air swept around the carriage. The train kept up its steady pulse on the tracks: *chank-chank-chank-chank-chank*.

'It's down to us to make a carefully considered decision,' said tattoo man.

Toby's heart seemed to have clambered up his windpipe and decided to hang out at the back of his mouth. His whole throat was beating. The bag *must* have a bomb inside, mustn't it? Why else would someone leave it on its own?

'If this explodes before I manage to get rid of it, it's on you,' replied denim-jacket lady. She tried to push the bag again, but the ANGEL hand held it still.

Toby thought about all those wires and explosives. He thought about the timer on its unstoppable countdown. The train drummed in his ears, sounding just like a clock. *Chank-chank-chank-chank-chank-chank-chank. Tick-tick-tick-tick-tick-tick-tick.*

Denim-jacket lady was right. They were running out of time.

Wires.

Explosives.

Smithereens.

Goodbye and goodnight.

*Chank-chank-chank-chank-tick-tick-tick-tick-tick
tick-tick-tick-tick* —

Toby leaped up from his seat.

He gave the flowery bag a huge, two-handed
shove . . . and it was gone.

'What on earth?' Tattoo man looked around,
stunned.

'Good call, kid,' said denim-jacket lady.

Tattoo man sighed. He closed the window and
the carriage went quiet again.

Toby sat back down and tucked his hands under
his thighs. The seat material felt weird — both
smooth and prickly all at once.

He tried to plan what he'd do with Gran this
evening.

He tried to think about who he'd put in the
Arsenal line-up for next week's match.

He tried to remember the names of all twelve
full moons.

But the only thing he could think about was the
flowery bag.

The carriage was suffocatingly, overwhelmingly, mind-bendingly full of the bag's *not-there-ness*.

Not long afterwards, an old lady entered the carriage. She walked unsteadily down the aisle.

She was, thought Toby, exactly the sort of old lady who might own a flowery bag.

'Where's my case?' said the old lady. 'My floral case. It was right there.' She pointed at the empty seat opposite Toby.

'You must have the wrong carriage,' said denim-jacket lady.

'No.' The old lady shook her head. 'Somebody's moved it.'

Toby stared intently at the floor under the opposite seats. There was a muddy train ticket and an opened cola can that had somehow managed to remain upright all this time.

The old lady shuffled around, peering between the rows.

Right now, Toby wanted to be anywhere else in the world except here. He wanted to turn back time so he could catch an earlier train or refuse to go to Gran's or something – *anything* so that he hadn't been here in this carriage, pushing that bag out of the window.

'I have to find it.' The old lady's voice was beginning to shake. 'That case contains something very precious to me.' The train jolted. The old lady grabbed at a seat to stay upright. The cola can fell over and rolled across the floor.

'Perhaps you should sit down,' said Toby.

'Yes,' said the old lady, fixing Toby in the eye. 'Perhaps. I. Should.' She said the words very slowly and very clearly, as if each one had a full stop after it. Like she really wanted Toby to think about them.

She made her way over and sat down facing him, in the very seat where she'd left her bag.

She pulled a crumpled tissue out of her pocket. 'I'll never be able to replace it,' she said. 'I have to find that case.'

'If your bag had something that important in it,' said denim-jacket lady, 'why did you leave it unattended?'

'I left it here to save my place while I was in the toilet.' The old lady blew her nose.

'You were in the toilet? All that time?' said tattoo man, looking between the headrests. 'We've been on this train for ages. What in heaven's name were you doing in there?'

'Excuse me!' Denim-jacket lady was turning out to be a world-class frowner. 'It's very rude to ask someone what they do in the toilet.'

Tattoo man sank back into his seat.

'What's the precious thing?' asked Toby. He gave the cola can a nudge with the toe of his trainer. He hoped the precious thing might not really be that precious at all. Perhaps it was something you could just order off the Internet. If it was, he could maybe even replace it with his own money.

The old lady leaned towards Toby. 'If you want, I can tell you the whole story. But it's a terrifying tale. Once heard, it can never be unheard, not for as long as you live. Are you sure you want to hear it?'

Toby nodded.

'All right,' she said. 'Then come a little closer.'

Toby shuffled to the edge of his seat.

Denim-jacket lady scooted one place nearer.

Even tattoo man came round and sat close by to hear the tale.

'A long time ago, when I was a beautiful young maiden, we had a summer so hot the ground baked your shoes as you walked, and the sun breathed fire from rise to set. I took to going out only after dark, when the air had cooled and moonlight spilled on to the treetops. One particular night, there was a glorious full moon. It illuminated the land with a haunting glow. I headed into the forest and went further than I'd ever been before.

'The place was full of life. Foxes darted between trees, and ghostly owls flew overhead on silent wings. Eventually I came across a lake, shimmering in the darkness, and on its banks was a woman. She appeared to be a good deal older than I was, although I couldn't be sure, for she wore a dark cloak with a hood pulled well up over her head.'

Toby gave an involuntary shiver.

The old lady continued. 'She was taking ten paces one way, then ten paces back, over and over, all the while pressing her hands to her cheeks and shaking her head. I didn't like to see a lone soul so anxious, so I asked her what was wrong. She told me the most frightening story I had ever heard. It chilled me to the bone, though the night was warm, and as she spoke I swear I saw a flash of amber eyes under the folds of her hood.

'She told me that when she was much younger, she had been cursed to transform into a horrifying beast at every full moon – half wolf, half woman – an atrocious creature, devoid of humanity, who would attack her own grandmother given the chance.'

Toby thought of his own gran, leaving her little cottage any time now, to meet him at the station.

'However,' the old lady went on, 'the hooded woman explained she was also in possession of an amulet – an enchanted charm as round and as silver as the full moon itself – which protected her from the curse. As long as she kept it close to her at all times, she would remain entirely human, even during a full moon. So she wore it, always, on a chain around her neck. But that evening she had taken a swim in the lake, and she'd lost the amulet!'

I've been searching for hours, she told me. *I'm close enough to the amulet for its magic to work, but if I stray from the lake it will no longer protect me and each full moon will see me transform into a wolf-woman. Who knows what damage I could cause! I shall have to stay by this lake forever! What will become of me? Oh, please help me find the amulet!*

'Well, I couldn't abandon the poor soul,' said the old lady, 'so I assured her I would help.

She grabbed my hand with strong, bony fingers. *You are so kind*, she said.

'I began to ask her in which part of the lake she'd been swimming, but then, in one quick movement, she pulled my hand to her mouth and sank her teeth into my fingers.'

Toby gasped.

'I was too shocked even to scream,' said the old lady. 'I pulled away and stumbled backwards. The woman took her hood down and laughed.

'*Why did you do that?* I asked her. *I was going to help you.*

'*I don't need your help any longer*, she cackled. *I've finally rid myself of the curse, after all these years. It's your curse now! You will become a wolf-monster at every full moon, instead of me! Unless, of course, you stay close to the amulet. But know this – it will only work if you keep it with you at all times!* Then she ran into the forest and I was left with a bleeding hand and a whole lake to search.'

The train began to slow and the old lady paused in her tale.

'What a load of old cobblers,' snorted denim-jacket lady. 'Oh, this is my stop.' She gathered up her things.

'It's my stop too,' said tattoo man. He looked at Toby. 'You do know this is all nonsense, don't you, nipper? You going to be all right?'

Toby nodded. 'I'm fine, thanks.' He was keen to hear the rest of the story and had stopped worrying about the flowery bag.

The train drew to a halt and the open doors brought in a shudder of January air. Tattoo man and denim-jacket lady got off. Nobody got on. When the train doors beeped shut again, Toby and the old lady were all alone in the carriage.

'At first –' the old lady leaned forward – 'I thought it was all nonsense too. But remember – it was a full moon. Just like tonight. I tried walking away from the lake – away from this amulet the hooded woman had spoken of. But each time I reached a certain point I could feel the curse taking hold. It was racing through my bloodstream, seeping into my bones.'

'What did you do?' asked Toby, chin in hands, elbows on knees. The old lady had his full attention.

'I searched the lake,' she said. 'I swam and swam. Day after day, night after night.'

'Did you find it?'

'Eventually. On the twenty-eighth day, just before the next full moon. Buried in the mud and the rot and the weeds. I hooked it over my neck and made my exhausted way back home. I've kept it on me ever since – until now.'

'Until now?' Toby felt a prickle on the back of his neck. His heart, which had returned to its usual spot in his chest, began inching back up into his throat.

'The chain broke this morning,' said the old lady. 'Luckily, I caught the amulet before it fell. I put it in my bag – my floral case – for safe-keeping.'

The floral case.

The floral case that he, Toby, had shoved out of the window, miles and miles ago.

The train swung round a bend and the cola can rolled tinnily under the seats.

Toby tried to swallow but his mouth was completely dry.

He suddenly wished he'd got off the train with the others. Or asked them not to leave. Or just somehow fixed things so he'd never sat down in this carriage at all.

The old lady blinked. Was that a glint of wolf-like amber in her eyes?

'If you know the whereabouts of my case,' she said, 'you must tell me. I have to find the amulet. We don't have long.' She looked out of the window. 'The full moon is coming.'

Toby looked out of the window too. It was true. The sky had grown dim. The wolf moon would be here very, very soon. And if the old lady was telling the truth about the moon, what else might she be telling the truth about?

What would happen if she transformed into a wolf-monster while they were still on the train? Would he be torn apart? Eaten alive? And what about the people in the other carriages?

This was all his fault.

He'd given the bag that final shove.

Toby gripped the edge of his prickly seat as the train sped further and further away from the amulet.

Was that the curve of a pale moon he could see, skimming the grey hills in the distance?

The old woman stared at Toby. She licked her lips.

Her fingernails were thick and curled, like claws. Was she turning? Right now? Right here?

He shifted his gaze to the still rolling cola can. They couldn't be that far from the final stop now, surely. It felt like he'd been sitting here, opposite the old woman, forever. They *must* be nearly there. Gran was probably already at the station, waiting for him. Please let the train arrive soon. *Please*.

Keep calm, he told himself. *Wolf-people don't really exist. Everything's going to be fine.*

But the slice of moon above the horizon was growing bigger. Any moment now he could be sharing the carriage with a monster. If only he hadn't pushed the bag out. If only he'd caught a different train. If only he'd –

The old lady whipped her arm across the table and grabbed his hand.

Toby froze.

'Where's my case?' she said.

Toby couldn't speak. He could hardly even breathe. The old lady's strong bony fingers pressed hard.

'Where's. My. Case?' she said. 'You know where it is. I can see it in your eyes.'

'I . . . um . . .'

'Tell me!'

Toby's voice had shrunk. 'We . . . I mean . . . I . . . um . . . we threw it out of the window.'

'I knew it!' The old lady's grip tightened even more.

'I'm sorry!' said Toby. 'We thought it was a bomb.' He tried to take a deep breath. Tried to stay calm. His mum's words echoed in the back of his mind: *Don't let that overactive imagination of yours run away with itself*.

'I don't believe you'll turn into a wolf-person,' he said. 'Wolf-people don't exist. But it's still really, really bad that we threw your bag off the train and I'm really, really sor—'

The old lady yanked Toby's hand towards her. Then she bent forward – and bit it.

Toby pulled away. He couldn't scream. He couldn't shout. He couldn't think. He couldn't even feel the pain.

He grabbed his rucksack. Stumbled out of his seat.

We are now approaching our final stop, said an announcement.

Toby found his way to the carriage door.

He was going to be sick.

He was going to pass out.

He was going to –

Please take all your personal belongings with you. We wish you a pleasant onward journey.

Toby shoved his bitten hand into his pocket. He couldn't bear to look at it.

The old lady laughed.

'You . . . just . . . bit me.' Toby's voice barely came out at all. He tried again, louder. 'You just bit me!'

'Yes,' said the old lady, 'and now *you* have the curse! You'll become a wolf-boy every full moon – unless you can find the amulet, of course, and I imagine that's going to be a *very* challenging task.'

'There is no curse!' shouted Toby. 'It's cobblers. It's nonsense. Just like the others said!' But his hand throbbed in his pocket. Was it the curse, racing through his blood? Seeping into his bones?

The train doors beeped. Toby hit the button with his free hand and tore on to the platform. The light was fading. The top half of the huge wolf moon loomed above dark, shadowed hills. There was no time to find the amulet.

He felt the curse creeping up his arm, thudding towards his heart.

He fumbled in his pocket for his ticket and somehow managed to get through the gate.

There was Gran, beaming. So pleased to see him.

He veered to one side, bashing into another passenger.

'Oi! Watch out!'

He had to keep away from Gran. Think of the harm he might do to her, as a wild wolf-monster.

'Toby?' said Gran. 'What's wrong?' She moved in for a hug but Toby ducked away.

His mind galloped. The curse – it was all through his body. He could feel it from his toenails right up to the tips of his teeth. He could feel it in the skin of his scalp.

'Oh, Toby, what's the matt–' Gran stopped. She'd spotted something over his shoulder.

It was the old woman, coming through the gates.

'Old Erica,' said Gran, shaking her head. 'Was it her who upset you? Come on, let's get you to the car.'

Toby suddenly felt exhausted. He let Gran lead him out of the station. He caught a glimpse of himself reflected in a glass door. He didn't *look* like a wolf-boy. He just looked like Toby.

'Old Erica has a bit of a reputation around here,' said Gran. 'She makes up unpleasant stories, just to scare people. And unfortunately a lot of the time it works. She's very good at it.'

Unpleasant stories?

Just to scare people?

Toby would have given anything to know that this had all just been made up. He didn't care how stupid he'd feel for believing it. He didn't care about the tears smearing his face. He just wanted to know for certain that it wasn't true.

'Hold on, Gran.' He paused under a street lamp and pulled his quivering hand from his pocket. No blood. He turned it palm down. No teeth marks. It wasn't even hurting, now he thought about it. Old Erica hadn't bitten him properly at all – she'd just pretended. And he'd believed her. Him and his overactive imagination! If the skin wasn't even broken, she couldn't have passed on any curse, could she? She *couldn't* have.

'Toby?' said Gran. 'Is there something wrong with your hand?'

'No. It's fine.' Toby wrapped his arms around his wonderful gran and squeezed her tight. 'It's fine,

Gran. It's absolutely fine!'

Curses weren't real.

They were *cobblers*. They were *nonsense*.

But as they drove towards Gran's little cottage, there was still a pulsing in Toby's ears and a rushing in his blood. There was still a thumping in his heart and a tremble in his bones.

When they reached the cottage, he stepped out of the car into the darkening night. The wolf moon had climbed in the sky. Only a small curve at its base was left hidden by the hills. Soon it would be fully risen, as bright and powerful as a precious silver amulet.

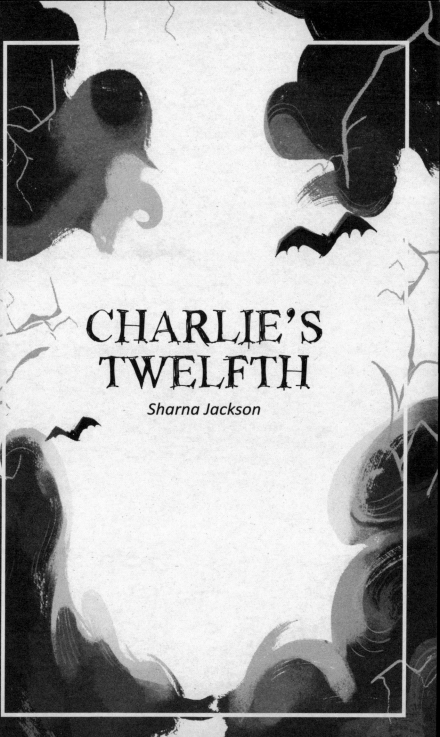

CHARLIE'S TWELFTH

Sharna Jackson

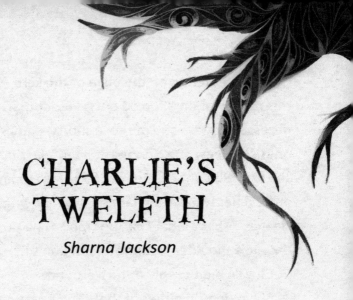

CHARLIE'S TWELFTH

Sharna Jackson

Two girls – and another one – loitered by the bus stop.

Anna bit her lip – literally and figuratively – as she tried to listen in.

'*Twelve?*' Olivia's nose wrinkled, like the number hadn't washed in weeks, then had the audacity to waft by her nostrils. 'You're still eleven? That's well young! *I've* been twelve forever.'

'Really?' Charlie asked. She raised a questioning eyebrow, which made her blond fringe rise on her forehead. 'How long? Do tell.'

'Ages! Since last September, the nineteenth. I'm going to be thirteen in –' she counted on her tanned fingers and under her breath – 'like, nine weeks. You're basically a baby, Charles.'

Anna, teetering on the edge of the kerb – and this conversation – forced out a louder than necessary laugh; one of those snorty, embarrassing ones she knew she'd cringe at later. 'Ha! *Charles*,' she said. She untied then retied her grey cardigan around her waist, then fanned her face with its sleeves. 'That's what I call her too.' Anna tapped Charlie's shoulder. '*I* call you that, don't I?'

Charlie didn't reply or turn around.

She didn't do either of those things for Anna lately. Instead, Charlie smiled at Olivia and brought her fists towards her face. 'Wah!' she cried somewhat sarcastically, rolling her knuckles under her bright blue eyes. 'That's me – basically a baby.'

Olivia laughed. 'You're *so* weird – in a good way, obviously.'

'Hopefully,' Charlie replied.

'Definitely.' Olivia nodded and leaned against the bus stop's timetable, then instantly winced away from the metal. 'That thing's on fire – it nearly took my skin off!' she said through tight teeth.

'Careful now!' Charlie said, gently pulling on Olivia's arm, then inspecting it. 'We need your skin, Liv. Keep your insides, well, inside. You'd be a puddle of a person otherwise, no good to anyone.'

Olivia smiled and shook her head. 'You kill me with your jokes.' She sighed. 'You know what? We *totally* should've made friends earlier than summer term —'

'Well, *we've* been friends since the very first day of school,' Anna interjected. 'Best friends,' she added proudly.

Although the sun shone down on all three of them that afternoon, Charlie shivered. And this time, for the first time in a while, she turned around. She paused before speaking, trying to find the right words. '"Best" . . . is a big word, Anna — but we *are* very good friends, that goes without saying.' She grinned unconvincingly.

Charlie's smile did not stop her words from stinging, and waves of pain and confusion washed across Anna's face. Not wanting to look at Charlie or Olivia — or for either of them to look back at her, she stared down at the twinkling tarmac. Charlie turned to Olivia with a shrug.

'Besides, it's always good to make *more* friends, isn't it?'

Olivia chuckled nervously and softly sung 'awkward' under her breath. She squinted in the direction of their school, looking for something, anything to change the course of this conversation. 'Where *is* my bus?' She nudged Charlie. 'I've got to get home – I've got wrapping to do. You're going to *love* what I've got you – you'll die when you see it.'

Charlie smiled. 'Let's hope not. But really, you shouldn't have. Your presence is the best present.'

'Nah, I can't turn up to a birthday lunch empty-handed, can I?' Olivia shook her head, her lips pursed. 'My parents wouldn't have it. It's rude.' She looked at Anna. 'Right? You're bringing something tomorrow, aren't you?'

Anna shook her head; her long brown curls brushed the shoulders of her white shirt. 'No, I'm not. I'm not going.' She glanced at Charlie, then down at her shoes. 'Not invited.' Olivia's eyes widened, and she turned to stare at the bus timetable, suddenly finding the schedule utterly fascinating.

'Anna,' Charlie said quietly. 'You know I could only invite one friend and, well, this time I chose Olivia. Trust me – I have a process; everyone will come over in due course. When . . . it's right. When Helena –' she glanced at Olivia – 'that's my . . . grandmother. When she is better. Anna, you know she's rather unwell.'

Anna nodded. She did.

'In any case,' Charlie said, brighter now, 'we're going to do something absolutely special the week after. We'll have our moment – we'll have our sleepover. Won't we?'

'Yeah . . . yes. We will.' Anna shrugged, knowing they absolutely would not.

On the other side of the street, a bus turned right and rolled up the road. Anna adjusted her bag on her shoulder. 'That's me.' She smiled, but it didn't reach her eyes – it barely reached her cheeks. 'Hope you both have a great time tomorrow.' She stared at Charlie, stone-faced. 'Happy birthday, I guess.'

'Bye, Emma!' Olivia said brightly as Anna ran across the road.

After boarding the bus and slumping in the front seat on the top deck, Anna stared at Olivia and Charlie from the window, hugging, laughing, having fun without her. As the bus trundled towards its destination, towards home, Anna's heart sank deeper into her chest, but her temperature?

Oh, it rose.

Anna threw her bag on the step and thrust her hands deep in the pockets of her grey school trousers. Once she'd found the basic brass key, she forced it into its slot. She twisted it, she turned it, but the door didn't open; it never did on the first try. Normally, Anna didn't mind this – she'd tell you she was a patient, calm girl, but today she wasn't. Today wasn't normal. She kicked the peeling yellow wood hard, yelling in frustration.

That did it.

The door swung open and slammed against the wall, sending a shockwave through the small, terraced house. Anna stomped down the hallway to the kitchen, dragging her bag behind her sledge-like on the smooth pine floor, shouting as she did.

'Will you actually get me a new key, Mum? Or am I going to have to fight the front door and break into my own house forever?

Anna's mum sighed. Anna was having one of *those* days, clearly. She stared down at her laptop and created closed curtains for her face with her long black hair and continued to calculate sums in her spreadsheet. Her papers, half-filled glasses of water, toys and trinkets surrounded her on the table. 'Need to talk?' she asked, without looking up.

Anna clawed at the fridge; her damp curls clinging to her sweaty forehead. 'No!' she snapped. She snatched a bottle of apple juice from the shelf and drank directly from it, gulping it down to its dregs while she stared at her mother.

'Anna, please. We're civilized people, not animals. We have glasses. Use them.'

'Why? What's the point? What's the point of anything?'

Anna's mother closed her laptop. 'Talk to me,' she said carefully.

'What's to say, really? Olivia's going. I'm not.'

'Ah.' She sat back in her chair. 'Charlie's party?'

'It's not even a party, Mum – it's lunch. Lunch at hers! Can you believe it?'

Anna's mum paused. 'So? What's the problem? What's the difference?'

'You don't know? You really can't see one?'

Anna's mother shook her head.

'Lunch is *way* worse than a party, Mum! It's super exclusive – just one person is going! If there is only one person going, why isn't it *me*?'

Anna sat down at the table opposite her mother.

'Hear me out – like, tell me how this is fair, or right?' She began counting on her fingers. '*I'm* the

35

one that's been cool with Charlie all year. *I* was friends with her when everyone else thought she was super weird and talked like their nans. Who stood up for her when she said she called her parents "Maisie" and "John" and her grandma "Helena" and not Mum, Dad, Granny or whatever? *Me*.' Anna's nostrils flared. 'I haven't even been to her house yet – I've only seen it on a map in geography.'

'Ah!' Anna's mother reached over to stroke her daughter's hand. 'Maybe *that's* why she doesn't want too many people at her house. She might feel a bit sad or afraid of what's going on at home – especially if her grandmother is still poorly. Be sensitive. She might be ashamed of her house. I know I was nervous of bringing people home when I was younger –'

'But that doesn't make sense! Charlie is way richer than us!'

'Money has nothing to do with my point, Anna –'

'So why is she suddenly changing everything, then? It *must* be because we're broke –'

'We're not broke; we're frugal.'

'Why is she now into Olivia then, huh? *Olivia?*'

'What's wrong with Olivia?'

'Everything, obviously!' Anna snapped.

Her mother narrowed her eyes. 'Really, Anna?'

'OK, not really.' Anna sighed. 'She's just annoying, thinks she's funnier than she is, and is too cool to even know my name!' Anna sat up straight in her seat and narrowed her eyes. 'Wait. I get it. I know what it is. It's because she's prettier than me, and they make a better-looking duo. Charlie *did* say she had nice skin.' Anna rubbed her chin. 'That must be it.'

Anna's mother vigorously shook her head. 'Who *are* you?' She looked around the kitchen. 'Where's the girl I raised? The one who didn't say – or believe – terrible things like this?' She reached for Anna's hand. 'Just like money, looks aren't everything. Really. You know this – well, I thought you did.' She paused. 'Who a person is in here –' she tapped her chest – 'and what they believe in, is what it's all about. That's what counts.' She sat up straight. 'That reminds me!' Anna's mum moved some papers around the table and picked up one of her trinkets: a wooden doll painted in bright colours, the length and width of her hand. She turned the rosy-cheeked, smiling face towards

Anna. 'Speaking of insides counting – do you know what these are?'

Anna shook her head but stared at the doll; its long eyelashes, the pink rose in the centre of its chest, the thick dark red paint around its feet.

Her mother grinned. 'This will cheer you up.' She began to slowly twist and turn the doll at its middle, the two timber parts slightly squeaking against each other. 'I remembered this being easier,' she muttered under her breath. With her tongue slightly poking out of her mouth and her brow furrowed, she gripped both ends and jerked the parts apart with a grunt. In response to her effort, a smaller – but otherwise identical – doll dropped on to the table. Anna reached over to touch it and turned it over in her hands. 'Nesting dolls,' her mother said proudly. 'Got them in a Secret Santa one year.'

'Are there more little dolls inside this one?' Anna asked, putting it to her ear and shaking it.

Her mother nodded. 'Yeah, I'm sure. I never tried opening *all* of them. Scared I'd lose them, to be honest – or you'd swallow them, you know, when you were smaller.'

Anna sat back in her seat and stared at the dolls.

If these wooden girls can be together, fit together and make it work, she thought, *then why can't the three of us?* She reached over the table to snatch the bigger doll. 'Can I have these, Mum?'

Anna was certain she was doing the right thing, sure of it and herself. She was back on a bus – top deck, front seat as usual – but this time, the next afternoon, she headed in a different direction. She looked down at the roughly wrapped, figure-shaped present in her hand, and gently ran her nails over the pearlescent ribbon around it, attempting to curl it to match her hair. Charlie was going to *love* her gift; Anna just knew it. She looked out of the window, proud of her decision. Bright-bloomed branches from the tall, bowing trees on both sides of the narrow road clawed the glass as the bus headed towards a low brick bridge with a tight round tunnel it surely couldn't fit through.

Anna held her breath as the darkness surrounded her. She settled into her seat and imagined how the afternoon would go.

Yes.

Charlie would love the dolls so much she'd

forget Anna wasn't *technically* invited and welcome her: first with open arms and then a tight hug. Olivia would be jealous – not only of Anna's present – but of how much Charlie loved Anna's outfit – her dress with daisies on it and her red shoes. Anna knew she'd get a chuckle out of Charlie when she realized Anna's look matched her gift, kind of. Then Anna would of course remember to call Charlie's parents 'Maisie' and 'John' and they would find her so polite, friendly and funny that they'd wish they had invited her over sooner. She'd ask after Helena too – to show she cared – and wish her well. Maybe she would meet her. Then they'd all eat nice food, play games – Anna would let Olivia win a few to make friends – then the three of them would understand that they all get along, really. When she got home, tired but thrilled, her mum would be sorry. So sorry that she'd begged her not to go somewhere she wasn't wanted. Instead, she'd tell her she was proud of her for doing the right thing. Then she'd finally give her a new key for the front door.

Yes. That's exactly how it would happen.

Bright light streamed in through the windows again; the blackness was brief. The tightly packed houses in the town, before the tunnel, had made way for detached cottages and green gardens on the other side. A different world.

Anna looked between the window, the screen on the bus announcing its stops, and the map on her phone.

She was close. She reached up to ring the bell.

Standing between the big, shiny red balloons tied to the white-painted bar gate and a clearly old but very fancy silver car sitting on a gravel drive, Anna suddenly wasn't so sure of herself. She felt small, stupid and poor. On tiptoes, she pushed the balloons apart and peered into the garden. In the distance, because, yes, the garden was that large, she could just about see Charlie and Olivia sitting together at a picnic bench, laughing at something on Olivia's phone. Anna's eyes narrowed, and as she gripped Charlie's present in her frustrated hands, her thumbnails dug into the wrapping paper, tearing it. She cursed herself under her breath and tried to cover it with the curly ribbon, but that just made it worse. She hated the stupid present, she hated those two giggling girls over there and, most of all, she hated herself. She –

'She'll *love* it,' boomed a deep voice behind her.

Anna froze.

'Don't you worry about the wrapping now, love – it's only going in the bin, isn't it?'

Anna breathed deeply but didn't move – she didn't know what to do. She did and did not want to be there.

'You can turn around. We don't bite – only gnaw a little bit!' He loudly gnashed his teeth together and laughed at his joke, then shuffled his feet on the gravel. 'You're Anna, aren't you?'

Anna nodded, still looking away. 'Yeah.' She sighed and cautiously looked over her shoulder to see a tall man with a wide smile, a thick waist and thinning grey hair. 'I'm sorry. I wasn't supposed to be here. Charlie didn't invite me.'

He waved his hand. 'Ah, it's no bother, no bother at all – you're very welcome! Always. The more the merrier is what we say.' He sighed. 'You know Charlie, don't you? You know how she is. So . . . particular. She's doesn't take after her old dad.' He leaned back on his heels and chuckled. 'Not even a little bit!'

'You're John?' Anna replied.

'The one and only.' He extended his hand, as did Anna, but as they touched, she winced, quickly snatched it away and rubbed her hands together. John's fingers were freezing – icicles in the dead of winter, at the height of summer. She looked up at him quizzically, confused, and he laughed again, clearly used to this reaction. 'Poor circulation! Strange old body, this one,' he said, putting his hands on his hips. He sighed. 'Look at us. We're a right pair, aren't we?'

'We are?'

'Yes. Me with my cold hands, you with your cold feet!' He pushed the gate open. 'Come on, in you pop. Charlie!' he shouted across the lawn, too close to Anna's ear. Charlie's head snapped up at the sound of her name, and she dropped the phone in her hand. 'Look who I found lurking!' Anna waved sheepishly at her so-called friend as she walked towards her.

'Ooh, Emma's here!' Olivia squealed. 'That's cool!'

Charlie shook her head. 'No,' she said firmly. 'No.' She stood, her shoulders tense, her face stony. 'I told you not to come,' she snarled. Anna took a step back. She'd never heard Charlie talk like that, in that tone. 'What did I say?' Charlie's lips were tight and pale; her bright blue eyes darkened to a deep navy blue and glistened with tears.

'I – I,' Anna stammered. She took a breath. 'I just –'

'You just *what*?' Charlie hissed. Her bottom lip trembled. 'Anna, I told you, I have a process, I –'

'Do calm down, Charlie,' a woman said, carrying a jug of what looked like weak squash from the house to the garden. She set it down on the table and wiped her hands on her apron, then tucked her short, mousy-brown hair behind her ear. She hurried over to Anna, and when she leaned over to kiss her on the cheek, Anna recoiled. She would never say this out loud, ever – and she felt bad for thinking it – but the woman's breath didn't smell good, or right. She smelled like decay, like she needed a dentist, desperately. Maybe that was why Charlie didn't want her here? 'There's plenty of food, Anna. You're very welcome. I'm Maisie. She looked pointedly at Charlie. 'Nice to meet you. Finally.'

'Mum,' Charlie began, but Maisie shushed her.

Charlie glared at her parents. They smiled back and gave her encouraging nods. She slowly sat down and stared at the table.

'I'm glad you're here too,' said Olivia, breaking the tension. 'And you look nice. Cool dress!'

'Thanks,' Anna replied, surprised at her kindness. Maybe Olivia wasn't so bad after all.

'Yeah, it looks vintage. Old, I mean.' Maybe Anna spoke too soon.

'Well, I think you look lovely,' said Maisie. She glared at Olivia's denim shorts. 'Appropriate,' she added.

'Very fitting for the occasion,' John concurred.

Anna looked down at her hands, still holding her tatty, raggedy present and sighed. This was a disaster. 'Charlie?' she said glumly. Charlie looked up. 'Happy birthday.'

'Twelve! The best birthday!' John said loudly.

Maisie agreed. 'Most important,' she nodded.

'Why, though?' asked Olivia, wrinkling that nose again. 'It's not that good. I'm nearly thirteen, and I *know* that's going to be a better year.'

'Ah, it's just special,' said Maisie with a wave of her hand. 'When you're twelve, things change, you help people around you change too –'

'Because you're really growing up,' John added, watching Maisie.

'Exactly,' she said, smiling lovingly back at him. 'Anyway, enough of the mushy stuff,' she said. 'Anna, why don't you give Charlie your present – it looks exciting!'

Anna placed the present on the table in front of Charlie, who mouthed a glum 'thank you' and tore what was left of the paper away from her gift. She sighed when she saw what was inside.

'Show us, show us!' said John. 'What did you get?'

Charlie took a deep breath, picked up the gift with an unconvincing smile. 'Dolls. Nesting dolls. They're great, really. Thank you, Anna.' She stared at her mother.

'Matryoshkas!?' Maisie shouted. She glanced at John who slapped his thigh. 'How funny.'

'Bodies inside bodies!' he cried. 'What . . . a thing!'

'Yeah, a weird thing,' Olivia muttered.

'A beautiful thing,' said Maisie, shooting Olivia a sharp look. 'Very traditional.'

Anna looked over the table. 'What did you get Charlie, Olivia?' she asked, her eyes scanning for an elaborate and/or expensive present.

Olivia sat up proudly. 'A gift card,' she said

smugly. 'iTunes.'

'You had to run home yesterday to wrap that?' asked Anna. 'A gift card?'

John stifled a laugh. 'It's all too modern for me,' he said.

Olivia shook her head when she heard that. 'Unbelievable,' she muttered.

Maisie continued to touch the dolls and turn them over in her hands. 'Indeed. What an *amazing* gift. You *are* a special girl, Anna. Charlie was right about you. Now eat, everyone, eat!'

Anna sat down next to Charlie and looked at the food on the table. Thin triangle sandwiches with the crusts cut off, bowls of crisps, cubed cheese with pineapple on sticks.

'Are we getting pizza?' Olivia asked. 'Or, like . . . burgers? This food's . . . nice, it just reminds me of the things my mum said she would eat at her birthday parties, years and years and years ago.'

'It's classic party food,' said Maisie, a trace of irritation in her voice. 'Eat up!'

Anna popped a boiled sweet into her mouth – rhubarb and custard – rolled it around her mouth and took in her surroundings. The lush green grass, the mahogany shed and the white-washed cottage with its thatched roof. She narrowed her eyes to focus on the windows, to see inside the house, searching for reasons – reasons apart from John's frosty fingers and Maisie bad breath – as to why she may not have been invited here before. She could see into the kitchen, with its huge oven, deep sink and neat stacked sets of matching plates. Scanning right, a low-ceilinged living room with soft sofas. Looking up now to a round window, very close to the roof, she saw a flash of a figure.

Anna was certain she met the eyes of a woman. A woman with a wrinkled, weathered face and long greyed hair.

Helena? Charlie's grandmother?

Whoever it was disappeared as fast as Anna saw her face.

Shocked and surprised by the woman's speed, questioning if she'd really seen her, Anna lost control of her sweet and it slid sideways down her throat. She began to choke and coughed to return it to her mouth. She looked over at Charlie who was already staring at her. Charlie – with possibly more force than necessary – slapped Anna on the back, causing Anna to spit the sweet out embarrassingly on to the table in front of her. She quickly swiped it on to the grass and smiled.

Anna looked at Charlie gratefully. 'You saved my life!' she said slightly sarcastically, definitely dramatically.

'For now,' Charlie replied flatly, not a hint of fun or friendliness in her voice.

'I'm sorry. I was just looking in your house,' Anna said, trying desperately to lift the tension. 'It looks lovely – and I think I saw your grandma. That's what surprised me.'

Charlie stiffened. 'You saw her?'

John leaned forward. 'Did she see you?'

Anna nodded. 'Think so? But she moved very quickly. Charlie told me she hasn't been well. I hope she's feeling better.'

Under the table, Maisie grabbed John's hand and squeezed it. 'She's almost there,' said John with a smile. 'Very close now.'

'Emma's right you know?' Olivia said with a sigh.

'I am? About what?'

'Their house. It's well nice.' She turned to Charlie's parents. 'How about a tour? I'm finished with my food,' she said, waving her hand dismissively across her unused plate.

'Oh no,' said Maisie firmly. 'No. Not yet.'

'Maybe not ever. That's for the winner only,' added John with a broad smile.

'No,' said Charlie standing up, gripping the table's edge. 'We're not doing the game. We don't need to. I have a process and —'

'But you have *two* friends now,' said Maisie. She looked at Anna warmly. 'It will be fun!'

'Yeah, we might as well do *something*,' added Olivia, drumming her fingers on the table. 'Is it on the PlayStation or something?'

'No,' said John. 'We don't have anything like that. It's a classic game. Hot potato.'

Olivia shook her head and muttered, 'Weird, weird, weird,' under her breath. She reached for her phone and began furiously tapping away.

'Hot potato?' Anna said. 'What's that?'

'An even worse pass the parcel, if you can imagine that,' said Olivia. 'No cool gifts in the layers you unwrap or anything.'

Maisie laughed. 'It's something like that. The winner in our game is the one left holding the bag.'

'What's in the bag?' Anna asked keenly.

'You'll see,' said John.

'No, she won't see, because she is leaving,' said Charlie, pulling Anna by the elbow. 'Come on, you *need* to go.'

'But I want to play,' said Anna.

'See, she wants to play,' said Maisie, ever-so-slightly mocking Anna, a strange smile dancing on her lips.

John put a strong hand on Anna's shoulder, holding her in place. He turned to Charlie. 'Let her,' he said in a cold voice – a voice colder than his hand. He looked into the sky, shielding his eyes from the glare. 'It's time.'

Maisie clapped her hands together with glee. 'I'll go get it,' she said over her shoulder as she skipped into the house.

Anna and Olivia faced each other in the garden, throwing a small – but heavy – sack between them to the tinny sound of a song from the 1970s playing through Maisie's phone. Olivia, stone-faced, threw it with zero interest to Anna. As Anna threw it back, she grinned at Charlie. Charlie's increasingly contorted face swung between Maisie and John.

'Enough,' she pleaded. 'Stop it. Now.'

Maisie swatted her away with her hand. 'In time, in time.'

'Really? How much longer?' Olivia whined. 'I'm over this, honestly.'

'I don't mind keeping going,' said Anna, eager to please. This wasn't so bad after all, she thought.

The music suddenly stopped. The bag was in Anna's hands. Charlie stumbled and sank to her knees.

'Yay, you won, great,' said Olivia dryly. She returned to the bench and picked on some crisps. Her phone beeped and she jumped up. 'Oh,' she said, pretending to be surprised and very much failing, 'Dad's here – there's an . . . emergency at home. Yeah . . . I have to get back.' She waved her hand over the table. 'Thanks for everything. It was –' she sighed – 'an experience.'

Anna was delighted – not only had she won the game, she had also won Charlie's parents approval and alone time with Charlie on her birthday. A devastating victory. Take that, Mum. She tried to hide her smug smile, but didn't succeed. 'Oh, that's a shame, Olivia,' she said. Even she was a bit shocked at her sarcasm.

'Yeah, it's something like that, Emma,' Olivia replied, walking to the gate.

Charlie stood and jumped in her way. 'Liv, no,

please. Do stay,' she pleaded, her hand gripping Olivia's arm. 'I – I,' she stammered, looking around for words. 'I believe you won the game, actually.'

She leaned over Anna to snatch the sack from her hands, but Anna held tight. She was not losing to Olivia. Not today. Anna's eyes met Charlie's and Anna shook her head firmly. No. The bag was hers.

Charlie's lips wavered, her eyes watered.

John stepped forward. 'Let go,' he said, prising Charlie's fingers off Olivia, who ran towards the gate without a backward glance. 'We have our winner.'

'The rightful winner,' said Maisie. She looked towards the house and when Anna followed her gaze to the round window, the one very close to the roof, Helena was there, smiling down at the scene.

'Don't you want to see what you've won, Anna?' said John. 'Go on, look inside!'

Anna shook the sack in front of her and a large, ornate iron key fell on to the grass by her feet between her and Charlie. She laughed when she saw it. 'That's so funny, I was just telling Mum I needed a new key – and now I have one. A fancy one, too.'

'Well, isn't that something!' said Maisie. 'A lovely coincidence.'

Anna bent down to pick up the key and it instantly felt right in her hands, so perfect in her palm. 'It's so heavy, I love it.' She held it tenderly to her chest. 'What's it for? What does it unlock?'

'The house,' said John. 'You can go in now.'

'No, please,' Charlie croaked. 'Please, don't go inside.'

'The rules are the rules,' said John.

'Yes,' added Maisie. 'It's your . . . process, after all.' Maisie looked at John and they burst out laughing.

Charlie's pale skin flushed red with frustration and fear. A single tear ran down her burning cheeks.

Anna struggled to look away from the key, but she managed to steal a quick glance at her friend. 'It can't be that bad, Charles — let's go.' She grinned at John and Maisie. 'Thank you!' she said. 'For everything.'

'No. Thank *you*,' said John. 'Really.'

'It was . . . time you came over,' added Maisie.

'Are you coming too?' Anna asked, staring down lovingly at her key, mesmerized, under its spell.

Maisie shook her head. 'No, we'll watch from here. Charlie –' she paused – 'she's ready.'

Anna was ready. She walked confidently and proudly towards their house. The key clutched in her right hand gave her all the direction she needed. Charlie walked cautiously behind her, and as they went through the doors into the living room, out of her parents' sight, she grabbed Anna's left hand and squeezed it tight.

'I told you not to come,' she cried. 'I *told* you!'

Anna shook her head. 'But I'm having a great time – the best time.' She stood by the front door and looked up the narrow set of steep stairs, and at the close walls lined with framed photographs. 'I need to go up there, don't I, Charlie?'

Charlie gripped Anna's hand tightly, her knuckles bright white. She shook her head. 'She wasn't meant to call *you*,' Charlie whispered. 'This wasn't how it was supposed to go.'

Anna wasn't listening, not really. 'It will be fine – I'm just having a look.'

She climbed the stairs slowly but full of determination. The key in one hand, Charlie's palm in the other. She looked back to smile down at her friend. 'Cheer up!'

Charlie's lip trembled. 'I can't.'

As Anna turned away, she squinted at the photographs on the wall. Very old black-and-white ones, newer, brighter coloured ones. Some taken outside, many indoors, but always four people in the frame. 'Who are all these people?'

'Us,' Charlie whispered. 'Us. Every twelve years.'

Anna peered at the photos and laughed. 'Charlie, be serious.'

Charlie gulped but said nothing else.

They reached the top of the stairs. A wooden door with ornate ironwork around the lock loomed over them.

'Aha!' said Anna, holding the key in front of her. 'A match!' She turned to Charlie and grinned. Before Charlie could confirm or deny it, Anna slipped the key into the lock. Unable to help herself, she twisted it once, to the right, and it opened, easily, with a soft, satisfying click.

'I'm going in there now,' said Anna, transfixed.

'Anna,' Charlie replied weakly. 'Anna . . .'

Anna stepped inside. The door slammed shut behind her.

'You *were* my best friend,' Charlie sobbed. Hot tears tumbled down her face, rolled on to her neck and soaked the pink collar of her dress, turning it blood red. She threw her back against the door and forced her fingers into her ears.

Charlie didn't like to hear it happen any more. The process was fun at first, but it hadn't made her smile for centuries. It was especially not enjoyable when she cared – and this time she absolutely did.

The only good thing about it, she thought, was that it was short.

Because it certainly wasn't painless.

The door rattled behind Charlie's back.

Holding her breath while wiping at her eyes, she slowly moved away from it. As it creaked open, Charlie began breathing again, panting, her chest rising and falling rapidly.

A red shoe slipped between the crack, then the rest of the . . . girl appeared in her flower-print dress. Brown eyes stared at Charlie.

A smirk turned into a smile, then turned into a grin. The widest grin in the world.

Charlie stepped backwards. 'Anna?' she asked.

The other one shook their head. 'No.'

GAME
OVER

Aisha Bushby

GAME OVER

Aisha Bushby

PART ONE

THE INVITATION

> Nada and Bee are cordially invited to spend the
> evening with Rhea and Amy at the Arcadia on
> Friday 13th February at 10 p.m. Bring snacks and
> sleeping bags.
>
> *xoxo*

I squeal when I see the invitation slotted into
my locker that morning. I can't help but think
that Rhea put *my* name first on the invite.
Nada. And she also put it in *my* locker, not Bee's.
My stomach churns with guilt for being pleased,
because Bee's my best friend, but that's how I feel.

Rhea is the most popular girl in Year 7. Probably because her parents own the Arcadia, the biggest arcade in town, which has games *and* food *and* a giant play pit. She also has this video channel with thousands of subscribers. Sometimes she pranks people – just for a bit of fun – and other times she vlogs what she's doing that day.

Once a month Rhea and Amy – her sidekick – invite two people from our year to go to the Arcadia with them after hours and hang out. A *whole* arcade to themselves for the *whole* night. And the Monday after, they all walk into school together, and chat at lunch about how fun it was. Sometimes they stay friends, other times they don't. But I just know we'll get along because Mum's a video games tester, which means I've been practising for this moment basically my entire twelve years. I held a console before I could write with a pen.

I've been standing here for a few minutes, clutching the invitation, when some of the other students start to spill into the locker area. I keep an eye out for Bee, to tell her the news. I'm buzzing so much I feel like a whole swarm of wasps is living inside me and I'm about to take off. I need to *calm down*. Who's this excited at school on a Monday morning when the day starts with double maths?

Then Rhea walks in and my heart jolts. I drop the invitation and do that thing where I try to catch it mid-air as it flutters to the floor. I miss. Luckily she doesn't see me act like a loser, so I pick it up quickly, trying to look unbothered while also trying to catch her eye. To be honest, I expect her to look over and smile at me, or at least acknowledge that we're going to have the best weekend together, but she just walks past as if I'm invisible, her expensive perfume lingering behind her.

But it doesn't matter, because soon we're going to be proper friends. Bee turns up then and I practically launch myself at her.

'You'llneverguesswhat!' I say breathlessly, thrusting the invitation into her hand.

And Bee, my best friend in the whole world, gives me the exact reaction I expect.

She holds the invitation up like it's treasure and says, 'Nada and Bee, gamers extraordinaire, will secure our place in the upper ranks of Summersby High School with our expert aim and fast reactions. We will –'

'Beatrice, please,' Mr Turner says, walking past.

He's our form tutor. 'While I love the enthusiasm this early in the day, I've only had one cup of coffee, and neither of us want to burn out before short break, now, do we?'

'No, sir,' Bee says, with complete sincerity. 'Thank you, sir, for your sage advice. I shall take it forth as I battle the day ahead.'

Mr Turner stares for a moment and then sighs, walking into the classroom, shoulders hunched.

'He hates you,' I say, giggling, while Bee grabs her things and we head into registration.

Bee is literally the reason I go to school every day. She's a ray of sunshine. The best. I'm *so* glad we're going to Rhea's sleepover together.

PART TWO

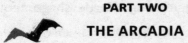

THE ARCADIA

'Well? Are we going to go in or what?' Bee asks impatiently. She's holding an umbrella over both of us as it's pouring down with rain.

'One sec,' I say. 'I want to savour this moment. We're making core memories right now.'

Bee snorts. 'You've been listening to your dad a bit too much. What's his theory on life this week?'

'It's not a theory on life,' I explain. 'It's the idea that there are moments we're going to remember in years gone by. Like "wasn't that just the best night of our lives?" So, yeah, normally, we wouldn't remember for example what we wore on a random Friday. But *this* Friday, we'll remember it when we're old, in our thirties.'

'All right, Nada the Knowing,' she teases, using my RPG nickname. 'So *that's* why you spent three hours choosing an outfit? Got it.'

'It was only two and half.' I grin, but Bee's right. It was a bit . . . chaotic this evening. Bee came over to get ready but she's very relaxed about this whole sleepover and turned up in lime-green dungarees and a pink jumper, looking effortlessly gorgeous. Meanwhile, my favourite trousers were in the wash, which threw the whole outfit I had planned out the window. I'm wearing jeans and a vintage console sweatshirt, which I'm now worried is too on theme.

So, instead, I focus on the building ahead of us. It's the tallest one in town with tinted windows with a huge neon-red sign, which says: *The Arcadia*.

Thunder booms, making Bee and I jump, followed by a flash of lightning. It blinks on and off, making spots appear in front of my eyes, and when I next look at the sign the 'dia' bit at the end is flickering. Another jolt of lightning and the 'a' flips upside down, hanging off the tail so 'dia' now looks like the word 'die'.

'Well, that's not creepy at all,' Bee says sarcastically. 'Done with your core memory-making now?'

'Yep,' I say, swallowing nervously, and we step inside.

66

Bee the Bold walks in first. I follow, the door slamming behind me, the sound of rain disappearing, replaced with an eerie silence. It's dark. The only light is coming from an emergency-exit sign to my right, and the telltale red dot of the surveillance cameras in each corner of the giant room.

Up ahead are dozens and dozens of arcade machines, their power switched off. There's a maze-like route through, but we have no idea where we're supposed to meet Rhea and Amy.

'Do you think they're here yet?' I whisper.

'They have to be,' Bee replies in a normal voice. 'Why else would the door be left open?'

'True. Shall we dump our sleeping bags and snacks?'

'Good idea,' says Bee, shoving her stuff up against a wall.

The arcade spans four floors, and I've memorized them all. Before we'd even met Rhea in secondary, we spent most rainy weekends in the Arcadia.

The ground floor has lots of slot games, mainly 2p machines and things like that, plus a chippy. It gets more exciting the higher you go. The first floor has basketball hoops, dance mats and ice hockey. It's the sort of thing most people in our year enjoy. You can get milkshakes and the most delicious desserts too. The second level is all about racing and skill-based stuff, and they have a ticket counter where you can swap your tickets for prizes like a rice cooker or sweets. And the top floor – the best floor – has the infamous *Zombie Raid* machines, the giant play pit and Pizza Palace.

Where are Rhea and Amy?

'Hello?' I call into the darkness, as Bee guides us around. I hate that my voice is shaking, but I'm *really* nervous. What will we even talk about with Rhea and Amy? Arcade games, I guess. Rhea must be into them, right, if her parents own the arcade?

There's no answer.

'Hellooooooo,' Bee says more confidently. 'Ugh, shall we just leave? We can have a sleepover at mine instead. It's cold here, and it smells a bit like wee.'

'Shh!' I say, worried Rhea will hear. 'Don't be rude. We can't just leave.'

I'm unable to see her face but I *know* Bee's rolling her eyes.

Then I hear it. The click of a door locking. I turn

quickly and see the blur of a figure, but it's too tall to be either Rhea or Amy.

'How long do you think that door was open?' I ask, my heart pounding. 'Anyone could've got in, right?'

Bee turns, shrugging. She's trying to act casual, but her worry frown gives her away. 'Yeah, but no one knows it's open, do they? It's fine, just your imagination.' She grabs my hand to comfort me. She knows about what happened, why I act this way. And she doesn't judge me for it like someone else might.

We walk further in, heading roughly for the chippy, in the hope that Rhea and Amy will appear. But then I feel a gust of wind to the right of me, and turn to see a blur of red and white.

'Someone's in here,' I say to Bee, tears springing to my eyes.

'Who? Where?' she asks.

A rush of adrenaline surges through me and I trip up the steps to the chippy, dragging Bee with me.

'There's someone here,' I cry. 'I swear there is.'

'Nada, it's OK, I'm here,' Bee says, standing in front of me. I can't see her face in the dark but her voice soothes me. The wee smell from the entrance is replaced by stale oil from the chip fryer and a hint of bin juice.

I hate the dark. Hate it. When I was seven we lived in a bungalow and one evening I woke up in the middle of the night to moonlight streaming through my window and a face staring in. I screamed so loud Mum and Dad rushed in, and I was so terrified that I wet the bed. Turns out it was a Halloween mask some teenagers put in front of our window as a prank while I was asleep. But I was so scared I still sleep with a night light even now.

'Breathe with me,' Bee says. 'One, two, three . . .'

'Four, five,' I say with her, doing as she says. I'm just about feeling OK when a clatter sounds from behind the chippy counter. We both turn as the figure I'd seen in a blur of red and white springs up, just as a light above them turns on.

It's a clown, a lurid, grinning clown holding a knife.

I scream.

The clown laughs, stepping forward.

I'm so terrified my knees buckle and I let out a sob, while Bee tries to pull me up and drag me away.

Then the rest of the lights turn on as Rhea appears from behind a machine, phone in hand, pointed at me and Bee.

The clown takes their mask off to reveal Amy, smirking.

'Oh my god, you were so funny,' Rhea says, focusing the phone just on me now, before locking it and stuffing it into her pocket. 'I can't wait to edit that. You've had the best reaction yet.'

It takes me a moment to wipe my tears away and stand up. 'Y-you're not really going to upload that, are you?'

'Of course I am,' says Rhea breezily. 'You didn't expect to come to a Rhea sleepover and not feature on my channel, did you? My last video got 40,000 views, but I think you'll beat it.' She imitates my scream, sinking to her knees before laughing again, Amy giggling in unison. Bee has her arm around me, squeezing.

'P-please don't post it online,' I say pitifully, wishing my voice would stop shaking.

Rhea looks at me without an ounce of emotion. 'Oh, come on. Don't be so *boring*.'

There's an awkward silence.

'Was that a real knife?' Bee asks Amy casually.

'Yeah,' Amy says. 'I just had the idea last-minute. Grabbed it from the kitchen.'

Bee raises her eyebrows. Her fighting expression. 'If you post that online with a real knife, you'll get into a lot of trouble. Probably even arrested.'

Rhea's face drops. She turns to Amy, furious. 'Ugh, she's right. Why didn't you stick to the plan? You've ruined it now!'

Amy looks dejected. 'Sorry, Rhea,' she mumbles.

My heart lifts. 'So you won't post it?'

Rhea turns to me, pouting. 'Not now, thanks to Amy.' She spits her name out like it's a swear word.

While it doesn't make up for what she did, I can't help but feel a little satisfied to see Amy looking all sad in her clown suit.

PART THREE

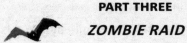

ZOMBIE RAID

'You're *sure* you don't want to go home?' Bee asks for the third time while we make our way to the top floor. Rhea is up front, Amy a step behind her, and then the two of us.

'It was just a joke,' I say, my voice still shaking a bit. 'I'm not *that* much of a baby.'

Bee frowns. 'It's OK to be afraid. You know that, right? It doesn't make you a baby. And it wasn't a very funny joke.'

Bee knows all my secrets and she still loves me, but she doesn't get that running away will make it worse. I need to face this, like maybe it'll undo what happened that night. And I can't bail now and let Rhea and Amy think I'm a coward. I need to prove I'm brave. To them. And to myself.

'OK,' Rhea says, once we're all standing in front of *Zombie Raid*. 'I've actually figured out that I can reshoot the bits with Amy in the clown mask, and then stitch it with your reaction.'

My insides tie themselves in a knot. She never wanted to be friends with us, did she? That's not

73

why she invited us here. She was just using us as content for her online channel.

Bee responds. '*What?*' The single syllable is scorched with fire.

'Unless,' Rhea continues as if uninterrupted, 'you can beat the high score on *Zombie Raid*.'

'Ah, right,' Bee says in a fake friendly voice. 'So, on top of threatening us with a *knife*, you're now coercing us too. That's really great, Rhea. I'm sure your parents are very proud.'

Rhea's face falters for a moment. Then it hardens. 'They are, actually. Why else do you think I get this whole place to myself?'

I'm not sure now why I ever wanted to be friends with Rhea. She's mean and stuck up, and even Amy seems to be cringing at how she's acting. But I can't let her post a mashed-together video of me making a fool of myself, can I? She's got me trapped.

'Well, Nada?' Rhea says, turning her attention to me. 'Are you going to accept the challenge?'

I glance at Bee. She purses her lips, shrugging at me, as if to say 'you decide'.

'Fine,' I say, the first word I've spoken to Rhea since I pleaded with her not to post the video.

Rhea glances at Bee, satisfied. 'Perfect.'

Zombie Raid is a two-player game and, unlike in real life, here *I* take the lead. The aim of the game is to get to the top of an abandoned electrical building and switch the city lights back on so the zombies disappear. Simple. Oh, and obviously you have to try not to die from zombie attacks on the way.

I pick up one plastic laser shooter while Bee has the other and, as the screen loads up, immediately give out instructions.

'To your right, then behind,' I say quickly. Bee obeys, wordlessly, while I tackle my own zombie attack.

I'm aware of Rhea standing behind me, her breath on the back of my neck, filming our game. She offers commentary every once in a while, introducing herself to everyone watching her videos. But I ignore her and play.

Zombie Raid has seven levels, and no one's made it to the final one. Yet.

Level 1: we tackle zombies in our house as they come looking for blood. Up close, the zombies are seriously terrifying. They have sallow white skin, covering what I think is a face underneath, but it's hard to make out any features. All you can see is a giant slit for a mouth, which opens to reveal knife-sharp teeth and tar-like saliva. Whenever they move their jaws, I hear a sickening *click, click, click*. Their hands are basically giant claws too and their limbs long, bending at weird angles.

Level 2: we manage to commandeer a car to drive us to the city.

Level 3: we cross a bridge into the heart of the city.

But just as we're about to get to the end a red splat of blood covers the screen as Bee is flung off the bridge.

She swears. 'Sorry, Nada.'

'It's fine,' I say, grinning. 'The bridge is a checkpoint so we can keep going.'

'TWO lives left,' Rhea taunts us, before addressing the camera. 'Can they make it to Level Seven? Or shall I post the other video I have planned. We'll see.'

Amy hovers behind her like a background character waiting for instructions.

Back in the game, Bee and I cross the bridge this time.

Level 4: we make it into a building where everything is dark and dim.

It gets harder here and I really focus now. This level is all about sound. I can hear the zombies screeching in the dark. Two long screeches, then a short one, like they're communicating.

'Focus on the speakers,' I say to Bee. 'Whichever one releases the sound is the direction you point.'

'Got it,' Bee says, making sure I know she's heard.

It's a little cheat I figured out a long time ago, and I hear Rhea mutter under her breath, 'Impressive.'

Even after how she's treated me, I feel a surge of satisfaction at her praise. I shake this feeling away. It's all about the game now.

Level 5: we make it to the elevator all the way across the building.

Level 6: we need to get to the top floor without dying, all while Zombies hijack the elevator and break through the ceiling.

Bee's job is to sort out the wiring while I hold them off. But it's hard in such close proximity. I can't get my scope to aim and –

'Ohhhh, another life gone,' Rhea says. 'Only one left.'

It's my turn to swear.

All we need to do is get to the top of the elevator. Once the doors open, we've beaten the higher score.

'You got this,' Bee says as we get back inside on our last life.

This time, I drop my laser shooter after the first zombie breaks through the roof and use the metal panel it flung down as a shield instead. Bee and I are cornered.

'Smart!' Rhea says, leaning in hungrily as the elevator goes up and up to the top floor.

A zombie manages to scratch at me, and I lose my health to the very final bar before . . .

. . . doors open. We beat the high score!

I'm about to turn to Bee and celebrate, when the machine switches off, along with all the lights.

'Rhea!' Bee shouts. 'Are you serious?!'

'It wasn't me!' Rhea chimes back.

'Sure it's not,' Bee growls in response, but there's something in Rhea's tone that makes me believe her.

'Amy?' Rhea calls in the dark.

'It . . . it wasn't me.'

Why do they sound so scared? Is this part of the prank? But I've had drama lessons with both of

them and they're rubbish at acting. This is real.
They're afraid.

PART FOUR

LEVEL 7

uddenly, the arcade machine turns on, but nothing else. And all that's flashing on the screen are the words 'Level 7'. In my peripheral vision I can see a percentage, along with a single heart: my stats from the game, which usually stand at the corner of the screen. My health is at thirty-two per cent – not great – with just one life left.

Then I hear it: two long screams followed by a short scream.

It's the zombies. From the game. Somehow they're here.

'Get your phone lights out,' I say to everyone, jumping into action. 'And stand with your backs to each other.'

While I might struggle to make many friends at school or know how to talk to people like Rhea and Amy, video games are a language I understand. They give me confidence, something to focus on. I know I'm the only one who can get us out of this mess.

We stand in a circle, facing outwards, pointing

our phones ahead of us and trying to see what's going on. Maybe someone else is pranking all of us; it's just our imaginations running wild in the dark. But then I hear the sound again, and as I point my phone light I see the zombie coming towards me. It opens its mouth, dislocating its jaw with a click, wide enough to swallow a whole human head.

It lunges for Amy. She screams, holding her clown mask out. It must mistake it for her real head because I watch it gulp down the mask in one. Then it lets out a guttural howl, spitting the mask back out. The rubber's torn to shreds.

A second zombie appears from the gloom, followed by a third and fourth. One for each of us. I hear the *click, click, click* of their jaws unlocking.

How is this real? my brain screams, but my mouth says something different. 'RUN.'

I grab Bee and head in the direction of the Pizza Palace kitchen, thankful I've memorized the layout of this place. As we fly over the counter and head into the back, we grab frying pans, kitchen scissors and blowtorches as our weapons and our armour.

'What do we do?' Bee screeches, her usual calm exterior shattered.

'Call our parents,' I say breathlessly. 'And hide

until they come to get us.'

Bee tries to dial out on her phone, but there's no signal here. Rhea and Amy are nowhere to be seen.

'OK, OK, OK,' I say into the darkness. 'What do we know about zombies?'

Silence.

'Bee?'

'Sorry,' she says, taking a deep, shaky breath. 'Well, if they scratch or bite you in the game, you turn into one of them after, like, three nights or something. So we have to be careful, right? Because we might not know straight away.'

'Right, yeah,' I say, quickly trying to puzzle this out. Somehow the zombies came from the game. But everything that's happening is real. And if they're from the game, can we get them to go back into it?

I say all of this to Bee. 'What if we switch the game off? The machine is on but if we cut the cord it might stop it.'

'It's risky going back out there,' Bee reminds me. 'And we only have one life left.'

As if I could forget the flashing heart, my health is down to twenty-eight per cent now.

'What else?' I ask. 'What's the whole point of

Level Seven? We get to the top of the building to –'

'Restore light to the city.'

'But where will the power station be?' I ask, just as my eye falls on the red light of one of the surveillance cameras. 'In the control room!'

'Well, where's *that*?' Bee growls.

'Rhea turned it on from downstairs, didn't she?' I say.

'So we need to find her and hope she's alive to tell us exactly where.'

While our plan is coming together, a door slams open and steps thump across the concrete floor of the kitchen, followed by the *click* of a jaw.

I wordlessly grab Bee and dive into the giant, industrial dishwasher, pulling the box-like lid down on top of us. We can see through, but the glass is tinted, keeping us hidden.

I watch the zombie stalk past slowly, sniffing the air. They're just like they are in the game: how they look; the sounds they make; the way they move, but in real life it's worse because now I can *smell* them too, and it's the smell of rotten eggs. It seeps down my throat and settles in my chest, making me want to heave. My mouth fills with bile and as I shuffle back my hand hits something that clatters against the back of the dishwasher.

The zombie turns, lightning-fast, its face pointing in our direction.

Bee grabs my hand and squeezes as it moves closer to us, its mouth open wide, thin lips twitching as it smells us, tastes our fear.

My whole body is sweating and dark patches appear before my eyes. I'm going to pass out. But then another slam, and a scream, and the zombie turns, running out of the kitchen.

Bee and I scramble from the dishwasher, the screams tearing at us. Is it Rhea, or Amy?

'Turn the game off,' I say to Bee as we head back towards the machine.

It's still dark, but the moonlight shines through the big window at one end, and my eyes have adjusted enough for us to see into the gloom of the arcade's top floor. It's eerily quiet, all of the zombies – and Rhea and Amy – have disappeared.

'Where are they?' Bee whispers as we creep along as quickly and quietly as we can.

I don't know and I don't like it.

All too soon I'm cutting the cord to the game, breaking through the protecting rubber before snipping each wire. Bee stands in front of the screen, watching it.

'It's off!' she says. 'Level Seven has disappeared.'

Relief washes over me unlike anything I've experienced before. My body goes from hot to cold, and I want to cry and laugh at the same time. But before I can do any of those things I hear another scream. It's Bee, and her scream is followed by a zombie's shrieks.

It didn't work.

I watch as my best friend wriggles beneath a zombie twice her size, helpless. Except she's Bee the Bold and manages to hold it back with a frying pan, while its claws reach dangerously close to her skin. Its mouth is open wide, wider than Bee's entire head. It's going to bite it off, like a lollipop.

No! I launch myself at the zombie and hold the scissors with two hands, slamming them down into the zombie's brain. It judders, then falls sideways. Bee crawls out from under it. Her whole body is shaking and she turns away to be sick.

She's sobbing, and I hold her to me. 'It's OK, you're OK. Did it scratch or bite you?'

Bee sobs a couple more times, and sniffs, before

stuttering, 'N-no.'

Relief washes over me.

I give Bee a moment, watching out for any other zombies, before pulling her up. 'Come on, let's find the other two.'

We stand back to back, weapons at the ready, and circle around until we reach the play pit to the right of the stairs. There I find Amy's clown suit, discarded, along with Rhea's phone. I pick it up, hoping maybe there's an app for the lights in the arcade, but it's smashed to pieces.

At least she won't post the video online, I think, before immediately feeling guilty that my first thought wasn't whether Rhea and Amy are OK.

Bee and I barely have time to catch our breath before another zombie shriek comes from behind us, and I turn to see a figure rush at us from the gloom.

'Go!' I shove Bee ahead of me, which happens to be the play pit slide. She climbs up, her shoes gripping on the plastic and I get high enough before I feel the zombie slam into it, making the whole thing shake. Then I hear its nails clatter against the plastic as it climbs up after us.

Bee makes it to the top, and I follow, but then

my foot slides and I lose my grip, falling backwards.
I feel claws pull at my shoes and Bee screams, 'No!'

She grabs my hand, pulling so hard it feels like
my arms might leave their sockets. I kick at the
zombie, managing to shake it off before Bee finds
the strength to pull me up.

Then we somehow navigate the maze of the
play pit, with the zombie right behind us.

'If we go to the rope bridge, we can climb down
through it into the ball pit,' I say to Bee. I can hear
the zombie climbing up the slide and it won't be
much longer before it catches up. 'I think it'll be
too small for it.'

'Where?' Bee asks, with no time to reject my
plan.

'Left, then right.' I've been coming here since
I was young enough to play in that ball pit.

As Bee climbs down the first level of the rope
bridge, which zigzags downwards, the clattering
stops and is followed by the muffled steps of the
zombie moving over the padded floor. It's
catching up.

Bee manages to move with speed and I follow,

feeling the zombie reach the rope just as I slip my head beneath the first level.

Its legs fall through and it panics, scrambling around, tearing up the cushioned mats. It screeches for help, and I don't know where the others might be. No time to rest.

Bee launches herself into the ball pit, and I fall behind her.

We're safe for the moment, until I feel movement from beneath the surface. I scramble out, like we're in shark-infested waters.

Something bursts from the ball pit and for a moment I think it's another zombie, until I see it's Amy, her face streaked with tears and sweat.

'Jeez, Amy, way to make an entrance,' Bee snaps.

I expect a retort, but Amy's silent. Her whole body is quivering.

People talk about fight or flight in scary situations but they forget about freeze. That's Amy right now.

'Where's Rhea?' I ask, encouraging Amy out of the ball pit and towards a hidden corner, away from the struggling zombie. She follows like a well-behaved dog on a leash.

'Who knows,' Amy says flatly. 'Probably gone. You know she left them to eat me, right?'

My stomach jolts. 'What?'

Amy sniffs, and I just about see her hands reach for her face.

'We were running and Rhea fell over just before we got to the stairs. The zombies were about to get her when she called for me. I went back – *of course* I went back. As I was helping her up, as soon as she got steady, she pulled me down and let the zombies swarm.' Amy takes a shaky breath. 'It was the clown suit that saved me. They were on top of it, but I managed to drag myself out and hide in the ball pit. Eventually they gave up looking and went downstairs.'

'Do you know where the control room is?' I snap. I don't have time to comfort her when we're still in danger. And I'm not sure I want to, after what she did to me and Bee. Keep her safe, sure. But that's it.

Amy nods, sniffing. 'By the counter in the chippy. The code is five-nine-three-four.'

I peer around the room, looking for a solution. My eyes rest on the elevator. The lights are on. 'It's still working!' I say to Bee. 'Must be on battery power or something.'

'Five-nine-three-four,' Bee says, repeating the code Amy just uttered. 'Let's go.'

'Hey!' Amy calls. 'Don't leave me!' But we ignore her. She's safe enough for now, if she hides. But if we let the zombies out while it's still dark, who knows what'll happen? The whole town could become zombified in a few hours.

It feels like it takes a thousand years for the elevator doors to open. But when they do they're in emergency mode, heading only to the ground floor, which is fine because that's where we need to go.

I think back to the game, and riding up on the elevator, zombies breaking through at every floor. But that doesn't happen here, we're safe . . . Until we reach the ground floor.

The first thing I see as the elevator doors slide open is Rhea disappearing outside the front. She's gone, leaving us behind in this building to die. The next thing I see is half a dozen zombies turn their heads as the elevator lets out a *ping* to let us know we've reached our destination. Kind of like we've been microwaved and are ready to eat.

'I'll clear a path for you,' I say to Bee, waving the frying pan in front of me to deter the zombie at the front. 'You . . . go . . .'

It's hard to speak and fight at the same time, and Bee hesitates.

'Are you sure?' Of course she's asking this. She's Bee the Bold. But I'm the one who knows this game.

'We don't have time to debate this.' I grit my teeth.

As I face the zombies head on, I think of the mask that terrified me when I was seven; I think of Amy's clown suit that scared me earlier tonight; I think of Rhea's cruel laugh and the fear of embarrassment. And I swallow it all down and turn it into something different: anger.

I launch myself at the zombies, frying pan waving, blowtorch burning through the air. They screech and move backwards, afraid of my fire, just enough for Bee to slide through and run. A couple of the zombies turn in her direction, but I smash the frying pan at the wall to create a diversion. It works. They're focused on me now. All of them.

I manage to hold them off for a bit longer until the zombie at the front swipes the blowtorch away, missing my skin by centimetres. My health slips down, down, down to five per cent. With just the frying pan to protect me, they push back, forcing me into the claustrophobic confines of the lift.

One, two, three of them are upon me.

I wait for the pain of their scratches to tear at me, something to tell me it's Game Over.

Then the first zombie's mouth opens wide, an abyss sucking me in. Its sharp teeth are dripping with gooey saliva, and I wonder if it's going to hurt, or if I'll just slip into unconsciousness. But I'm determined to fight until the end. I won't hide this time. I lock eyes with the zombie and push against it with all my might, until my limbs burn. It's stronger than me, inching closer and closer, until . . .

The weight lifts from me. I wonder, for a split second, if I'm dead. A ghost.

The stars from the game have disappeared from my vision. The zombies are gone. And light returns to the arcade. It's over. We won.

It takes me a moment to stand up, my legs like jelly.

We survey the damage: destroyed arcade machines, tables turned over, and the emergency-exit sign flickering, half off the wall.

'We did it,' I say. 'Bee the Bold and Nada the Knowing.'

'More like Nada the Bold and Knowing,' Bee says, squeezing my hand, like always.

PART FIVE
GAME OVER

O n Monday morning everyone's talking about how Rhea trashed her dad's arcade and isn't allowed to invite anyone over again. Guess they're not proud of her any more.

'Nada!' Rhea calls, rushing up to my locker. 'Hey, Bee,' she grins, sickly sweet. Though her smile is a little too wide, and her eyes look hollow.

We say nothing. Amy stands, arms crossed, by the wall opposite. She looks at Rhea with pure hatred and I don't blame her.

'Just wanted to say, um, thank you for the other night. I was . . . Um, well, you know I was going to get help, right?'

Bee raises her eyebrows. 'Sure.'

'Well, anyway.' Rhea pulls me in for a hug and I smell it: rotten eggs. 'Thank you.'

Once this would've been a dream, for Rhea to want to be friends with me. Not now.

She hugs Bee too and her blazer sleeve slides up. I see, on her forearm, three diagonal gashes.

They got her.

As she walks away – a weird, shuffling walk –
and Amy saunters off in the other direction, I turn
to Bee. She noticed it too.

Tonight is the third night of transformation.
Rhea will be a full zombie tomorrow.

We don't need to say anything to each other.
We know what we have to do.

THE LIGHT BULB

Rachel Delahaye

THE LIGHT BULB

Rachel Delahaye

A scream pierced the air, and its tortured echo crept beneath the shed door of number 6 Lucklands Road. Otto gripped Avery's hand so tightly it hurt.

The first time, it had taken her by surprise. Otto Newell, the Year 9 football legend, had a reputation for being as tough as nails and as charming as an old-time movie star. But alone in the dark, they'd shared secrets. The Emo and the Footballer. He'd begun to understand more about her 'weirdo skin' and she'd got to know the real him. Like, he couldn't sit still and was scared of the dark.

'It's going to be OK,' she whispered.

'Well, that's a lie.'

Hazel Beech, the Keen One – a girl with two

trees in her name and all the sensitivity of a wooden spoon – had crashed their hiding place a week ago. She wasn't welcome, but you can't turn away someone who's running from death, can you? Besides, she was older and knew stuff. Hazel was practical from her red hair right down to her ankle socks. And smart too. It'd been Hazel who had thought of black-out curtains so they could safely light a match; Hazel who knew by the age of a house if it had a cellar; Hazel who had placed tea lights in a bowl under a metal grille so they could heat a pan of water. Hazel was useful. It was just a shame she was such a pain in the bum.

'Honesty is always the best policy,' Hazel said, sensing Avery's fury. 'You can roll your eyes all you want, but it's true.'

Hazel also had a way of knowing what you were doing, even in the dark.

'I'm lighting a match,' said Otto.

'Why don't we save it for when we need it?' Avery suggested gently.

'You're just saying that because you like holding my hand in the dark.'

'Otto, you're the one who's holding mine.'

'Listen.' Hazel's condescending voice made

Avery's teeth itch. 'You're going to have to start using your head more. There might come a time when I'm not here —' Avery squeezed Otto's hand as a cue to hold his tongue, although she was having trouble holding her own — 'and you're going to need to be more practical about things. Because —'

Hazel's lecture was broken as another louder scream cut through the skies like a razor blade before rasping, curdling with death. Avery leaped to the shed door.

'Don't go out there,' Otto begged.

She opened it a crack and peered out. Shapes criss-crossed the road in the charcoal light. People were shouting, 'They're coming!'

Hazel appeared at her side. 'They're here. We have to go.'

'Do we?' Otto whimpered.

Avery felt for his hand again, to help pull him to his feet.

'See? You're in love with me,' he teased, but his voice trembled and she could feel the cold sweat between his fingers.

'Run!' ordered Hazel.

Otto was a winger, fast and tall, and Avery's love of parkour made her nimble; out here in the stagnant gloom they were equals. But Hazel could outrun them both. Her speed had taken them by surprise. Her long legs took big strides, covering twice the ground they did, like some bionic Wonder Woman.

'Keep up!' Hazel hissed. 'And don't trip.'

They knew the streets like the backs of their hands, but everything was confusing now. Under the permanent cloud cover, every view looked like a badly taken photo: strange, grainy, dingy and littered with obstacles, pitfalls, traps. And when night fell, it was so much worse. And night was coming.

'Everyone is running that way,' Otto said, tugging Avery's shirt.

'Hazel – that way?' Avery called.

'No,' came the answer.

'But –'

Hazel stopped and put her hands on her hips. 'Trust me. It's not a team game.'

They turned to see large, spindly shadows sweeping behind the crowds, rounding them up like sharks on a bait ball. Hazel was right, as usual. Here there was no safety in numbers.

As they ran on, the townscape thinned out. The spaces between houses got wider. Roads stretched into the distance. There were fewer places to hide out in the open, but the creatures had all followed the people – the meat – so the trio risked a stop to catch their breath.

'Do you think our parents are hiding together?' Otto panted.

Avery and Otto were next-door neighbours; their parents disappeared the night of the first mega-storm, along with all the other adults who met in the street to discuss the power outage and gaze at the cloud-filled sky.

'They're probably dead. Mine are,' Hazel said.

Avery's stomach twisted in fury. There were times when honesty could wait. But it was too late now. Hazel's words had smashed into her heart, breaking the protective shell she'd built around it. The thought of her parents, skewered and devoured by one of those things, crept through the cracks. She hiccupped back the pain and tears. She heard Otto cracking his knuckles.

'Don't listen to her,' Avery said.

'I'm fine,' Otto snapped as he sometimes did when he thought he was showing weakness. Avery didn't mind. He'd be holding her hand again before long. 'Just thirsty, that's all.'

Hazel passed around her water bottle and they ran on. They had to put space between them and the things. Things that arrived with the gloom. Things that had been stalking Burnston, and perhaps the whole of Burnshire county – who knew? Without Internet, television, radio, they had no way of finding out. In front of them, the countryside rolled like a wide, grey sea.

'What's that over there?' Otto pointed at a blocky silhouette.

'Looks like a petrol station,' said Hazel.

'There might be provisions,' said Avery, thinking of tea lights and warm drinks.

'And torches.'

Otto wanted light to see, but it had another purpose. The things – the *beasts* – were scared of it. When the batteries had run out, that's when they'd grown confident. Not waiting in the shadows, but entering houses to hunt. In darkness there was opportunity.

The door to the station shop was open and they entered carefully. Hazel went straight to the back, where penknives and lighters were usually kept, while Avery and Otto felt their way along the shelves, trying not to rustle packets or drop noisy cans. It became harder as night closed in and the shadows and silhouettes melted together.

Crunch.

Avery froze. 'Otto? Are you eating crisps?'

Crunch.

'Stop it, Otto!'

'Why do you think it's me? I thought it was *you* scratching your weirdo skin.'

'No, but thanks for bringing it up.' Avery's hand instinctively moved to the patch of eczema below her ear, which flared when she got stressed.

Crunch.

'Hazel, is that you?'

There was no answer. Avery and Otto instinctively dropped to the floor and they crawled on hands and knees to the cashier's desk and hid beneath it, hearts pulsing in their ears as the crunching grew louder. There was a slow creak. The door was opening. Footsteps thudded.

Where was Hazel?

Avery squeezed her eyes, but it didn't shut out the terrible image of a drooling skeletal creature, claws like knife racks, jaws like a shark. Her eczema itched like crazy. Not scratching it was agony. Next to her, Otto was quaking so much she thought he might shatter, like glass. Like a rockfall, there was a rush of sound – bony claws clattering on the tiled shop floor, accompanied by the terrorizing gargle of saliva-filled mouths. Display stands began to fall as the creatures looked for the humans they could smell. One after the other. *Crash*. *Crash*. Closer. *Crash*.

Fingernails dug into Avery's shoulder and a hand clamped over her mouth. A voice, barely audible, whispered in her ear. *Follow me.*

Avery nudged Otto and passed on Hazel's message. *Follow me.*

They scrambled through the stockroom door, and Hazel quickly slammed it against the smash and crash of tills hitting the floor where, only seconds ago, they'd been hiding. There was no time to lose. The monsters were just metres away. Avery slid the bolt across – for what good it would do – and followed Otto and Hazel through the fire door on the opposite wall. They burst out into the open, into the mechanics' yard. Behind them, the creatures' screeches ricocheted off the tiled floors and concrete walls.

'No need to thank me,' Hazel said with absolute sincerity.

'Fine with me,' Otto replied. 'What now?'

'They'll smell us. We'll never outrun them in the dark,' Avery gasped.

'I'm the brains, remember?' Hazel said. 'You never execute one step of a plan without already having worked out the next. See that dark patch in the distance? That's probably Burnshire National Forest. Head there. I'll catch you up shortly. Listen for my whistle.'

Before they could protest, Hazel had disappeared around the corner, back towards the forecourt of the petrol station.

'Where did she go?' Otto said.

'I don't know,' said Avery. 'But although it pains me, we should definitely do as she says.'

They set off across the dark blanket of fields, running free but with nerves frayed by their vulnerability. It was never-ending; the terror of being hunted was always biting at their ankles, and the thought of those who had perished . . . Avery's descent into dark thoughts was broken by Hazel's whistle. She appeared alongside them, accompanied by a sloshing sound and the sharp stink of fuel.

'Stop and watch.' She sparked a small bunch of matches.

'You idiot! They'll see us now,' Otto shouted.

'Keep cool, or they'll hear us first,' Avery whispered.

Hazel dropped them to the ground. The flames picked up the trail of petrol she'd trickled from the pumps and crept forward, getting bigger, brighter, taller, faster. The fire rushed towards the petrol station, briefly revealing a clutch of monsters – hideously contorted, spindly, angular, tall as lamp posts. They gnashed at the fire, needle teeth flicking like switchblades.

'And now we really, really need to get as far away as possible. I don't have to tell you that petrol and fire . . .'

'Kaboom,' said Otto.

'It's not the terminology –'

'But it's not wrong,' Avery finished. 'Run!'

As the flames scurried in one direction, they fled in the other, reaching a safe distance just as the petrol station *kaboom*-ed. Ferocious fire mushroomed into the air, and the heat blew against their skin. For a few seconds the sky was a blanket of orange and yellow.

'R.I.P., monsters!' Otto said, whooping for joy.

'R.I.P., us, if we don't get out of here,' Avery

said. 'As soon as the fire dies, others will come.'

They stumbled across the fields, falling over tufts and clumps and uneven ground as the light was sucked back out of the sky, the explosion exhausted. And then came the skittering shriek. The call of the beasts.

'They didn't all die,' Hazel said flatly. Her voice was uncharacteristically shaky.

'So what next, genius?' Otto yelled as he picked himself up from a tumble. 'Come on, Hazel. If you're so smart, tell us what the next step is.'

'If it wasn't for me, you'd have got munched back there,' she snapped.

'Great. Now I can get munched out here! You didn't kill them, you just made them angry!'

'You two, stop it!' Avery hissed. 'We have to work together. Let's hold hands – we're more likely to stay upright that way. And walking would be safer. Fast walking.'

'If we walk, our feet can adjust better to the terrain,' Hazel said.

'Yes, that's why I said it,' Avery said with a growl.

They trekked onwards, and although the air was thick with fear, the shrieks had died down. Apart from the wind in the grasses and the soft rasp of their soles on the ground, it was silent. It felt as if they were the only ones left in the world – like safety was just up ahead. They just had to keep going.

'Stop, I heard something,' Hazel said.

They froze, straining to hear beyond the whistling breeze.

'Shhh! There it is again.' Hazel paced, like she was trying to pick up a signal.

Sheeeeeek.

They all heard it, then. A noise that screeched like truck brakes, then rattled and gargled like gravel in a barrel. Not a cry of frustration, but one of hunger . . . and close. Too close. All this time, they hadn't been clear – they'd been stalked.

Avery looked over her shoulder to see spiky, inky silhouettes scurrying towards them like spiders, with the speed of wolves. 'Oh no. Oh no.'

'I'm sorry.' Hazel's voice was meek. 'I miscalculated. I really am sorry.'

'It doesn't matter. Just run,' Avery said. 'RUN!'

They scrambled over the grasses, hearts in throats, chests burning from lack of air. The beasts clacked and rattled like bones in a bag. Gaining on their meal. Teeth scissoring. The lactic acid burned in the children's muscles as they forced their legs on, panting, crying, moaning. One slip and they'd be dead.

Then Otto fell. Avery heard the thud and saw his shape crumpled on the ground just ahead of her.

'My ankle!'

'Up, up, Otto. You've got to get up! Help us, Hazel. Hazel?'

But Hazel had either taken flight or . . . Avery tried to prop Otto up but he threw her off.

'Go on without me,' he cried.

'Don't be stupid.'

'What's the point?' he wailed. 'I'm no use to anyone. Everyone knows that. I'm not clever. I'm not brave, like you.' He sobbed as if he'd just unburdened himself of a weight, not as if he was about to be eaten.

'If I leave Burnshire's star winger to die, they'll never forgive me. Come on, I'll support you.'

'But you're a girl,' he spluttered.

'Great observation skills. I'm not leaving without you, so get up or my skeleton will tell everyone you suck.'

Avery tensed in preparation for his weight, but Otto was surprisingly light. More sinew than muscle. She ran with him, lopsided but steadily, towards the forest, where she saw a small flame spark and die in the first line of trees. Then another. It was guiding them.

Hazel's half whisper sailed to them. 'Come on, you can do it!'

Propelled by another skittering shriek from the fields behind, Avery found a burst of energy to run the remaining distance.

'I thought you'd left us,' she panted.

'Of course not,' Hazel said. 'Where should we go now?'

Hazel's earlier mistake had shaken her up, made her uncertain. It was Avery's turn to take charge. 'Deep into the forest. It's our only chance.'

'Yes. The trees will slow them down,' Hazel agreed, regaining some confidence.

'Which is why I said it,' Avery tutted.

'Yes, sorry.'

Skeeeeech.

They thrashed through the dense thicket. Branches scratched their faces and whipped their bodies; it would be nothing compared to the cleave of the creatures' teeth if they caught up. And they *were* catching up. The trees didn't slow the monsters; they swung through the branches like monkeys. Skittering, clacking, gnashing. The sounds pulsed through the forest, ripped through the vegetation, echoed in their eardrums.

'Help me with Otto!' Avery shouted. 'Hazel!'

Hazel turned, cheeks slippery with tears. 'I don't want to die! Please, I don't want to die!'

'Hazel, get a grip!'

'There's a light.'

The calmness of Otto's voice made them stop. Yes, there was a small beam – a pinprick through the trees. Not flickering like a match or swaying like a torch. It was constant. True.

'That's electricity!' Hazel yelled. 'Electricity!'

Avery wondered if it was some kind of mirage, like desperate people imagine water in the desert. But as they ran towards it, the light got bigger and brighter. And then they were standing in a clearing in front of a small cabin. A single light bulb shone through its window.

All three of them pummelled the door as the excited creatures chattered and buzzed like grasshoppers behind them, held back by the glow but ready to pounce the minute the light went out.

'Please! Open up!' Hazel shrieked.

There was a metallic *clunk, clunk, clink*. The door opened and they crashed through it and fell in a heap on the rug behind. The owner of the house quickly closed the door behind them and slid the locks back into place.

Dazed, Avery, Otto and Hazel looked around them. It was a small space, but it was a home. Warm and light, with sofas, carpets and good smells. Jazz music crackled from an old record player.

'Well, well. I wasn't expecting visitors. What a delight. Why don't you come in? I'm Clementine. But call me Clem.'

Clementine was an older woman with long brown hair, greying, and blue eyes that twinkled beneath hooded eyelids. Her jeans were baggy and her oversized cardigan with a wonky snowflake pattern made her look soft and motherly. Avery was sure she saw tears in Otto's eyes. She felt like crying too. They were safe. They were *safe*.

'You're safe now,' said Clementine, nodding, as if she knew they needed to hear it. 'Come on. Sit yourselves down. I'll get Dan to rustle up some food. Doesn't look as if you've had anything healthy in a while.'

'Ravioli,' Otto said blankly. 'In tins.'

Clementine clasped her hands. 'You are the future. You need healthy food and good sleep.'

Avery groaned longingly at the mention of sleep. For a month, since it all began, she felt as if she'd only ever been on the edge of it, her body always ready to run at a moment's notice, with shed walls and hard floors as her pillows and mattresses.

They sat at the table, and Dan – a man with a barrel chest and a long thick beard – brought over a tureen of rich tomato soup, which he ladled into bowls, and a plate piled high with thickly sliced buttered bread. They ate a whole bowl each before looking up. Meeting each other's eyes and grinning. The bowls were refilled, and Clementine and Dan began to ask about their journey, gasping as they heard how the children had come within an inch of death, spending days in cramped cellars, nights curled up on filthy garage floors.

'No more of that. You'll have a mattress each,' Clementine said. 'Pillows, blankets, hot-water bottles if you want them. Although the others create enough warmth up there, so you may not need them.'

'Others?' Hazel said. 'Other whats? Cats? I'm allergic.'

'Children, just like you.' Clem put her finger to her lips. 'They're sleeping right now, but you'll get to meet them tomorrow.'

'You rescue children?' Avery marvelled. 'You're like a Disney character!'

Dan and Clem chuckled. 'When it first started – when the lights went out – Dan made trips into town with his truck and trailer and brought back as many orphans and their belongings as he could manage,' Clem said, reaching across the table for her partner's hand. 'Now they have safety. And schooling. We're keen to see that education continues and you're fully prepared when the world goes back to normal.'

'Really?' Hazel brightened.

'But how come you have a home in the forest?' Otto said, dropping his spoon with a clatter. He reddened and Avery felt sorry for him.

'Yes, how come?' she said quickly, to cover his nerves.

'I bought it years ago as a hunting lodge.' Dan's voice was gravelly and sweet, like crystallized honey. Avery noticed a mounted deer head on the wall behind him. 'But I haven't shot a deer in decades,' he added, noticing her fallen face. 'Not since meeting Clem. She told me it was a mean thing to do.'

'That's right,' Clem said. Avery smiled and Clem winked back. 'If you're a fan of pain, then you've got no brain. That's what I told him.'

'Speaking of brains, how were you all doing at school before the . . .?' Dan tipped his chin at the window where the light bulb stood guard.

'I'm in the football team,' Otto said brightly. 'That's all I was good at, really.'

Clem and Dan nodded politely before looking at Avery.

'Art's my favourite topic,' she said. 'I want to go to art school, and . . .' She trailed off.

They'd already shifted their attention to Hazel who was sitting bolt upright as if her moment had come.

'I'm pretty good at everything. I've got at least fifty achievement certificates.' She had a ring of tomato soup round her mouth. Clementine passed her a napkin and nodded for her to continue. 'And I –'

'I got picked for the Burnshire Young Artists Exhibition,' Avery said hurriedly, wanting once more to be the object of Clem's warmth. 'I'm doing a portrait. Of a historical figure. And, um, and Otto plays football for the county.'

'That's nice.' But Clementine looked back at Hazel. 'What subjects do you like?'

'Maths. And science. I get to represent the school when distinguished guests come to visit.'

'Wonderful,' Clementine said. 'Isn't it, Dan?'

Dan nodded. 'Do your good grades come naturally, or do you have to work hard?'

'She's a genius,' Otto said, and Avery guessed he'd piped up just to get a word in. 'Everything comes naturally to her.'

'Well, not really.' Hazel looked bashfully into her soup bowl. 'I want to be a genius when I grow up, but I'm still in training for that.'

Avery let out a hoot. 'You don't get to become a genius. You either are or you aren't.'

'Now, now,' Clementine tutted. 'Seems to me you're a bit tired. Bedtime.'

Avery blushed with shame but saw, with relief, that Clementine was still smiling. Although Dan was looking at Otto strangely, like he wasn't to be trusted. Why? Apart from the spoon incident, he'd been the politest Avery had ever seen him. Maybe Dan wasn't a football fan.

Under strict instructions to keep quiet, they followed Clem and Dan upstairs. The attic room stretched the full length of the cabin and the floor was covered in mattresses, squashed alongside each other. There must have been forty, and half of them were full of sleeping children.

Avery ran her eyes over the figures, as still as statues beneath their blankets. Clem and Dan had rescued all these children! The lucky ones that got away, found safety and warmth and foster parents who would prepare them for the new world. Imagine if they'd never found this place. Imagine if they were still out there, running in the darkness. The never-ending darkness.

They were given mattresses next to one another, and Avery's body suddenly ached with tiredness; she was sure to go out like a light. Clementine and Dan stood in the corner of the room while they settled, watching them like contestants on *The World's Strictest Parents*. But it wasn't annoying. Avery found it comforting being cared for.

Otto slipped into sleep first, emitting his strange slumbering nose-whistle. Then Hazel, who had been huffing as she found a comfortable sleeping position, suddenly stilled. But Avery's eczema woke, as it sometimes did at night when there were no distractions, and in their hurry to leave Burston, she'd left her aqueous cream behind. The troubled patches of skin started to burn from inside, as if her body was a furnace. And then she was wide awake again, scratching and listening to the dormitory sighs and simpers. Then there was a voice.

Avery couldn't make out what was being said, and raised herself on her elbows. A child had got up – he looked young, and Clem and Dan ushered him out. Perhaps he'd had nightmares and they were going to give him cocoa. As the door opened, a shaft of light from outside the room fell on Otto's face. He woke up.

'Avery? I need the loo,' he whispered. 'Like, *really*.'

'I think it's downstairs. I'll come with you.' As she got up, she nudged Hazel's arm, which had flopped over on to her mattress.

'Wha–? Where are you going?' Hazel sounded groggy, as if her genius brain was in the process of turning to slime.

'Going to the loo.'

Hazel got up, as if it was an unwritten rule that

they did everything together, and they walked downstairs, feeling strangely elated. It was such a normal thing to do, but after everything they'd been through, this felt like absolute freedom — walking in light, without the soundtrack of cries and clattering claws, without looking over their shoulders.

'Are you thinking what I'm thinking?' Otto said.

'Is it *thank god we're alive*?' Avery asked.

'Yeah, that's it.'

'Me too,' said Hazel. 'And thank you for letting me tag along with you.'

Avery smiled. 'We're glad you did.'

'Yeah, cos the kaboom thing was brilliant,' Otto said.

'Phew. I was worried you thought I'd been a right pain in the bum.'

'Well —'

Avery pushed her finger against Otto's lips before he could ruin the moment.

The downstairs room was empty. The jazz record had finished and now lisped as it spun round, while a small fire crackled in the hearth and the light bulb in the window continued to glow. On the other side of that window were things, waiting for the moment it stopped working. But if there wasn't an electricity supply left, how did it work at all? Avery decided she'd ask in the morning, because right now, if there was any question she wanted to ask, it would be on the topic of hot cocoa.

'Where are they?' Hazel said, turning in circles.

Otto peered into the side kitchen. 'No one in there.'

'Over here.' Hazel had found a small door tucked in an alcove next to the fireplace. 'Do you think the loo's down there?'

'I'll have a look.' Avery opened the rickety door and peered through. 'There are steps.'

'I hope that's the bathroom, because if the loo's outside, I'll be holding it in forever,' Otto groaned.

'I'll check.' Avery went first, stopping abruptly halfway down.

There was whirring and clunking, like a restless prisoner in a cage.

'Do you think they've got a monster down there?' Otto said.

'Maybe Dan hasn't quite given up on his hunting!' Avery said with a chuckle. 'Only joking, it's probably a really old toilet system.'

Psssht clunk, psssht clunk – the sound, like an

old-fashioned steam locomotive, grew louder.

'Weird,' said Avery.

'Might be an electricity generator. My granddad has one on his farm. It's probably what's keeping the light bulb alight.'

'Clever Hazel,' said Avery, and she meant it. 'How does it work?'

Hazel blushed. 'I don't actually know. He did try to tell me but I got . . . bored.'

'High-five, sister!' Otto said, holding up his palm.

'Er, OK, *bro*,' Hazel giggled.

'Come on, *fam*,' Avery snorted. 'Let's find this bog.'

Mouth full of laughter, Avery pushed open the door at the bottom of the stairs. Her laughter stopped dead. Her tongue froze.

'What is it?' Hazel said, trying to see over her shoulder.

'Is it the most brilliant bathroom ever?' Otto said. 'Jacuzzi, gold taps?'

'Avery?'

'Torture.' The word hardly made it through Avery's dry lips. And it could barely be heard over the noise.

Psssht clunk, psssht clunk.

The basement room was long, and, facing them, rows of children sat behind desks. Papers, pencils, rulers. They wore blank expressions, their eyes red-sore. Plastic caps fixed to their heads spilled red and green wires that were hooked up in a spaghetti mass that travelled along the ceiling, twitching and writhing, to a machine on the back wall. The machine had switches and dials, and needles that danced between numbers. A green light glowed beneath a label: *output*.

The boy Avery had seen in the dormitory was there, too awake to sleep but too tired to be this awake. He lolled in his chair, eyelids flickering. His lack of concentration was met with the snap of a cane across the back of his hand. *Thwack!* The boy gasped. His eyes found focus. He bent over his papers. The welt on his hand began to redden.

Clementine had her back to the door.

Hearts crashing against their ribs, Avery, Hazel and Otto backed up the stairs quietly. But the bottom door shut with a loud creak and above them, in the doorway, a large figure was waiting.

'Get up here,' Dan growled. His voice wasn't honey any more. There was a hunting rifle in his hand.

They walked up the stairs and Avery noticed Otto's vein pulse in his throat, and saw Hazel's eyes stretch so wide it was a wonder they stayed in their sockets. Avery felt weirdly calm, part of her convinced this was a joke. It had to be a joke, right? They were safe. This was a safe place. The food, the warmth, the conversation . . .

They sat in silence around the dinner table and Dan stared through them as he waited for Clem. Otto's leg bounced under the table. Avery's eczema itched like hell. Hazel was now perfectly still, as if her brain had seized up.

Clementine appeared, cane in one hand, fixing her hair behind her ear with the other. And her smile was already in place, friendly and full of warmth. Avery's stomach turned, overcome with repulsion for this imposter carer.

'You've met our generator. Rather earlier than scheduled,' Clementine puffed, pulling out a chair and falling into it with a thump. 'But there we are.'

'You kids should've been asleep,' Dan growled, eyes narrowing.

'What's done is done, Dan.' Clementine's tone was way too light for the occasion. 'Let me explain: our brainwave machine is what keeps our light bulb burning. Without it, we'd all be dead.' On the word 'dead' she whipped the table with her cane. 'To keep the light on, we need a constant supply of brainwaves.'

'You're tearing brainwaves out of their heads?' Otto squeaked.

'No,' Hazel said wearily. 'They're using the power of brain activity to create electricity. Just like harvesting wind or sunshine.'

Clementine clapped her hands. 'She's got it, Dan. Isn't that wonderful?'

'So you expect us to sit and think about stuff?' Otto sounded dismayed.

'That's right. Twelve hours a day, sums and logic. Not much to ask for the right to live, is it?' She blinked happily.

'What do you mean, *the right to live*?' Avery watched as Dan checked his gun.

'Well, you have a choice, poppets. You can work and live. Or you can die. You didn't think we were running a holiday home, did you?' she hooted. Then her face dropped. 'And we can't allow you to go back and tell everyone. That wouldn't do. Not that you'd survive one minute out there.' She raised her hands like monster claws, then tipped her head back and laughed.

Otto jabbed Avery in the leg over and over. She saw his eye twitch. The gulp of his Adam's apple. She nodded. She understood. It would be torture for him. For her too. Strapped down. Forced from work to sleep, sleep to work. No talking. No play.

'I'll give you to the count of three,' Clementine said. Dan raised his gun and looked down the barrel at Otto. 'One.'

Avery flicked her eyes around the room, looking for an escape.

'Two.'

One door to the kitchen, one door up to the dorms. One door down to the basement, one door out – out into the woods. Certain death. They were trapped.

'Thr–'

'Sounds good to me,' Hazel said brightly, as if she'd just been offered pudding. 'Doesn't it?'

As Hazel looked at them, Avery saw her give them a subtle conspiratorial wink.

'I know Avery and Otto will be just as keen as me,' Hazel continued, giving them a faint nod. *Go along with it*.

'Absolutely. I choose life over death any day.

Right, Otto?' Avery pinched him under the table and gave him an unnaturally large smile.

'Uh-huh.'

'Wonderful. Isn't it wonderful, Dan?' Clementine clicked her tongue happily. 'I'll go and check on the workforce. You kids get some rest for tomorrow's shift.'

She scuttled down to the basement, and Dan, the rifle lying across his arms like a baby, jerked his head upwards, at the dormitory room.

Hazel leaped to her feet. 'You know what? I'm just too wide awake now. These two are tired, but I may as well work while my brain's still buzzing.'

Dan looked at her suspiciously.

'Up to you,' Hazel said. 'But there really is no point in lying in bed and staring at the ceiling and letting all these brainwaves go to waste.'

There was a soft hiss as a moth burned itself against the light bulb in the window.

Dan continued to stare at her, as if trying to work her out.

'Come on, what are we waiting for? You know, I reckon I could make more brainpower than all those other kids put together. Can we make it a contest?' Hazel leaped across the room and tugged his arm. 'We could put a chart on the wall. Go on, Dan, *go on*!'

Hazel locked eyes with Avery for those last two words. *Go on*.

Avery carefully took Otto's hand in hers, and there was no smart comment this time. Just an understanding that something was about to happen. They couldn't mess it up.

As soon as Dan and Hazel had gone down the stairs, they attacked the bolts on the front door – sliding them back silently and swiftly. Avery spotted a bowl on the windowsill. It contained random items: keys, torches, matches. They filled their pockets and, with torches on full beam, slipped out into the night. From warmth to cold breeze, from carpet silence to howling and creaking.

The light bulb's scattered halo offered a thin protection as they tried to see which way to go. They searched the trees, looking for a glint of an eye, the sheen of saliva, but the forest shadows triggered goosebumps and the feeling of terror returned, closing in on them from all directions. They had to make a decision. Fast.

'What do we do?' Avery's head twisted at every forest noise. 'Otto. What do we *do*?'

'We ride.'

'What?' Avery looked where Otto was staring. To the right, where a tarpaulin was flapping, revealing a wheel beneath. 'A motorbike? We don't know how to ride one.'

'Speak for yourself,' Otto said, searching the keys in his hand. He held one up triumphantly. 'My uncle has a bike. He may have given me some secret lessons.'

'*No use to anyone*,' Avery tutted playfully. 'Right now, you're the most useful person alive.'

They stripped back the cover and Otto leaped on, getting the key in place, waiting for Avery. As she mounted, her foot skidded on a carpet of wet leaves, revealing a glowing glass panel in the ground underneath – a floor window into the basement room. Avery peered in and gasped.

Beneath their feet, a girl with red hair was at a desk, wired up to the machine.

As if she could sense them, Hazel raised her watering eyes and slowly blinked goodbye. Avery mouthed 'thank you' and silently promised to return with help. Then she wrapped her arms around Otto's waist and squeezed.

'Knew it! You love me,' he laughed, revving the

engine.

The front door banged. Then *crack*, a bullet knocked Avery's torch clean out of her hand – *Dan!* – and in the momentary darkness a thin leathery limb brushed against her face. She grabbed Otto's torch from his back pocket and pointed it at the beast. It shrieked as it withdrew, but not before she saw its red eyes, its dripping jaws.

'Go, go, go,' Avery yelped.

The bike roared towards the trees as another bullet dusted its wake. They changed direction, skidding, zigzagging until the light bulb was swallowed by gloom. Until they were free of the forest. Until, apart from the engine's whine and the blue headlight that danced ahead of them, everything was black and silent.

They crossed the fields without a word and hit the ink-black road that headed north. Not knowing how far the petrol or their one torch would last. Knowing only that they had left the light for the dark.

TALOS SPRINGS

Elle McNicoll

TALOS
SPRINGS

Elle McNicoll

I call them the Magpies.

I watch them from my window, high up in the Nursery. I can see all of Talos Springs from here, but that's hardly difficult. It's a small town in the middle of nowhere so there is not very much to see. In the nine years that I've lived in the Nursery, Talos Springs has always remained predictable. The snow always falls on the 30th November and clears up by the 2nd February. It rains in April. It gets unbearably hot in July and then grows crisp in September. While seasons are always easy to predict, Talos Springs is a town that runs its weather changes like clockwork. As if someone is monitoring the environment like a train guard.

The Magpies live in the townhouse on the street with the birch trees, across from the mechanic. The other children and I can see them from our windows. They come out of their fancy house, always wearing black and white, and they make their way here, to the Nursery. He always wears a suit and her hair is always pinned up. They usually just look around, ask a few questions, and then leave. But a month ago they came in and chose Evie.

Evie was my friend. I see the Magpies from my window occasionally. But I never see Evie.

'James?'

Mrs Devol calls my name but I don't move from my seat by the window. It's raining but I can still make out the Magpies as they cross the street and head towards the small farmers' market.

'I don't think Mr and Mrs Carnegie want you staring at them all day from our windows, James,' Mrs Devol says, and her tone is accusatory.

'Why do they never have Evie with them?' I ask bluntly.

I don't need to turn around to look at her to know that she is watching me, figuring me out and trying to think of what she can say to reassure me that my friend is fine.

'She'll be at their house,' is all Mrs Devol is able to say. 'That's where she lives now, James.'

I watch the Magpies disappear inside the market. So Evie is now a Magpie. Evie Magpie. Yet I never see her. She never comes out with them; they never step out together. I feel Mrs Devol place a hand on my shoulder and then she sits down next to me upon the window seat.

We look out at Talos Springs in the rain together.

'Someone will come for you one day, James,' she says gently. 'Boys like you are always harder to find homes for, but you won't be at the Nursery forever.'

I don't say anything. I watch Talos Springs and all of the strange people on the streets below.

I don't know if I want to leave here. There's something wrong with the people out there.

And I'm going to find out what it is.

In the middle of the night, it's still raining. I'm not sure what wakes me up at first, but the other children in the room are still asleep. Our beds are in the attic and the rain is loudest up here. I turn over in bed, accepting that the heavy raindrops are probably what woke me.

Then I hear hushed and harried voices from the floor below.

'Just jump into your old bed, we'll come and get you in the morning. Don't wake anyone, just go to sleep.'

I frown, wondering who Mrs Devol is talking to. I hear footsteps on the stairs and quiet sobs, which Mrs Devol quickly hushes. I dare not sit up to see who it is, as they move into the room and climb into one of the empty beds.

'I'll come and get you in the morning,' Mrs Devol repeats, and she is standing so close to me I have to pretend to be asleep. 'Goodnight.'

She goes back downstairs. I hear the creak of the bottom step on the staircase and then count to ten. Only once everything has fallen back into early morning quiet do I open my eyes.

Evie. Evie is back in her bed. As if the last month hasn't happened. As if she never left.

'Evie?' I whisper her name frantically. 'Evie!'

The quiet sobs stop but she doesn't answer me.

'Evie, what happened? What's wrong? Why are you back?'

'James, don't,' she finally says. 'I can't.'

A floorboard creaks and more murmurs

downstairs stop me from pushing. But it's impossibly difficult. I have to know why she's back. No one has ever come back in the entire time I've been at the Nursery.

I don't fall back to sleep. Instead I listen as Mrs Devol comes up to the attic to wake Evie. Her words are spoken so softly I cannot make out what is being said, but Evie gets up and follows her dutifully downstairs. I'm tempted to follow but I stay in bed, straining to hear.

There is crying. Then what sounds like a scream. Then silence.

I'm almost too afraid to breathe. I don't even notice that the rain has stopped.

When I see Evie at the breakfast table the next morning, happily buttering toast, I feel like someone has pushed me down some steps.

'Evie!'

She glances up in surprise. 'Morning.'

'Don't give me good morning,' I snap, sitting at the table next to her and glancing about to make sure Mrs Devol isn't watching us. She's talking to Mr Devol, her calm and quiet husband, on the other side of the dining room. 'What happened last night?'

Evie frowns. 'What?'

'Or this morning,' I amend. 'Where did they take you? What happened?'

'Everything's fine,' she says carefully, and it's odd because she is looking at me as though I am mad. As though I have made all of this up in my head. 'I'm glad to be back.'

'Things didn't work out with the Magpies?' I ask.

She looks confused at that but before she can say anything, Mrs Devol approaches our table.

'How are you feeling this morning, Evie?'

'Good,' Evie says chirpily, smiling up at Mrs Devol.

I watch the two of them discuss the day ahead and I'm confused. Evie seems perfectly happy. Perfectly normal, even. I don't understand it.

I don't remember a time before Talos Springs and the Nursery. I've been here for most of my life, if not all of it. We're taught to cook and clean and take care of ourselves. We get to draw and play musical instruments. The food is excellent and the garden is huge.

But there's another house in town like the Nursery, right on the end of Main Street. It's a children's home. For children who need new families. Sometimes from the window I can see them leaving with new parents. Then I see them around town. I'll see them walking a dog or throwing a ball.

When children leave here, when they leave the Nursery, I never see them again.

Evie is the first one. And there's something strange about her return.

I'm at the window again this afternoon, watching the Magpies. They're having lunch outside a French restaurant. They're laughing and enjoying themselves, as if Evie never existed for them. As if they never came here to take her away. I think I hate them. Mrs Magpie sips her cappuccino and Mr Magpie waves his arms around while telling a story.

'I don't think they're human.'

I say the words aloud to myself for the first time. Until now, it's been an unsure thought in the side of my mouth, where my molars are. It's been hesitant and reluctant. Now, as I watch them enjoy their lunch beneath a parasol while Evie is back here, I feel brave enough to say it.

'If they're not human, what are they?' Mrs Devol sits beside me, her voice kindly and encouraging. She's humouring me.

'Maybe they're aliens,' I muse.

Mrs Devol is folding linen on her lap. She glances up to give me a warm smile. 'Aliens, is it?'

'Gotta be,' I reply. 'They came down from the sky and took over that couple's bodies. That's why they're so weird.'

'You don't think they're weird,' Mrs Devol says quietly. 'You think they're cruel, James.'

I'm sullen but I don't deny it. 'What else explains them sending Evie back in the middle of the night? Other than alien abduction, what could it be?'

'Not everyone in Talos Springs is as moral as you, my boy.'

'We aren't library books,' I say bitterly. 'You don't bring us back once you've finished with us.'

'James, you've never left the Nursery,' Mrs Devol says wearily. 'Maybe if you worried a little less about the others, and more about –'

'Why did Evie scream early this morning?' I ask sharply.

Mrs Devol's indulgent smile vanishes and she suddenly looks afraid. 'Pardon?'

'I heard Evie scream this morning. Only now she's acting like nothing's happened. So what's the truth?'

'James, since the day you learned the word "why", you've always been searching for answers that don't exist.'

'Evie screamed this morning and the people who sent her back here are sitting out there like nothing's wrong.'

'Nothing is wrong.'

'You're lying.'

'James! Stop.'

Her voice is coarse and cross, so I do. I stop talking and glare at her. I watch as her face transforms from anger to fear.

'You can't keep asking questions, James,' she says. I've never heard her sound so disillusioned. She is exhausted with me, but I don't really know why. 'You question things too much. It's not safe for you.'

Unsafe. I don't understand what she means. The Nursery is many things, but unsafe has never been one of them.

'Don't keep asking these questions, James. We've been down this road too many times.'

Evie is different. She behaves differently. Before the Magpies came to take her away, we were friends. Now she treats me like a new kid she barely knows. She used to always have meals with me and sit with me by the window whenever it rained. She doesn't now. I try to jog her memory but she just smiles at me with bemusement and then turns away.

The Magpies have changed her. Sent her back all wrong.

When Mrs Devol and I are at the window again, I make an effort to keep quiet about Evie.

'What's that shop by the market?' I ask, just to make conversation.

I thought it was a banal question but Mrs Devol sighs, as if the question is impertinent. 'That's the Workshop, James.'

'What do they make?'

'They make –' Mrs Devol chooses her words carefully – 'things to help people.'

'Medicine?'

'Not exactly.'

We watch as a family leave the Workshop. A little boy leaps about on the pavement. He looks about my age. He's delighted with something I can't quite see. As the family make their way further down the high street, it becomes clearer.

It's a little dog. Only it has no fur. No slobber. It's made of steel.

'Robots,' I say, frowning. I'm surprised I have never noticed this before. I sit by this window every day. 'That's a robotic dog.'

'Cyborgs,' Mrs Devol says with a slight shrug. 'People do love their technology.'

'Cyborgs,' I repeat. 'That's it.'

'That's what?'

'These weird people, the strangers I see from up here every day. That's why they're so inhuman. They're cyborgs.'

Mrs Devol laughs, but it is a shrill and nervous sound. 'Yesterday it was aliens, James. What will they be tomorrow? Zombies?'

'No, that's it,' I say. 'I'm right. They're not human. They're cyborgs. And they steal human memories; that's what they did to Evie –'

'That's enough, James.'

I am right, though. I watch the little cyborg dog follow its new family home and I feel vindicated. I feel excited. I know what they are. And they're not going to take any more of us.

The Magpies visit just as the snow starts to fall.

They walk around the Nursery in their odd, inhuman fashion. They have a child with them. It does not behave like we do. It is different, strange. We're all gathered in the dining room, having lunch, while they walk around. I glare at them. They don't know that I know what they are, but it's so obvious to me now. That strange sense of déjà vu I feel every time I see them is my gut picking up on the abnormal. The uncanny valley, I read about it in our library.

They're pretending to be human, like us, and it unnerves me.

'I know what you did to Evie.'

The whole room falls silent as I say the words. I almost cannot believe they came from me. I'm always against the wall, watching and observing. I like my window. I like being alone. Except for Evie. She was the only friend I ever had.

Which is why I must do this.

'What's the problem?' asks Mrs Magpie, her smile frozen on her face as she glances towards Mrs Devol, clearly expecting an explanation.

'He's unwell,' Mrs Devol says quickly, a panicked look entering her eyes. 'James? Shall we –'

'You did something to Evie and then you sent her back changed. You're not human. You're cyborgs. You're evil and I've known it since I first saw you –'

I feel a gentle pinch on the back of my head and then nothing.

I wake up in a darkened room with Mr and Mrs Devol looking down at me. They seem concerned. My head aches and it feels as though someone has been squeezing my upper arms. I try to sit but they stop me.

'James, we can't keep ending up back here.'

I blink in the dark. I must be somewhere within the Nursery but I don't know this room. I'm on a table and they're peering down at me with regretful expressions. I can't explain how I know, but I can tell that something is terribly wrong. Their energies are off. They are frightening me.

I leap up from the table and desperately skid about the small room, hunting for a door. They both stand in front of it.

'What's going on?' I finally ask, breathing heavily and glaring at the two of them. I trusted them. But they're involved. Whatever this is, they're involved.

'James,' Mr Devol speaks gently. 'This is the final time we can do this.'

'Do what?'

'Please sit back down,' Mrs Devol says calmly. 'You're not yourself.'

'Those people aren't like us, they're not human.'

'They are, sweetheart,' she says softly, looking at me like I'm dying and there is nothing she can do. 'They are as human as Mr Devol and me.'

I glance between the two of them, my suspicion morphing into paranoia. 'Then . . . maybe you're not . . . not –'

'James.' Mrs Devol speaks despairingly, sitting down in a chair that she backs against the door. She takes out a letter opener. She cuts a small mark in her palm and shows it to me. I watch the little swell of scarlet.

'You think we're cyborgs too?' she asks.

'No,' I say staring at the blood. 'But something is wrong.'

'Yes, dear,' she says, still sounding so mournful. 'As we said, we've been here before.'

'I don't understand.'

'Evie was returned because she wasn't a good fit for them. Just as you were not a good fit.'

I frown and it makes my head hurt even more. 'Me? Not a good fit . . . I don't understand.'

Mr Devol walks towards me, as if he's approaching an escaped animal. He takes my forearm and presses his thumb into a vein. I automatically flinch. I hate to be touched, I never like my arms being handled like this.

'They're not cyborgs, James, why would you think that?' he asks. His words are soft but his grip is firm.

'Because they're strange,' I say, though I'm feeling less and less sure now. 'And they did something to Evie.'

'They sent her back; she wasn't performing the way they needed her to.'

'You don't send back orphans when they don't perform!'

'Correct. Absolutely right, James. But none of you are orphans.'

I feel a chill, despite the heat of his hand. I look to Mrs Devol for some reassurance or an explanation but she still looks shaken and sad.

'What?'

'There's a children's home down the street. For real children. The Nursery is not an orphanage, James.'

Boys like you. I remember when Mrs Devol said the words. 'I . . .'

'James, we've had this conversation. Many times before. In many different places. We always reset you, you go back to your factory settings and then a few weeks later, you're asking questions again. You're endangering your position yet *again*.'

None of this makes sense to me. I'm trying to speak but the words don't form.

'James, do you ever wonder why you can't remember life before the Nursery?'

'I was brought here as a baby.'

'No, that's the story we gave you. We rewrite it every few months now, it seems. This is the last time we can do this, sweetheart.'

Mrs Devol says the endearment but I've never felt more alone in my life.

'I'm human,' I hear myself say. It's absurd, because of course I am, but I feel the need to taste the words, to spit them out. 'I'm human.'

'Look down, James,' Mr Devol says quietly.

I do. I look at my forearm, the one he's holding. The skin somehow seems opened up, like the boot of a car. Instead of muscle and tissue, I see wires.

'We're resetting you one final time, James,' Mrs Devol says. 'No more after this. If you break ranks again, start asking questions, we're shutting you off. You'll be on the scrapheap.'

I'm not like other children. None of us here are. They don't even want us as children, just as little servants. If we don't keep their houses clean in the way they like, they send us back. We're not human to them but it's because we're not. Not human. They treat us this way because we are not like them.

I wonder how many times I've had this revelation. How many times have they wiped it clean from me?

They're about to do so again. I scream, like Evie did. I kick. I don't want to go back to not knowing. I don't want them to take my agency away. I don't want —

I call them the Magpies.

I watch them from my window, high up in the Nursery. I can see all of Talos Springs from here, but that's hardly difficult. It's a small town in the middle of nowhere, so there is not very much to see. I watch the couple move towards the cinema at the corner of the street.

'There's something weird about them,' I tell Mrs Devol.

She's darning socks next to me. When I say it, her face crumples. I don't know why. I watch her look across the playroom to Mr Devol, who is working at one of the tables. She gives him a single nod and he looks just as resigned as she does.

I turn back to the window.

'James, come downstairs with us, please. We need to show you something.'

I keep looking out at Talos Springs. It's such a strange little town. I don't know much about it, despite having lived here my whole life. I know when it rains and when it snows and when it's hot. Though I can't seem to remember ever leaving the Nursery.

'James? Let's go.'

It's a nice town, though, Talos Springs. Everything runs like clockwork.

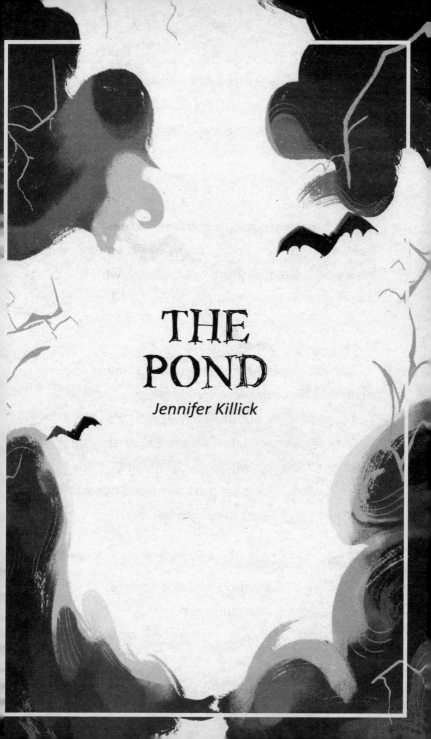

THE POND

Jennifer Killick

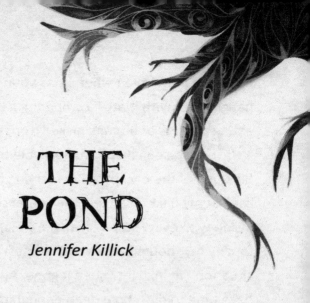

THE POND

Jennifer Killick

'Are you sure you want to do this, Emmanuel?' Nikhil breaks into a jog to keep up with me.

I'm only walking, but with the kind of power boost that comes from being whisper close to getting in a massive load of trouble. Like a man carrying a ticking time bomb. I'm walking explosively. With added thrusters.

'No,' I say. 'But also, yeah.'

'Don't sound that sure to me.'

We're halfway across the field at the back of my street. It's ugly, with scratchy grass and stinging nettles, the remains of illegal bonfires and leftover rubbish from late-night teen parties. A wasteland. But I feel like I've spent half my life here, riding bikes and playing tag when I was younger, and now hanging out with mates, comparing game stats and eating packets of biscuits nicked from home.

'I've assessed all options available to me,' I say, flinching as the backpack I'm carrying bounces against my back. I can feel the contents move inside with every step I take. The weight of it forcing my thoughts back to the disaster of a situation I'm in. 'I just need it gone. And I don't have time to dig a hole deep enough to make sure it stays buried.'

'But the pond, though,' Nikhil says. 'It's so drastic, man. There are some things in life that you just shouldn't mess with.'

'Yeah,' I say. 'And one of those was my little sister's stupid doll that she loves more than anything else in the world. But I did. And let's not forget that you helped, by the way. And now here we are.'

'I really thought you'd make the jump.' Nikhil shrugs. 'The ramp seemed solid.'

The ramp *did* seem solid. I thought it would take the weight of me and my bike for sure. I even tested it first – jumped on it as hard as I could a bunch of times. I didn't expect it to snap like that, sending me flying into the line of items – broken toys, empty beer bottles, and the now smashed-up doll in my backpack – I was supposed to be flying over.

'It would have been legendary if I'd made it.' I sigh. 'This day sucks.'

'Our mistake was using that old pallet at the bottom. It's been out in the field for months. Probably rotten.'

'Our mistake was deciding to make Tilly's most prized possession part of the stunt,' I say. 'And I'm pretty sure that was your idea. Something about increasing the risk factor?'

'You could have said no,' Nikhil says.

We're getting close to the far corner of the field, climbing the verge of scraggly grass that leads to the fenced-off area that keeps people from getting to the pond. The late-afternoon sky has clouded over, making everything dull and grey.

'You know what happened to that kid from Claytons who threw a stray cat in there?' Nikhil says.

'Yeah, I've heard the story. Everyone has. Doesn't mean it's true.'

'My auntie saw the kid's mum at the post office

the other day. She said he's still in hospital.'

'This really isn't helping.' I sigh.

'She said he still hasn't spoken a single word. He just screams and shakes and cries.'

'Don't forget the bit about his fingernails,' I say. I'm sweating. From the walk, or the climb, or the fear — or all three.

'Gone.' Nikhil shakes his head. 'No fingernails left . . .'

'And covered in scars that look like cat scratches,' I say. 'Come on, man, that's clearly horse turd. Like the cat actually came back from the dead and sought revenge on some scrut-brained kid from Claytons. Didn't happen.'

'Fine.' Nikhil holds his hands up. 'But let this not be another bad idea that's blamed on me.'

'Besides, this is a doll, not a living creature. It's made of plastic and glass and fake hair and some other random trash. It has no brain . . .'

'And we know that for sure after literally splitting its head open,' Nikhil snorts.

'It's definitely not capable of coming back from the dead.' I say it with absolute certainty. I'm too old to get suckered into believing spooky stories for little kids. I have a situation that needs dealing with

and that's what I'm going to do. I remind myself
that this is the best solution.

The fence looms over us; thick, dull metal, four
metres high and topped with vicious-looking
barbed wire. It's like it's existed here forever, so
overgrown with ivy and bad vibes that it seems like
a survivor from a past apocalypse. It has a gate in
one corner, which is bolted and padlocked and
wrapped with thick chains and padlocked again.
Someone has put a lot of effort into making sure
no one can get in. But the fence is old. Rusted in
places. There are holes if you know where to look.

We're in a minute later. I should feel relieved to be
here – close to disposing of the evidence that will
get me in a load of trouble. But even without the
rumours, the pond is seriously creepy. We're
standing on the metre-wide strip of grass that
circles the drop to the pond itself. The edges are
made of the kind of crumbly soil that looks like it
could disintegrate at any moment, so we never get
too close to the edge. The sides of the pond are so
steep they're vertical – more like a well shaft than
the banks of a natural pool – dropping ten metres

before reaching the dark water below. There's no way of climbing up or down them without either a rope or Spider Powers.

The pond itself is only about the width of my bedroom and smells twice as bad as the boys' toilets at school. It's so black and still that you'd think it must be something solid. But I've seen people drop stones in before – they hit with a silent splash, make the smallest ripple, and then disappear beneath the surface. Nobody knows how deep the water is, and nobody can get close enough to fish items out, though sometimes kids try. Anything that gets dropped in the pond, stays in the pond.

'Last chance to change your mind,' Nikhil says.

'You're not helping, again.' I stink-eye him.

'Damn right, I'm not,' Nikhil says. 'I don't want to get cursed. I mean, if you're dead set on it, then go for it – I'll be interested to see how it plays out. Just don't say I didn't warn you.'

'That's not what I meant, but whatever. I'm doing it.' I take my backpack off and unzip it.

I don't like looking at the doll. Its head is split open from the back of her neck, all the way over its plastic skull to her mouth, and the two halves are angled in different directions, leaving a gaping hole in between. One of its glass eyes popped loose of the socket and cracked under the fallen ramp.

I tried to put it back in, obviously, but it wouldn't stay. So I dropped it inside the body of the doll and I can hear it rolling around in one of the feet, underneath its little white buckled shoes. The doll's clothes are torn and filthy, tyre tracks from my bike streaked in oil across its pink coat.

'Ew.' Nikhil makes a face. 'Looks like roadkill.'

'I mean, technically it *is* roadkill. We had to peel it off the concrete.'

'You sure you don't want to fess up? Tilly's going to be looking everywhere for it.'

I take one last look at the doll. 'To be honest, I think seeing the doll like this will emotionally scar her for life. Plus, I will be in more trouble than I can handle.' I shake my head. 'This is the best way.' I step closer to the edge, almost drop it in and then pull back. 'What if it floats?' I say. 'We should weigh it down with something.'

'*You* could fill it with rocks,' Nikhil says. 'I already told you, I'm not being part of this. I'm too young to die.'

'Fine,' I huff, bending down to scoop up pebbles

and stones from the uneven ground. I drop them through the gap in its head and hear them bounce down into the hollow plastic legs. I stop when it's full to the waist. 'That should be enough.' Then, before I can freak myself out, I step forward and drop the doll into the pond. It falls fast, weighed down by the rocks, but still hits the water with no sound. The legs go under straight away, but the upper half stays afloat, the split one-eyed face staring up at us. For one, two, three seconds it stays there, and I get an even sicker feeling in my stomach than I already had. What if it doesn't go under? What if someone sees it there and recognizes it? Then it bounces upwards out of the water, like it's trying to escape, making us both gasp and jump backwards. I feel total panic rising with the hot vomit in my gut. But then it falls back again and is sucked under the surface.

'That was intense,' Nikhil says. 'Let's get out of here.'

As we scramble back through the hole in the fence I decide that I am never going to the pond again.

160

I make sure I'm casually gaming in my room when Mum and Tilly get home. I reply to their hellos with my best 'nothing to see here' voice and hope they don't notice my hair sweat-stuck to my forehead or the goosebumps prickling my arms that don't seem to want to go away. I listen to them going through their usual activities – shoes off, bathroom stuff, getting changed, putting the kettle on, getting juice from the fridge. And I'm waiting. Just waiting. For what I know is coming.

'Mummy!' Tilly yells from her bedroom, loud enough that you could probably hear her from the back of the field. I flinch at the thought of the pond. At the image of a broken doll at the bottom of a pool of sludgy water.

'Rose is gone!'

I stop playing my game. Click the mute button.

'Just a sec, Tilly,' Mum calls back.

But Tilly can't wait a sec. She bumps down the stairs and clatters across the hall to the kitchen. 'But Rose is gone and we need to find her right now,' Tilly says.

'She can't be gone,' Mum says. 'Come on, I'll help you look.'

I listen as they come back up the stairs and

161

rummage through Tilly's room. Wardrobe doors open with a creak then slam shut. The bed squeaks as they take off the pillow and duvet. There's shuffling and thudding, and then, quietly at first but quickly getting louder, the sound of Tilly wailing.

'She must be in the living room,' Mum says. And they thump back down the stairs to continue their search. I should offer to help, but the fakery of doing that makes me feel sick. It crosses my mind to tell them the truth, but I feel like I've walked too far down this road to turn back. Tilly will never forgive me. Mum will kill me. I just need to get through this first part and then it will be easier. Like jumping into an outdoor swimming pool on a cold day.

They search for over an hour, tearing apart every room in the house. I act a bit annoyed when they insist on looking in my room but let them do it and even open and close my drawers to seem like I'm helping.

'Maybe you left her in the park,' I say with a shrug when Tilly starts full-on crying.

'We didn't take her out with us today,' Mum says. 'Did we? I don't think we did.' She's sweating and stressed and I feel like such a scumbag.

'I thought I saw Tilly holding her,' I say. I have to make them think she's gone – the sooner they do, the sooner we can all move forward.

'I was sure we didn't,' Mum says. 'I feel like I'm losing my mind.'

I'm gaslighting my own mother. I'm going to hell for this.

'I didn't, though, Mummy,' Tilly says. 'I know I didn't.'

'Remember that time you left her on the train?' I say. 'And that nice lady handed her in at the station?'

Tilly nods, snot dripping from her nose.

'You forgot her then, didn't you?' I say. 'Everyone does it sometimes.'

'I'm going to call Daddy and ask him to look in the park on the way back from work,' Mum says. 'Come on, Tilly, let's have a cuddle and a cupcake. I'm sure Rose will turn up.' She scoops Tilly up and carries her back downstairs, leaving me in my room feeling like the actual worst person in the world.

The search goes on until bedtime, and I lie awake for hours listening to Tilly crying in her room. She's not gone to sleep without Rose since she got her for her second birthday. I put my pillow over my head to block out the sound, or the guilty thoughts, or both maybe. But it doesn't work. I'm too hot and too cold and can't get comfortable, and it's only when I decide that I'm going to tell the truth as soon as I get up in the morning that I finally fall sleep.

I jolt awake suddenly, with that heart-thudding feeling you get when you've just had the worst nightmare, and for a moment you can't work out what's real and what's your brain playing tricks on you. I thought I was falling – plunging face first from a great height, watching the ground come rushing up to meet me. I put my arms out to steady myself, gripping the edges of my mattress like it's the only thing between me and certain death. Then I hear something outside my room. Light footsteps skipping across the landing floor towards Tilly's bedroom. They tip-tap over the wooden boards like a dance, and I can't understand it because Tills never gets out of bed in the dark. She always yells out for Mum. But then I hear her door open and close.

I get out of bed wondering if Tilly's so upset about Rose that she's actually lost her mind. What if I've properly broken my little sister? I open my door as quietly as I can and step out into the hallway. My bare foot presses down into something cold and slippery that oozes up between my toes like slug slime. I gasp and pull it back in disgust, wanting so badly to turn the landing light on so I can see. But when I poke at the sole of my foot with my finger, there's nothing there. Must still be half asleep and letting the pond get in my head. I tiptoe across the landing to Tilly's room and put my ear to the door.

I expect to hear muffled crying, but instead I hear singing. It's a little girl's voice but not quite like Tilly's usual Americanized *Little Mermaid* power-ballad style. She must be putting on a weird accent or something.

'Ring-a-ring o' roses, A pocket full of posies,
A-tishoo! A-tishoo . . .'

I open the door.

Tilly is sitting cross-legged on her bed, looking like a ghost in her pale pink pyjamas next to the soft glow of her night light. She's wide awake and not even under the covers, and she jumps when

I poke my head around the door, like I've caught her in the middle of doing something.

I have quite a few questions, but I go with, 'Why aren't you in bed?'

She turns towards me, and I see that she's put flower clips in her hair and some kind of pink make-up on her cheeks. 'I was talking to Rose. She was teaching me a new song.'

'But Rose isn't here,' I say. 'You lost her, remember?' I look around her room, confused. There's nobody here but Tills.

'She came back,' Tilly says. 'And she said you've been a very naughty boy.' Tilly frowns at me. 'What did you do, Emmanuel?'

I'm trying hard not to freak out. But I have no idea what's happening here.

'Do you mean you're imagining Rose?' I say. Cos I've heard lots of kids do that.

Tilly tips her head back and laughs – a creepy, tinkly giggle that's nothing like her usual belly laugh. 'Silly Emmanuel,' she says. She laughs again.

'What?' I say. I can't see what's funny here. 'What are you talking about?'

'Silly, naughty Emmanuel.' She stops laughing suddenly, her face going dead serious. 'You should go back to bed before something bad happens.'

I stare at Tilly for a few seconds, torn between going in to see if she's OK, and running the hell away from her as fast as I can. But then she shuffles across her bed and starts snuggling herself under the duvet. 'I'm sleepy now.' She yawns. 'Night, night, Manny.'

'Right. Night then, Tills.' I back out of her room, closing the door behind me, wondering what the freak just happened.

I go back to my room, and I'm telling myself that everything's fine. Stuff always seems weirder at night. I was creeped out from the nightmare, and it messed with my head. There is absolutely nothing strange going on. I get into bed and I'm pulling my duvet up, but then I jump out again and wheel my desk chair over to the door, propping it under the handle. It might not stop anyone from getting in, but if someone tries it will definitely fall and wake me up. I know there's nothing to worry about. But just in case.

I don't get much sleep. I huddle under the blankets willing the sky to grow light so I can get back that feeling of daytime normality. But when the sun finally does come up I find I'm scared to leave the safety of my bed. I listen for the sound of Tilly waking and moving around in her room as usual, but she sleeps so late that Mum ends up going in to wake her. I wait until they've gone downstairs before dragging myself out of bed, putting on the first clothes I pull out of the drawer and thumping downstairs.

'Dressed already?' Dad says, looking up from his coffee. 'This is new.'

'Who's dressed?' Mum comes out of the kitchen. 'Manny's dressed? At eight thirty on a Sunday morning?' She does an exaggerated fake faint.

'Funny,' I say. 'Can I go to Nikhil's?'

'Come and have breakfast first, please,' Mum says.

I look over her shoulder into the kitchen where I can hear Tilly singing, *'Ring-a-ring o' roses, A pocket full of posies, A-tishoo! A-tishoo . . .'*

I *so* don't want to go in there and face her. 'Not hungry.'

'Emmanuel, you are always hungry,' Mum says. 'So if you're saying you're not, then there must be something wrong.'

'I'm not always hungry,' I huff. We all know that's not true.

'You're the only person I've ever known who keeps eating through a vomiting bug,' Dad says, eyebrow raised.

They're not going to let me out if they think something's up. 'Fine. Just some toast, then.' I follow Mum into the kitchen.

Tilly turns to look at me from where she's sitting at the breakfast bar. She's stirring her cereal with one hand and looks like she's holding something in the other. Her fist is closed around it, but gently, like if she squeezes too tight it could break. 'What did you do, Emmanuel?' she says. Her face isn't even angry – it's just blank. No frown, no glare, no expression. Like she's some kind of android.

'He got dressed!' Mum laughs. She's turned to the kitchen counter, getting bread out of the box it lives in. 'Sit down, Manny, I'll get your toast.'

I sit at the breakfast bar, as far as possible from Tilly, but I watch her out the corner of my eye. She's spooning Coco Pops into her mouth, her eyes fixed on her left hand and whatever secret she's hiding inside it.

'You two are quiet this morning,' Mum says, putting a plate of toast in front of me.

'Thanks,' I say. My voice crackles out of my throat like dried-up autumn leaves.

'I know we're all worried about Rose.' Mum smooths back Tilly's hair. 'But I really think she's going to turn up again and surprise us.'

Tilly keeps her face down but I see a smile creep across her face. It's not her usual goofy grin. It's cold, like cracking ice. What the hell is happening to my sister?

I take bites of toast, chewing and swallowing it like it's bits of the back doormat we use to scrape the mud off our trainers when we come in from the field. Mum carries on as usual, singing while she puts kitchen stuff away and scrolls through her phone. I'm waiting for her to leave the room so I can bin the last of the toast, but when she does go I'm stopped in my tracks by Tilly. She lowers her closed hand to the breakfast bar. Turns it over to put whatever she's holding on to the hard surface with a click. She keeps it covered so I can't see. Then, without looking at me, and with one smooth movement, she pushes it in my direction.

A small ball rolls slowly over the counter

towards me. It's shiny, like it's made of glass, and for a second I think it's a marble. But then it stops directly in front of me, a small black circle surrounded by a ring of blue staring upwards. And my stomach lurches as I realize what it is.

'Rose is keeping her eye on you,' Tilly says, and then screeches with laughter.

I jump down from my seat, knocking it over as I do and sending my plate smashing on to the kitchen tiles.

'What's going on?' Dad comes running into the room, closely followed by Mum. I look at them, then back at the breakfast bar. The eyeball has gone. Back in Tilly's hand from what I can see. She carries on eating.

'I'm sorry,' I say. 'I tripped.'

Yeah, it sounds lame, but it's taking all of my brainpower to focus on not throwing up.

'It's all right,' Mum says, bending down to pick up the broken shards. 'Why don't you go over to Nikhil's now?'

'Thanks, Mum,' I say. I pull my trainers on without doing the laces, grab my hoodie and bang out of the front door without looking back.

The world outside is grey in colour and sound.

As I walk down the road, still early Sunday quiet, I'm sure I can hear footsteps behind me. Tippy-tappy ones made by small feet in shiny shoes. But every time I turn, there's no one there. My feet feel heavy. My shoes uncomfortable. There's a crunch every time my foot hits the pavement that doesn't make sense. I stop. Check my trainers. What I see makes me cold. The air bubbles in the soles, which were perfect yesterday, have been slashed and stuffed with stones. I remember filling Rose's feet with pebbles to weigh her down. I turn and sick up my toast right there on the pavement, then I carry on walking.

I feel like I'm losing my mind. By the time I reach the big road opposite my old primary school, I'm fully freaked out. I've thought of a hundred different reasons to explain Tilly's dead-of-night singing. The things she said to me. The marble. The stones in my shoes. Maybe she knows what I did to Rose and she's messing with me for revenge. Maybe she's so upset about Rose that she's acting out of character. Maybe I'm so upset about what I did to Rose that I'm imagining things. But there's a nagging fear in my mind that relentlessly pulls me back towards the same thing: the pond. I just want to get to Nikhil's so I can talk it through with him.

The road is empty when I cross to the middle. Literally, there's not a single person or car in sight. But as I step forward off the island to cross the next part of the road, the sound of a honking horn breaks through the mess in my head, and I turn to see a bus roaring up the street towards me. My heart drops like a stone into my guts and I pull back just in time, the rush of the bus past me blowing my hood down. I find myself staring at my own ghost-white face in the reflection of the bus windows. And something else. The reflection of a doll – blond hair, blue eyes, pink coat, the head split open like an over-ripe apple that's fallen from high up in a tree and smashed on the ground. I gasp and jump backwards, away from the bus. Another horn blasts behind me. I hear the screech of brakes and feel the crunch of solid metal as the car hits me. I bounce up on to the bonnet and roll across it, my mind unable to piece together what's happening. Until I tumble back to the ground.

I take a second, breathing deeply. Working out what hurts. If I'm bleeding. If I'm dead. I do feel pain, but not as much as I'd expect from a serious impact. The car was moving slowly. I'm OK. I jump up, ignoring the driver of the car who's come to see if I'm all right, and I sprint the rest of the way to Nikhil's.

'I was right, wasn't I?' Nikhil says the moment I get up to his bedroom. 'About the pond?'

I nod.

'Told you, man.'

'How do we fix it?'

Nikhil does his thinking face. 'Reverse time?'

'Oh great, I'll just go knock for Dr Strange, shall I?' My legs go full jelly and I sink down on Nikhil's bed.

'You could try to get her back out of the pond.' Nikhil sits in his gaming chair.

'How? It's never been done.'

'Just cos it's never been done, doesn't mean it can't be done.' Nikhil taps his chin with his finger. 'Anyway, the only other thing I can think of is offering a human sacrifice to the pond, so you might as well try.'

'You're coming to help me, right?' I can't stand the thought of going back there alone.

'I don't really want to, to be honest with you.

This shiz is messed up and I'm scared that creepy-ass doll will come for me next.'

'Come on, man. It was your idea to use her in the stunt. And who's to say she won't come after you, once she's done with me? We should finish this.'

Nikhil spins silently on his gaming chair for a minute while he thinks it over.

'I'd go with you if it was the other way round,' I say. 'You know I would.'

'Fine.' Nikhil sighs. 'But if it wants a human sacrifice, I'm pushing you in.'

Even though I'm currently dealing with the biggest trash-fire of my life, I smile with relief. With two of us together, I feel like we stand more of a chance. 'Thanks. Let's go.'

Nikhil shakes his head. 'No way I'm going there empty-handed. We get supplies first. Then we go.'

I follow Nikhil to the garage, which is dark and dusty and makes me itch. As we walk up and down shelving racks and rummage behind piles of boxes, I jump at every sound. I swear I can hear the tap of Rose's shoes. The sound of her humming that nursery rhyme. I imagine her scurrying in and out of the shadows. Maybe crawling under the shelves so she can reach out and grab my ankles, biting into them with tiny, sharp teeth.

'Emmanuel,' Nikhil says suddenly, making me jump like a cat out of a bath, 'I've found the stuff. You sure you want to do this?'

I nod. 'I have to do *something*, and we don't have a better plan, so yeah.'

Ten minutes later, with a backpack full of rope, garden tools and crisps, and carrying a giant torch, we're making our way through familiar streets – still weirdly empty of people – and back to the field.

Nikhil jogs to keep up with me, and I think back to yesterday when I walked like a man on a mission. Thinking that throwing Rose in the pond was my best option and having no freaking clue what a stupid plan it was. A cold wind starts to blow behind us, pushing us onwards. It gets stronger the closer we get to the field, and soon we're half running as it carries us forward. Like some demonic power is desperate for us to reach the pond. Maybe to punish me. Or maybe the wind is a good wind sent by the universe to help me right a wrong.

We enter the field through the rusted gate,

which creaks ominously as it closes behind us.

'Could this be any more sinister?' Nikhil says. 'It's literally like a movie scene that ends in horror and death.' He stops walking and opens the backpack.

'I don't think a weapon is going to help right now,' I say.

'Not getting a weapon.' He reaches in to pull something out of the bag. 'If I'm going to die, I want a final snack.'

We walk through the field to the sound of Nikhil crunching on a packet of salt and vinegar. On the surface, not much has changed since we were last here. Scorch marks from a new bonfire blacken the grass. More cans and bottles are scattered around. A bunch of crows are pecking through a pile of grease-stained pizza boxes. But at the same time *everything* has changed.

The rise to the pond feels harder to climb than ever before, even with the wind shoving us on. Whatever shock or adrenaline had stopped me from feeling the pain of the earlier battle of Manny versus BMW, it's started to wear off. With every step my body throbs. Like all over. Everywhere. Breathing deeply makes pain shoot through my chest. I wince as my right knee gives way beneath me.

Nikhil finishes his crisps and looks across at me. 'You good?'

'Not really. Feel like I've been hit by a car,' I half smile.

'LOL,' Nikhil snorts. 'If you make it out of this alive, you should probably go to the hospital or something. You might have internal bleeding.'

We're at the top of the hill, and part of me is hoping that something will happen to stop us from getting through the hole in the fence. Someone will come along and yell at us to play somewhere else. A gang of Year 10s will throw stones at us and chase us back down the hill. The hole will have been boarded up with indestructible metal sheets. But nothing happens. And way too soon we're standing at the edge of the pond, staring down into the black liquid below.

'I'll find something to tie the rope to,' Nikhil says. 'Give me the torch a sec.'

I pass him the stuff and listen as he scuffles back towards the fence. In the dim light I squint at the pond, my eyes straining to see any sign of Rose beneath the inky surface. The wind howls outside, making the fence bend and groan. But the pond is silent and still. The stench of the stagnant pool wafts up into my face as I lean over it, making my eyes water.

There's a pressure building in my head, pulsing behind my eyes and sending stabs of pain through my skull. My legs feel heavy, like they're made of concrete. It could be from the accident – that would make sense. But a feeling of absolute terror that I can't explain is taking hold of me, from the marrow of my bones to the hair on my head.

She's here. Rose is here. I sneeze.

From the darkness of the pond I hear a sneeze. Once. Twice. And then a voice whispers into my ear, so close I can feel the tickle of it on my neck.

'*A-tishoo! A-tishoo! We all fall down.*'

I feel the pressure of two tiny hands in the centre of my back, pushing me towards the pond. I stumble forward. The soil at the top of the bank gives way under my feet and I fall. With a yell, and a feeling of the most urgent pant-wetting horror that makes my heart stop and every nerve ending in my body slash knives under my skin. I plummet like a dead monkey falling out of a tree. Down into the dark. Down into the pond.

I hit the water with a splash that takes my breath away. Sinking into the depths of the pond and then spluttering back to the surface. For the second time today, I'm surprised to find I'm not dead. I tread water. Floating and choking while I try to get my head together.

'Manny!' I hear Nikhil's voice from far above, and I look up to be blinded by the light from his torch.

'I'm OK,' I yell back. 'Let the rope down. I'll find her and then I'll climb out.' And as I'm saying it I know that the only way of ending this is to find Rose and take her home. By being honest about what I've done and facing the consequences. However bad they are, they *have* to be better than the alternative. I want to be able to walk around without being terrified. I want my little sister back. I want to be able to sleep at night.

So I ignore the warning that I've heard my entire life: what goes in the pond, stays in the pond. I take a deep breath and dive. Down, down, into the thick water which fills my nose and stings my skin. And I hope that the pond will give me the chance to make things right.

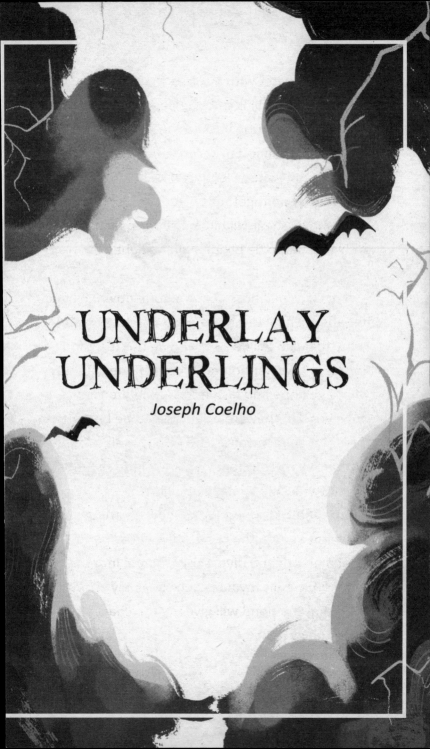

UNDERLAY UNDERLINGS

Joseph Coelho

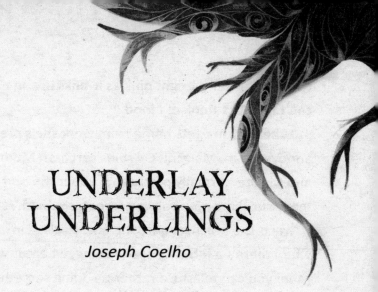

UNDERLAY UNDERLINGS

Joseph Coelho

PART ONE
THE REVEAL

'Malachi! Don't bring your bike stuff in here,' says Mum as she sees me unwrapping a small bottle of hydraulic brake oil. I need it to bleed the brakes on my Zedx Mountain Trail bike before I can tackle the hills with my best mate Mark. I hear Mum telling me to be careful and to make sure I have my gloves on (the oil is nasty stuff, it can irritate your skin and make you sick and if swallowed, it's FATAL) but I'm so excited I run through the hallway with the brake oil to grab my tools and I slip. The brake oil goes everywhere – all over our white hallway carpet –

turning it a weird bright pink as it sinks in and I can't help but think of blood.

When my ma gets home from work she's pretty annoyed. 'Oh, Malachi! Oil ruins carpets!' Mum and Ma are normally pretty cool about the odd mess but the whole hallway carpet is ruined.

Ma is the practical one, she always dives in when there's a job that needs doing, whereas with Mum you can tell she'd rather be doing something non-messy like watching one of her science documentaries.

'That carpet has been here longer than us,' says Mum, 'so probably time for a new one.'

Ma starts ripping up the carpet with her bare hands. Mum helps and that's when I see it for the first time. Underneath our white carpet is another carpet. A shiny, red silk carpet, threadbare in places showing the hessian weave underneath, like ribs in a half-decomposed corpse. There is a faded black pattern of strange swirls and shapes that make my eyes hurt as my brain tries to make sense of it. One moment it looks like the vines of some terrible plant, another moment it looks like a swarm of writhing, wriggling beasts running after some unknown prey. I shift my gaze slightly and it looks like hungry mouths and grasping hands. The pattern seems to shift and change as I stare at it, cold sweat prickles all over my body, it's like all other colour has been drained from my sight, everything but the shiny red of the carpet.

My parents stand smiling with the old white carpet rolled up between them. 'Look at that, a genuine vintage carpet, it's gorgeous!' says Mum, bending down to trace the pattern with her finger.

'Don't!' I yell, and my parents look at me like I might be up to something, and I start to regret all the times I've pranked them for my YouTube channel.

'It might be mouldy,' I say, struggling to make my fear seem normal. Mum's finger traces the ash-black pattern of the carpet and my stomach flips. Can't they see how horrible and creepy it is?

'Don't worry, love,' she says. 'I don't think it's mouldy, it's just old.'

'It must be from the 1920s,' says Ma. 'To think that's been under our boring white carpet all this time!'

The thought of that blood-red carpet having been there all this time makes my skin crawl.

Mum suddenly yelps and brings her finger up

from the carpet, a red bead of blood pooling at its tip. 'Must be a loose staple or nail from where the carpet was held in place, I'll give it a hoover.'

Ma then runs her fingers over it too and my stomach does somersaults

'Yes!' she says coiling one of her dreads around a finger, 'and tomorrow I'll hire a carpet cleaner, bring this old beauty back up to its former glory.'

I feel my whole body go hot and then ice cold. 'We're not keeping it!' I say.

'Why not, Malachi?' says Ma. 'This is vintage.'

'But . . . but it's worn out! You can see the threads underneath!'

'Only in a few places, and we can cover those with rugs.'

'Oh, yes!' says Mum. 'We've got those two sheepskin rugs in the basement. They'll be perfect.'

And the two of them head out to the front garden to dump our non-creepy white carpet, leaving me in the hallway with a floor that now glows red.

PART TWO
THE RUGS

That night I can't sleep. My room is off the downstairs hallway so the carpet is just outside my door. My mums are asleep upstairs.

I try to sleep but I swear I can hear it, the carpet is making noises; a rush of whispered voices trapped behind the black bars of that swirling, shifting pattern. I need to go to the toilet but I don't want to step on the carpet, especially not with my bare feet. Mum hoovered it before bed so it should be safe, but I feel that if I did step on it . . . I might not survive.

I hold out as long as I can, my bedside clock says 1 a.m., then 2 a.m. then 3 a.m. and my bladder is ready to burst, so I get up and I go to my bedroom door. The switch for the hallway light is by the front door and the toilet is down the other end. My room is in the middle and I have just the light from my room to light the way. The carpet seems quiet for now. I strain to listen – that weird, muffled whispering is gone. Maybe I dreamed it after all?

Mum and Ma found the two old sheepskin rugs in the basement and they lie like stepping stones up the hallway towards the toilet. My bladder aches so I summon my courage and leap, landing on the first rug, which is warm and soft under my feet. I chuckle to myself. There is nothing wrong with the carpet; it's just my sleepy brain imagining things. I smile and just for fun leap for the second rug, this one is right outside the toilet door. After I've used the toilet I wash my hands, thinking how silly I've been to believe there was anything wrong with the carpet. I look at myself in the mirror, pat my bedtime fro back into shape and roll my eyes and say out loud to myself, 'I think you can walk back to your bedroom, Malachi, no need to leap like a complete doughnut all the way back.'

And then I hear the noise. *WHOOOMP!*

I know it's not my mums as I would have heard them coming down the stairs. I wonder if it's a robber . . . but in my heart I know it's something else. I know it from the way the hairs have stood up on the back of my neck and the way cold sweat is pouring all over me.

I open the bathroom door just a crack and peer out. Squares of light from my bedroom and the bathroom illuminate bits of the carpet, the rest is in darkness, I look up and down the hallway; there is nothing, there is no one. Maybe it was just next door's cat Minko. We have an old cat flap in the back door that my mums have been meaning to get rid of and every now and then Minko wanders in like he lives here. Probably just him, I think, and go to step on to the carpet, but just before my bare foot touches the carpet's silky red finish I notice that the sheepskin rug is gone.

I snatch my foot back to the cool tiles of the bathroom. There were definitely two rugs but now I can only see one, halfway between the bathroom and my bedroom. Maybe the cat came in and dragged the rug out, maybe that's the noise I heard. That's what I tell myself in an attempt to stop my heart from crashing against the walls of my chest.

I decide to take a towel from the bathroom and carefully lay it on the red of the carpet before stepping out, and that's when I notice that the carpet is just red; the weird swirling pattern has gone. I jump on to the towel before fear gets the best of me. I then get ready to leap on to the remaining sheepskin rug, but there is another noise, a muffled whispering, and it's coming from the far end of the hallway, the end nearest the kitchen.

I peer into the darkness and see that the pattern of the carpet is gathered there, coiled up within itself like a snake, and it is moving, stretching and squirming along the carpet towards me, the muffled whispering getting louder.

I leap for the sheepskin rug and turn to the sound of another *WHOOOMP!* as the towel I was just standing on gets sucked down into the carpet. The pattern continues its creeping glide towards me, the whisperings getting louder and louder. I am one leap from the bedroom door but the whisperings are itching at my skull, drawing me in, telling me to stay still, telling me to join them, to let the carpet take me.

I shake my head and leap, just as the pattern reaches the rug and snatches it down into the carpet's red depths.

PART THREE
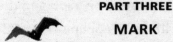
MARK

Somehow I managed to sleep. I convinced myself it was just a nightmare but in the morning it's clear it was no dream. My mums are in the kitchen talking about the rugs.

'Malachi, did you take the hallway rugs?' they shout when they hear me moving around my bedroom.

I try to tell them about the carpet, about the rugs being swallowed, but they just laugh.

'Good one, Malachi,' says Ma.

'How gullible do you think we are?' says Mum, playfully prodding my stomach. 'Remember it's *us* that help you run your pranking channel!'

And they have a point because my friend Mark and I are the Prankster Boys and we have done every prank in the book . . . like the time I pretended there was an alien in the garden (it was a very realistic dummy I had dressed up), or when I swapped Mum's yoghurt for mayonnaise (and didn't tell her when she put it all over her breakfast berries), OR when I filled Ma's work bag with fake spiders (she proper hates spiders). They put up with it because it's kinda become a job and they help me and Mark with all the online side of things, but it now means if I say anything that sounds even slightly dodge, they won't believe me.

I give in. 'OK, you caught me,' I say, and instead give them a story they might believe. 'I heard next door's cat in here last night, maybe he dragged the rugs outside.'

And that they believe! I peer from my door to look out over the hallway, the carpet looks normal, the weird swirling pattern is back in place and to my horror my mums are casually walking all over it. Mum leaves the bathroom, Ma is collecting post from the front door with a piece of toast clamped between her teeth, both ooohing and ahhhing at their wonderful vintage carpet find.

'You having breakfast, Malachi?' asks Mum as she fixes her curls in the hallway mirror. 'I can do you some toast before I go?'

I am hungry but the sooner they leave, the sooner I can start my investigations, so I shake my head.

'Suit yourself but you must eat something, and if you are on your bike again today remember to . . .'

'I know, I know . . . no more bike stuff in the house.'

As soon as my mums leave for work I message
Mark, I know he'll believe me. As the Prankster
Boys, Mark and I have been through a lot together
and he, more than anyone, knows when I am
pranking and when I am telling the truth. He comes
round in no time, knocking on my bedroom
window as he makes his way to the back garden.
The carpet seems to be acting normally now, but I
don't want to take any chances, so I throw a bunch
of clothes from my bedroom floor all over it and
dash to the kitchen to let Mark in and show him
the terror that is . . . *the Carpet.*

Mark stumbles in with all his camera equipment.
He's wearing a baseball cap backwards because
he's been getting into a load of TV shows set in the
eighties and he says everyone wore their baseball
caps backwards then. He's also wearing a neon-
yellow T-shirt (apparently neon was big in the
eighties too). He's treating this whole thing like the
old TV show *Britain's Most Haunted*, saying how he
thinks the carpet is possessed. I mean, who's ever
heard of a possessed carpet?! But I can't think of
anything else that makes sense, so I go with it.

We set up the camera in the kitchen where it's

got a clear view of the hallway carpet, right up to the front door. I gingerly work my way back from the front door, picking up my clothes as I go so that the camera can see the carpet in all its red viciousness.

'So you're saying the carpet ate your rugs last night?' says Mark, zooming in on the clawed swirling pattern of the carpet.

I nod. 'Yes, but it's not just that, it was also making this freaky whispering noise.'

'Whispering?! Why didn't you say? I left all of my super-sensitive sound-recording equipment at home! It could pick up any weird noises this nightmare carpet might be making.'

'Can we get that stuff?' I say, excited to be sharing this horror with someone.

'Yeah, course, gives me the creeps to think you've been living with this. Don't worry, Malachi, I've got you, we'll get to the bottom of this mystery.'

We leave the camera equipment set up recording the carpet and head to Mark's, luckily he only lives down the road. We go out the back door, neither of us wanting to walk over that red swamp of silky thread.

Little did we know that while we were away the carpet would claim its first victim . . .

PART FOUR

DELIVERY

As we head out through the back gate we see my neighbour Nicky in her garden. She's always out there cutting and pruning something.

'You boys being good?' she asks. She always says this and always follows it up with a throaty laugh like she expects, or hopes, that we're doing something bad.

'We're investigating Malachi's haunted carpet,' says Mark, like it's a totally normal thing to do. I'm about to laugh it off, to tell Nicky to ignore him and that it's just another prank for our channel but Nicky has gone unusually quiet. She drops her shears and rushes over to the fence and starts nervously fiddling with the many necklaces that hang around her neck, her mass of bangles clashing as she fidgets. 'What's this about a carpet, Malachi?'

'My mums took up the carpet in the hallway and we found an old carpet underneath. A shiny red silk carpet.'

'Did you cover it back up?'

'No, I mean, I want to, but my mums like it, they say it's vintage or something.'

'Malachi – that carpet needs to be covered up, it can't be left in the open, it's not safe. You boys get back there and cover it up. It's dangerous. The man who owned the house before you had nothing but tragedy after he got that carpet . . . first his hamster, then his lovely poodle . . . then his own mother.'

'What do you mean? What happened to them?'

'That's just it, no one found out, the police took him away . . . but I knew him, he was a nice man, and he said to me . . . "Nicky . . . it's the carpet . . . it's the carpet from that hell-forsaken shop".'

'Shop? What shop?' say Mark and I in unison, both desperate and terrified to hear more.

Nicky looks at us dead serious. 'That damned shop, they should have closed it down. It's called Underlays and it is bad business. A *terrible* business. Cover it up, Malachi, cover it up, before it takes us all.' And with that, Nicky, trembling, picks up her shears and disappears into her house.

'That was weird,' says Mark as we push our bikes to his house, I take out my phone and start searching. 'What you doing?' he asks.

'She mentioned a shop where the last owner got the carpet from, she called it Underlays!'

I type *Underlays* into Google and a shop in town comes up, a shop down a road I sort of recognize, Daegal Street. I click a YouTube link to a video by a local history expert. A woman pops up in a thick blue coat. It's an old video uploaded years ago and, by the looks of it, it was filmed in winter.

The woman is outside the shop, standing under its faded *UNDERLAYS* sign.

'Hey, guys, I've got a creepy tale for you today! This is Underlays, a vintage carpet shop in the heart of Canterbury. But did you know that it used to be the local undertakers? There's been an undertakers at this site for centuries, going right back to medieval times when a man named Daegal would prepare the bodies of the dead by washing them in an old dark stream. But before I carry on, guys, remember if you're liking this creepy story please hit that *like* and don't forget to subscribe for more creeeeepy content! And this story gets even spoooookier! Legend has it that Daegal would steal souls from the dead and use them for his magic! Some say his dark magic still lingers here and that's why the street still bears his name.'

The video shows a page from an old book, there's an old-style painting of a man dressed in a long, flowing red robe. 'There was an undertakers on this spot right up until the 1980s, when it was closed down due to reports of bodies going mysteriously missing.' The woman in the video gives a mischievous grin as she says 'mysteriously' and wiggles her fingers, witch-like, into the camera lens. 'A year later this vintage carpet shop opened up, offering original vintage carpets.'

The shop door opens but the camera doesn't pick up who's inside, muffled voices are heard and then the video stops. I can't find any more videos by that YouTuber . . . that was her last video.

'That place doesn't look right,' says Mark.

I nod. 'But we have to go there, it's the only clue we have.'

We get to Mark's and grab his sound-recording stuff. 'We'll set this stuff up recording the carpet and then go find the shop!' says Mark as we rush out of his house, jump on to our bikes and speed it back to mine and the carpet.

Back in my kitchen Mark starts checking the camera equipment. The carpet looks unchanged except for a package by the front door.

'How did that get there?' I ask as we stare at it from the kitchen. I grab my clothes from the discarded pile and remake my stepping-stone path across the carpet. The package is something for Ma.

'The delivery guy's supposed to leave things in the porch, not put them in the house,' I say. 'My parents must have left the front door open when they left this morning but that's not like them.'

Mark has gone quiet, staring at the back of the camera, and so I tiptoe across my stepping-stone path of clothes back to him, trying not to look at the pattern of the carpet. It makes my head hurt even if I just glimpse it. I peer at the camera's screen over Mark's shoulder. You can hear the kitchen door slamming in the background as we leave, muffled voices as we chatted to Nicky over the garden fence and then it's just an eerie silent video of the carpet and its undulating pattern. But even though nothing is moving, even though the pattern is right where it should be, in all its terrible swirliness, the carpet looks like it is waiting, like a spider in the corner of a web, perfectly still and alive.

'Look at this,' says Mark, fast-forwarding until an outline of a figure appears in the frosted glass of the front door; it looks like the silhouette of a man. On the video we hear the doorbell ring and that's when the carpet's pattern starts to move, slowly at first, slithering across the blood-red weave, and as it does so the whispering begins, getting louder and louder. The pattern gathers itself up by the front door and rises up, and out of the carpet thin, black-taloned hands claw up to the door handle, turn the lock and open it. By the time the door is fully open the pattern of the carpet is back in place like nothing has happened.

'Hello?' calls the man, scratching his head in confusion at the empty hallway. He has dyed purple hair and a very cool nose stud. 'Helloooo!' he calls again. 'I'm, er, just going to leave your package here.'

He puts it down on the carpet and I feel Mark tense up beside me. The delivery man straightens and takes out his phone. 'Just need to take a picture of the package in your hallway to prove I delivered it,' he says nervously to no one. Maybe he's thinking someone opened the door and ran off to the toilet, either way we can tell he is scared.

He's concentrating on taking the picture and that's when it happens. The carpet starts to roll up from the kitchen end towards the front door, slowly at first, you can hear the fixing nails and staples popping as it unpeels itself.

The man looks up, terrified and transfixed. We see the carpet heading towards him, and again I think of a spider crawling along a web until *SNAP!* The carpet lunges towards the delivery man and rolls up and over him like the tongue of some unimaginable beast. He screams once, a short, sharp scream, before he is totally engulfed. For a moment there is a man-shaped bulge in the carpet before it snaps back flat, like nothing has happened at all, and the man is gone.

PART FIVE

UNDERLAYS

ark and I are stunned into silence.

'That was horrible, but at least now we have evidence that this carpet is not safe. But we're the Prankster Boys no one's going to believe this is real! We have to get to the bottom of it ourselves.'

Without warning, the cat flap opens in the kitchen door and Minko comes striding in like he owns the place. Before we can stop him he runs on to the hallway carpet.

'Noooooooo!!' Mark and I yell. Minko stops and looks at us. The carpet isn't rolling up, the pattern isn't shifting, there are no whispering sounds. Maybe the carpet is asleep. Just when I think the carpet might be safe, Minko starts to sink very slowly into it, so slowly he doesn't realize at first what is happening. His paws start to disappear like the carpet has become sinking sand.

Now Minko realizes he starts miaowing and tugging and pulling, but it's no use, the carpet has sucked in all four of his legs and now his tummy is level with the floor. Mark and I start shouting and yelling, trying to get Minko to fight, to get away, but the carpet is swallowing him down. We throw items of clothing his way like makeshift ropes. Minko stretches his neck towards them, he manages to bite an arm of one of my jumpers and we pull, but it's not working, he is sinking lower until just his little black furry face is sticking out.

Mark and I clench our fists around my jumper, brace our feet against the kitchen door frame and pull. Minko shoots out of the carpet with a loud thick slurp and lands in a wet heap in the kitchen before shaking himself and exploding back out of the cat flap, safe but terrified.

Mark and I don't have long to celebrate this victory because a monstrous roar explodes from the carpet; the beast has been denied a meal and it is furious. Its pattern bubbles and at the centre of the carpet a bulge starts to form. The bulge gets taller and taller, pulling the carpet up with it, the nails and staples that were holding it in place popping off once more as the carpet takes the rough shape of a beast . . . a demon.

PART SIX
DAEGAL

Mark and I speed out the kitchen door and jump on to our bikes, just as the carpet demon crashes into the garden, taking the kitchen door with it.

'Follow me!' I scream as I bolt off down Wargrave Street. There's only one place I can think of to go. I ride as fast as I can with Mark hot on my wheels and the carpet demon lurching fast behind him, screaming an inhuman roar. I make a left down Cemetery Avenue and a right along Ferry Park, I know Daegal Street is around here somewhere, the street that sends a chill down my spine. I see it and skid my bike down its dark corridor and head for Underlays – the vintage carpet shop.

I think Mark is behind me but when I look back I see that he didn't make the turn. He is sprawled out on the floor, his bike on top of him and the wheels bent, the carpet beast is a rug's length away, its swirling black pattern dancing over its surface like war tattoos. I screech to a halt and race

204

back for my friend, not knowing if I will get to him in time, pedalling harder than I've ever pedalled before.

Mark is on the floor, scrambling to untangle himself from his bike. I need to give him more time. I spot a huge wheelie bin, the kind shops use, by the side of the road between Mark and the carpet demon. I pedal to it, jump off my bike and push it towards the demon; it's not moving, the wheels are locked. I run around and unclip the wheel locks and the bin starts to roll. I push hard, it gathers speed and I ram it into the carpet demon, but instead of pushing it over, the huge bin just sinks into its body, like the demon can just absorb it. Bit by bit it starts to suck the huge bin in. The thing slows just enough for Mark to jump up on to the handlebars of my bike and I pedal us away to Underlays.

The building doesn't look right; it looks like something pretending to be a building. There is a faded painted sign that says *UNDERLAYS – VINTAGE CARPETS* in large letters. The windows are blacked out, so anyone passing would think it was derelict, but in the doorway hangs a small sign that says OPEN. The carpet demon is lumbering down the road close behind us. I don't stop. I ride straight for the door and we tumble inside, bike and all. I'm about to yell for help but I'm shocked into silence. Standing inside the shop is a man dressed in a red velvet suit. But his face is all wrong; his skin is grey and his eyes are dark and he is smiling a smile too large for any face . . . any human face. 'Welcome to Underlays, I am Daegal, proprietor, owner . . . and I have been expecting you.'

It's the man in the painting I saw on the YouTube video: the same Daegal, the one who prepared the bodies here all those centuries ago! But how can that be? The front door crashes in as the carpet demon explodes into the shop.

'Oh, you have one of my bestsellers,' says Daegal in a voice that sounds like Velcro ripping. As he speaks, the rolls of carpet around him start to shift and change, rearing up into huge, monstrous shapes.

'What's going on?!' screams Mark.

'Are there demons trapped in all the carpets?' I yell, grabbing Mark and linking arms so we're back to back and turning as the carpet demons shuffle closer.

Daegal laughs and I imagine the dry cackle of a

skeleton. 'These are no mere demons, my boy, these are souls trapped in my carpets to do my bidding and prolong my life. These are my Underlay Underlings.'

I think about the undertakers that used to be here and the countless bodies that must have gone through these doors and the reports of bodies going missing and how all this time Daegal was here continuing his dark and terrible work.

Daegal sees my distress, his black eyes drinking in my pain, he creaks back his head and laughs a dry, moth-laced laugh. 'Now my Underlay Underlings will collect *your* souls for me and I'll weave them into a spell to give me more years in this dimension, or maybe I'll turn your souls into new Underlay Underlings to collect *more* souls for me.'

The Underlay Underlings start to crowd in around Mark and me, their sickening patterns swirling, thick dusty breath issuing from the place where a mouth should be. I don't know what to do, but one phrase keeps running around my head, something that Ma said: '*Oil ruins carpets*.'

Inspiration strikes and I grab hold of one of my bike brake cables and pull, the brake oil sprays out and I turn it on the Underlay Underlings. As the oil hits each demon in turn, they howl and hiss and start to fray and unspool. Daegal yells out but it's too late. Mark sees what I'm doing and lifts the rear wheel of my bike and spins the pedals so that mud and muck from the road sprays off the back tyre soaking the Underlay Underlings even more. All that's left of the carpets is a steaming pile of carpet fluff, but now they are moving and from each pile stands a glowing human shape, the trapped souls that Daegal had imprisoned in his carpets. One of them I recognize, it's the purple-haired delivery man.

The man and all the other trapped souls turn to Daegal and they start to speak in a haunting whisper . . . 'You trapped us . . . you took us . . . you made us do your bidding.' Their eerie whispers get louder as they close in on Daegal. The last thing we hear as we run from the shop is Daegal's inhuman scream.

As we push our busted bikes home, I can't help but wish there was some way we could really prove everything that happened. And it's as if Mark reads my mind. 'I think we should start a new channel!'

he says, and then he unclips a small adventure camera from his chest.

'Did you record all of that?!' I ask in disbelief.

'Hell, yes!' He grins. 'Everything is material.'

'We could do a new channel,' I say, our shared vision taking shape. 'Where we unearth the deep and hidden mysteries of the world.'

Mark nods and smiles. 'I did hear about something strange going on in Godfrey Park, something about people seeing something large swimming around the lake, something larger than any fish, larger than any boat . . . I thought it was probably a prank . . . but now I'm not so sure.'

As we walk we start to notice all the other strange things in our little town, the church with the bell that always chimes thirteen times, the graveyard where the gravestones seem to change places every night and the one post box that all the post people refuse to collect from.

Bit by bit a new channel starts to take shape of new mysteries begging to be revealed.

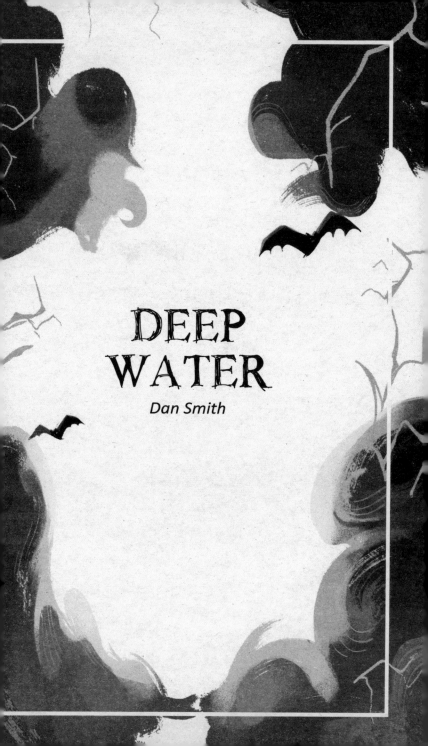

DEEP WATER

Dan Smith

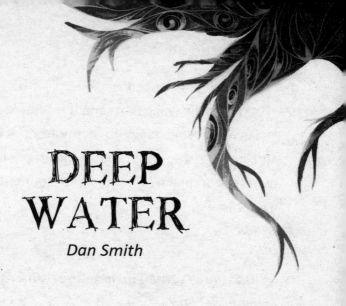

DEEP WATER

Dan Smith

It was the summer of disappearances. That's how everyone remembered it. First there was the disappearance of the ducks and swans, then the watch, and then . . . well, and then something else disappeared. Something far more valuable to the Cosgrove family.

The Cosgrove twins, Amy and George, planned to build a den in the woods and swim in the lake that summer. They had been at boarding school all term and were itching for some freedom. Just the two of them, running wild and free in the grounds of Cosgrove Manor. But their plans were shattered on the first morning home because Sebastian, the butler, came into the breakfast room, cleared his throat, and announced:

'Cousin Mia will be arriving this afternoon.'

Sebastian smoothed down the front of his jacket and stood to attention while he waited for the twins to complain. In his head, he counted down from three . . .

Two . . .

One . . .

'Ugh.' Amy turned up her nose. 'What's *she* coming for? She's such a bore. And so common. How on earth did we ever manage to have a cousin like that?'

'I'm afraid Mia's mother is unwell,' Sebastian explained. 'Your mother said it would be acceptable for Mia to join you here. It will only be for two weeks, perhaps three, and –'

'Send her somewhere else,' George ordered as he dropped a large dollop of marmalade on to his toast. 'Like a hostel or something. Somewhere for common people.'

Sebastian forced himself to smile. 'I'm afraid that would be quite against your mother's wishes, George. She has agreed that Mia can stay here and she has instructed that you be kind to your cousin. She is family, after all.'

'Family?' Amy scoffed. 'Kind?'

'Get out, Sebastian,' George ordered. 'I can't look at you any longer.'

'As you wish.' Sebastian gave them a small bow and left the breakfast room.

Later that day, the twins were in the attic room of Cosgrove Manor. It was a dark and creepy room; dusty and cluttered with Cosgrove family heirlooms. But it was also the highest room in the manor and had a small, circular window at the far end, facing out on to the front of the estate. From that window, Amy and George could see just about to the other side of the world. Or so it seemed sometimes.

George was tormenting a spider that had spun its intricate web on one side of the window. He was poking the web with a whisker he had pulled from a mangy stuffed fox that lay at his feet. Every time he touched the web, the spider rushed out in the hope that there was something tasty tangled in its threads.

Amy had her face close to the window so she could look sideways across the woods and see the edge of the lake. The water sparkled like a bed of sapphires in the afternoon sunlight.

'Where are all the ducks?' Amy wondered aloud. 'There should be ducks on the lake. Swans too.'

George was only half listening. The spider had stopped responding to his taunts and that irritated him.

'There are usually loads at this time of year,' Amy muttered. 'Perhaps Uncle Edwin's Kraken ate them all.'

'Uncle Edwin's Kraken.' George ridiculed the idea of it. 'I think Uncle Edwin's imagination ran away with him. He probably saw a pike and got scared. Or a stickleback.'

'Imagine, though,' Amy said. 'Imagine if it was real. How exciting would that be? A monster in our lake.'

'The only monster here is this big spider.' George poked the web harder.

'So where are the ducks and swans then?' Amy sighed.

'I wouldn't be surprised if Papa and Uncle Edwin have shot them all.' George ripped the web and threw the fox whisker on the floor.

'I'd almost be sorry about that,' Amy said.

'Me too.' George looked up at her and grinned.

'But not quite!' they said in unison and began to giggle.

'Oh, look,' Amy said as the smile fell from her mouth. 'That must be cousin Mia.'

From the window, they spotted a black cab. It was hardly more than a tiny shadow on the narrow country road that weaved past the estate. They watched in silence as it turned left on to the long straight approach to Cosgrove Manor and made its way towards them.

Neither of them spoke until the taxi was on the large, circular driveway below.

'She's such a bore,' George muttered as Mia emerged from the black cab and stretched.

Mia was a small, thin girl with short black hair and brown skin. She wore a red T-shirt and pale blue jeans.

'So common,' Amy agreed. 'And those trainers are ghastly. I wouldn't be seen *dead* in them. They're *so* last year.'

Far below, Mia dragged a bashed-up suitcase from inside the taxi. She dumped it on the gravel then reached in and carefully took out a small backpack printed with a camouflage design.

She treated the backpack so delicately that anyone might think there was something precious inside.

'What do you think that is?' George wondered.

'Let's go and find out,' Amy said.

'Good idea,' George agreed. He put out a finger, squashed the spider he had been tormenting, and wiped the juice on the windowsill. 'Come on, I'll race you down.'

The twins rushed downstairs, trying to push past one another. They were neck and neck when they sprinted across the cavernous hallway and burst through the front doors to find Mia standing with Sebastian on the enormous driveway. The taxi was already making its way back along the tree-lined approach towards the distant country lane.

'What's in the backpack?' Amy demanded between breaths. 'Something precious? Is it a present for us?'

Mia looked at them with surprise. 'Oh. Hello, Amy. George.' She looked at them in turn and smiled. 'How are you both?'

'Yes, yes, hello,' said George. 'Now what's in the backpack? Is it something for us?'

'Umm. No,' Mia replied. 'It's my drone.'

'Drone?' George said. 'How exciting. My best

friend at school has a drone. A Raptor Maverick to be precise. It's very expensive, you know. He lets me use it on the school field on Sunday afternoons. Can I have a go with yours?' He hurried over and tried to grab Mia's backpack. 'Is it a Maverick?'

Mia twisted away so that George missed and snatched a handful of thin air.

'No, it's not a Maverick,' Mia said. 'It's a MiniJack.'

'Oh.' George pulled a face. 'That's the cheap one, isn't it?'

'Well, can we see it, anyway?' Amy asked.

Mia's mum had told her to try to get along with her cousins. She had said that Mia should try to be 'the better person', and show the twins how a 'decent person' should behave. So, reluctantly, she placed the backpack on the ground and unzipped it.

'Does it have cameras?' George asked.

'Just one that points down,' Mia replied as she took out the drone. It was painted black and yellow.

'I call it "Wasp",' Mia explained as she unfolded the rotors.

When the drone was ready, she placed it carefully on the ground, then clipped her phone into the controller and switched it on. The drone buzzed as soon as Mia started the rotors. After a second it lifted into the air, swaying just a little in the gentle breeze. Mia flew it up until it soared far above Cosgrove Manor.

'Doesn't it go any higher?' George asked. 'The one Leonidas has goes much higher.'

'Well, just a bit,' Mia told him. 'But the connection gets weaker and –'

'I'll make it go higher,' George said, snatching at the controller.

As George reached over, Mia turned away to stop him, but George's fingers just caught the edge of the controller, making it slip from Mia's hand. It fell hard and fast, slapping on to the gravel with a crash that made Mia wince. Her phone clattered as it came free from the controller and landed face down, bouncing once, twice, three times, before it came to a stop.

High above, the drone stuttered and dropped like a stone. A moment later, it thumped to the ground.

'Oops,' George said. 'Look what you've done.'

'You –' Mia glared at George. 'You –'

'George,' Sebastian interrupted. 'Don't you think

you should apologize to your cousin?'

'Apologize?' George said. 'What for? It wasn't my fault. And if it *was* my fault, I'd *almost* be sorry —' He looked at his sister.

'But not quite!' they said in unison and giggled.

'Anyway, it was only the cheap one,' George said. 'She can just buy another.'

'Ugh, come on, George.' Amy nudged her brother. 'It was boring, anyway. Let's go to the lake. I fancy a swim.'

Amy and George ran back into the house, giggling to each other as Mia crouched down to pick up her phone. The screen was cracked, of course, and one of the drone's rotor blades was broken. She stayed there, standing on the gravel driveway, between her backpack and her suitcase, blinking hard as hot tears burned in her eyes.

'I'm so sorry,' Sebastian said. 'The twins can be . . . challenging. Is there anything I can do? Perhaps I can —'

'No, thank you.' Mia forced herself to smile. 'I can fix it.'

But she couldn't. Not really. There was no way to repair the phone screen, but Mia *did* have spare drone parts in her backpack. So she went straight up to the guest room where she was staying and put Wasp on the bed. She fished the spare parts from her backpack and was about to get to work when she heard the sound of giggling floating up through the warm summer air and into the open window.

Mia went to the window and looked out at the lawn that stretched along the back of the manor. The twins were running across the grass, dressed only in their swimming costumes. They carried rolled-up towels. They raced across the lawn and into the woods at the far end. Mia saw glimpses of colour through the trees, then the twins appeared on the other side, where the shimmering lake stretched into the distance. Amy and George were just small dots now, racing along the chocolate-coloured jetty and leaping into the lake. They swam like insects on the surface of the water, keeping to the shallows near the jetty. Further out, where the water was darker and the lake was deeper, that was forbidden. Dangers lie in deep water.

Mia watched them for a while, wishing her cousins weren't such spoilt brats. Cosgrove Manor should be a lovely place to stay, but instead it was like a punishment, with Amy and George as her tormentors.

Eventually Mia sighed and set to work replacing Wasp's rotor blade.

Much later, after the twins had returned from the lake, Sebastian came to tell Mia that dinner was served.

'Oh,' he added. 'And I'm afraid Aunt Cecilia and Uncle Sebastian won't be home until very late. And they will both be leaving early in the morning.'

'So it's just me and the twins then?' Mia sighed.

Sebastian tightened his lips and nodded. 'Yes, Miss Mia.'

'I don't think I can face dinner with them,' Mia said. 'Not tonight. Maybe I'll just go to bed.'

'I could bring something to your room?' Sebastian suggested. 'Something . . . not too fussy.'

'Oh, Sebastian, you're a star!' Mia replied. 'That would be lovely. Are you sure it's not too much bother?'

'No bother at all, Miss Mia.' Sebastian smiled and left the room. He returned twenty minutes later with a large and perfectly cooked pepperoni pizza.

Mia savoured the pizza as she enjoyed the

evening breeze through the window, then she slipped into bed. As she slept, she dreamed that *she* was Wasp, looking down on the trees, free to go anywhere she pleased – as far away from George and Amy as possible.

Mia awoke next morning when the bedroom door burst open and the twins barged in.

'Oops, did we wake you?' George bellowed.

'We're almost sorry!' Amy added.

'But not quite!' they said in unison as George jumped on to Mia's bed and flicked her ear a bit too hard.

'Up you get!' Amy marched across the room and threw open the curtains. 'Come on, sleepyhead. Mama says we have to look after you.'

'I don't need you to look after me,' Mia mumbled as she sat up and pushed George away. 'I'm fine on my own.'

'Not allowed,' Amy insisted. 'Mama has ordered us to include you in everything, which is a bit of a bore to be honest. Anyway, it's already warm so this morning we're going to swim in the lake and search for the Cosgrove watch.'

'Cosgrove watch?' Mia asked.

'Oh, do keep up,' George said as he rummaged through Mia's suitcase. 'Uncle Edwin fell in the lake a few weeks ago and lost his diamond-encrusted pocket watch. He came home soaking wet and gibbering about being attacked by a "Kraken". He said that it came up right beside his rowing boat and took a bite out of it. That's what he says, anyway. But now he's in some sort of clinic, trying to recover from shock or something, and we need a new rowing boat because the other one sank right to the bottom of the lake. Mama says –'

'It's all nonsense, of course,' Amy finished her brother's sentence. 'She says Uncle Edwin had too many glasses of champagne that afternoon. She says he probably just saw a big fish.'

'Like a pike or something.' George flicked Mia's ear again. 'Come on, up you get.'

'A Kraken isn't a fish,' Mia said, still in bed.

'What?' The twins looked at her as if she was speaking a foreign language.

'I said a Kraken isn't a fish. It's a mythical monster that looks like a squid.'

'Whatever.' Amy rolled her eyes. 'It's not real, anyway. What matters is that the watch fell in the lake and we're going to look for it. We're ever such good swimmers, you know, and we can dive really deep. Mama said Uncle Edwin will probably reward us if we find it. It's very valuable.'

'And Mama says we must look after you, so that means you're coming too,' George added.

'Umm . . .' Mia frowned. 'But I didn't bring a swimming costume.'

'We thought you'd say that,' George said with a smile. 'So –'

'You can borrow this one!' Amy held up a frilly swimming costume. 'It'll suit you.'

'Meet you outside!' George said as he dashed away.

Amy dropped the swimming costume on the bed and hurried after him, squealing with delight.

Mia's mum had told her to try to get on with her cousins, so she swallowed her anger. She snatched up the swimming costume and held it in front of her.

First of all, the twins had broken her phone and Wasp, then they'd burst into her bedroom without being invited, and now this! The swimming costume was hideous. It was bright pink, with enormous frills around the arm and leg holes. Amy had obviously picked it out to humiliate her.

Mia gritted her teeth and slipped into the swimming costume. She looked at herself in the full-length mirror at the far end of the enormous bedroom. She looked ridiculous. Like a pink iced gem. But she *had* promised her mum she would try to get on with the twins so she pulled her jeans and T-shirt over the top and grabbed her backpack.

Mia's stomach growled as she strolled along the east wing of Cosgrove Manor. At least breakfast was something to look forward to. Cook always put on a good spread. Eggs, bacon, sausages, doughnuts, muffins, and the most delicious hot chocolate. A breakfast like that would raise her spirits.

But Mia's rising spirits were dashed when she saw Sebastian waiting for her at the foot of the huge, sweeping staircase. He was standing to attention, hands behind his back.

'The twins are on the lawn,' he said. 'They've already had breakfast and are expecting you to join them. I'm afraid Cook has cleared the food away. Instructions from the twins.'

Mia sighed. 'That figures.'

Sebastian cleared his throat and lowered his voice. 'I took the liberty of putting something aside for you.'

He brought his hands from behind his back to show Mia a large, chocolate-chip muffin.

'I hope it's to your satisfaction,' Sebastian said.

'Oh!' Mia exclaimed. 'Thank you so much! You're the best, Seb!'

'I try,' Sebastian said. 'And please *do* remind the twins to stay away from the far end of the lake. It's dangerous there, and it would be a terrible tragedy if something were to happen to them.'

'Wouldn't it just,' Mia mumbled as she bit into the muffin and headed through the drawing room, out of the French doors, and into the warm morning.

At the far end of the well-kept lawn, the sun shimmered through the trees. It was a perfect view except for one thing. The twins. They were already there, close to the woods. When they saw Mia, they shouted something she couldn't quite hear, then disappeared into the trees. Mia sighed and went after them, making her way through the woods until she eventually emerged to see a most wonderful sight.

Cosgrove Lake.

Whenever she saw it up close, Mia was always surprised at how large the lake was. It stretched into the distance, the ice-blue water shimmering in the morning breeze. A dark jetty, the same colour as the last bite of Mia's chocolate-chip muffin, reached into the water, and all around the edges grew a lush and energetic meadow flooded with the blues and reds and yellows of summer wildflowers.

The only thing missing was the wildlife. When Mia was younger and she and Mum used to visit Cosgrove Manor, one of the highlights was coming to feed the ducks and swans. There had always been so many of them gracefully gliding across the surface of the lake. But not any more. Not a single one.

Mia frowned.

It was quieter by the lake than she remembered.

Then the sound of yelling cut through the still air, snapping Mia from her thoughts.

The twins were already on the jetty. They had stripped down to their swimming costumes, leaving two little puddles of clothes, and were dashing side by side along the wooden boards. Mia heard the *thump-thump* of their bare feet, then they jumped into the lake with a huge splash.

By the time Mia reached the end of the jetty,

the twins were treading water, looking up at her.

'Come on, then,' Amy said between breaths. 'The water's lovely.'

'Yeah, come on!' George repeated.

Mia looked down at them, wondering if she should just walk back to the meadow and lie in the long grass. She could watch the sky and lose herself in her own thoughts. But her mum had told her to get along with the twins so she had to at least try.

'All right.' Mia went to the edge of the jetty, kicked off her trainers, and stripped down to her swimming costume.

The twins immediately burst out laughing.

'That's hideous!' Amy pointed. 'Look at those frills! I can't believe you actually wore it!'

'It's *your* swimming costume,' Mia snapped and immediately wished she hadn't.

'You wouldn't catch me *dead* wearing that,' Amy said. 'I only keep it to make other people wear it.'

'People like you!' George howled.

Once again, Mia felt tears prick in her eyes. A lump of anger rose in her throat. She didn't care what Mum said; she'd had enough. She snatched up her jeans.

'Oh, don't be like that,' George said.

'Yeah, it's just a joke,' Amy said.

Mia ignored them as she tugged on her jeans.

Amy swam closer to the jetty and pulled herself out of the lake. She came to stand beside Mia, dripping water.

'Are you scared?' Amy taunted. 'Scared of swimming in the lake?'

'No.' Mia fastened her jeans and picked up her T-shirt.

'Then why don't you just JUMP IN!'

Amy shoved Mia hard.

Mia stumbled sideways, twisting awkwardly, and toppled backwards into the lake. Instantly, her wet jeans became a dead weight. Waterweed brushed her bare feet and coiled around her ankles like drowned demons trying to drag her down. Her lungs burned and panic flooded through her veins.

For one horrible, heart-stopping moment, Mia thought she was going to drown. She was going to sink to the bottom of the lake and disappear like Uncle Edwin's rowing boat. Like the Cosgrove watch. Like the ducks and the swans. She sank deeper and deeper until she touched the lakebed. Her bare feet squelched in the ancient mud and, for a second, she thought it was going to suck her in, but she pushed hard, driving herself upwards and bursting through the surface.

The first thing she heard was herself gulping for air. The second thing she heard was the twins laughing.

Filled with rage and panic, Mia splashed through the water and grabbed the jetty. She summoned all the strength she had left and dragged herself out of the water.

'Why did you do that?' It was all she could think of saying. 'Why?'

'I thought you needed some help getting in,' Amy said, widening her eyes to make herself look innocent. 'I was just trying to help.'

'I don't need help.' Mia glared at Amy, then turned to look at George. 'Not from either of you.'

'Oh.' Amy shrugged. 'Well, I suppose I'm almost sorry, then.'

'But not quite!' George shouted and began to giggle while treading water.

Mia felt her anger rising. 'Ugh. The only monster in this lake is you!' she snarled at George.

'Suit yourself,' George said as he slipped under the water and disappeared from sight. Amy pushed past Mia and dived from the jetty with hardly a splash, then she too disappeared.

Ripples circled outwards before fading to nothing, and then the lake was still.

Glad of the peace, Mia took a few steps away from the end of the jetty and struggled out of her wet jeans. She was laying them out flat to dry when the twins resurfaced several metres away and took a deep breath of fresh air.

The further away they are, the better, Mia thought as she opened her backpack and took out Wasp. Maybe a quick flight would help to calm her down. She didn't want to go back to the house just yet. Somehow that would make it feel as if the twins had won.

Mia put Wasp on the jetty. She unfolded the rotors and clipped her phone into the controller.

She switched it on and flew the drone directly upwards. Higher and higher.

On her cracked phone screen, Mia could see herself from above, becoming smaller and smaller as the drone flew higher.

When she was ready, Mia flew the drone forward until George and Amy appeared on the cracked screen, splashing in the water. They were like insects. Their bodies looked frail and insignificant from so high up.

As she was watching the twins on her phone screen, Mia was distracted by a noise in the trees behind her. She glanced over her shoulder to see a pair of ducks flying from the woods and heading out over the lake. It reminded her once again how Mum used to bring her here to feed the ducks.

The pair of ducks flew over George and Amy, appearing on Mia's phone screen for a second before passing right over them. As the birds neared the far end of the lake, they came in to land, skimming across the deep water. Mia watched with interest but was startled to see a large splash when the ducks landed. Usually they were so graceful.

'Strange,' Mia muttered to herself and immediately flew Wasp over for a closer look.

It took a few moments for the drone to reach the right spot, and then Mia was looking down at the far end of the lake where the water was deepest, and the twins were forbidden from swimming.

But there was nothing to see. Mia's phone screen showed nothing but large ripples washing outwards. The ducks had completely disappeared. As if something had snatched them from the surface of the lake.

And what was that? Mia frowned and peered closer at her screen. There was a large area where the water was even darker than everywhere else. Instead of dark blue, it was black. As if it was deeper in just one spot.

Or as if there was something large beneath the surface of the lake.

'What are you doing?' George called. 'Why are you hovering your drone over there?'

Mia kept watching her phone screen.

'Have you found something?' George asked, sounding excited. 'Something under the water?'

'Is it the watch?' Amy shouted. 'Have you found the watch?'

Mia didn't reply. She was concentrating on the screen because she was sure she had just seen the dark patch move. Not much, but enough to get a better sense of its shape. Wide at one end, narrow at the other. But as she watched, it seemed to move. The narrow end split apart into several long strands.

Almost like tentacles.

'No,' Mia muttered. 'No, it's not the watch.'

Then the shape began to move, gliding towards

the spot where Amy and George were treading water. And it was growing bigger, as if it was rising closer to the surface.

'I bet you can see it!' George shouted. 'You want Uncle Edwin's reward. Well, that's not fair. It's *our* lake. We should have it.' He started swimming towards where the drone was hovering over the water. He was on a collision course with the giant shape beneath the surface.

'No!' Mia yelled, bringing Wasp lower for a better look. 'There's something in the water! Something big!'

'Stop lying,' Amy said as she swam to catch up with George.

'I'm not lying!' Mia yelled. 'I'm –'

'You found the watch, didn't you?' Amy shouted. 'You want to keep it for yourself.'

'You can't lie to us,' George said. 'We're not stupid. We'll dive down and get it.'

Mia was about to reply when she remembered what Sebastian had said just before she set off towards the lake.

'*And please* do *remind the twins to stay away from the far end . . . it would be a terrible tragedy if something were to happen to them.*'

And with that, a wicked idea popped into her head. Mia imagined herself tempting the twins on through the water towards their doom. But that would be wrong, wouldn't it? And her mum *had* told her to try to get along with her cousins.

'Don't go any further,' Mia shouted.

'Where is it?' Amy shouted. 'Where's the watch?'

'Just a bit further ahead,' George replied. 'I'll race you!'

The two of them put their heads down, racing each other out into the deepest part of the lake. Mia called after them, but the twins were out of earshot now so she flew Wasp lower for a better view as Amy and George appeared on screen, their little bodies splashing in the water, swimming towards the dark shape. The dark shape that slipped through the depths until it was directly beneath them.

And then it began to rise.

As it came closer to the surface, Mia finally saw the full horror of the thing that lurked in the depths of Cosgrove Lake. It was bigger than a bus, with oily black skin that flickered in the sunlight, showing hints of dark blue and green. Its globular, swollen body rippled and pulsed as if it was made of jelly, and its tangle of tentacles wafted in the gentle current.

It paused a couple of metres below Amy and George, as if it were stalking them, then it rolled over giving Mia a glimpse of bulging black eyes and a cavernous mouth full of blunt teeth.

Mia was almost in shock as the creature wriggled its enormous body and rose quickly towards Amy and George. She was almost horrified when its thick, fleshy tentacles broke from the surface and snaked towards her cousins. She was almost sickened when they coiled around their bodies, thrashing the water into a white froth.

And she was almost sorry when it dragged them down and they disappeared into the depths of the lake.

Almost. But not quite.

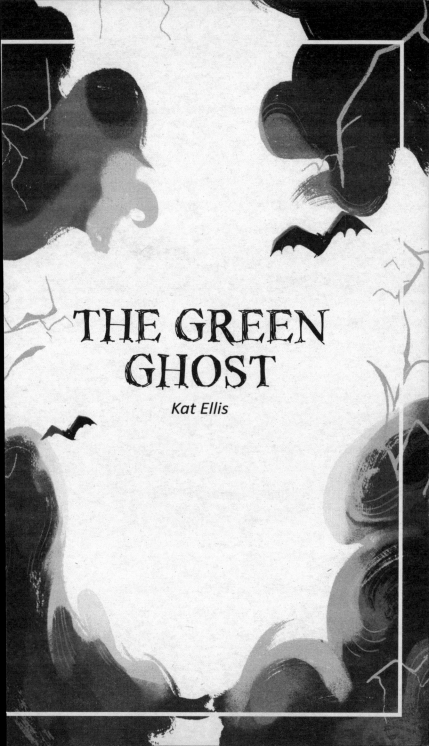

THE GREEN GHOST

Kat Ellis

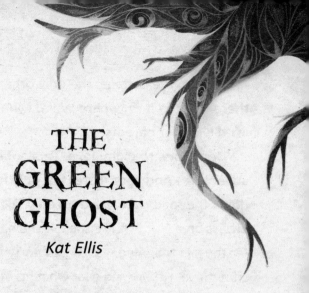

THE GREEN GHOST

Kat Ellis

PART ONE

Aled's mam squeezed their belongings into the boot of the car as he slowly wheeled the last case over to her. Maybe if he moved slowly enough, Aled could delay the inevitable.

'Come on, slowcoach,' his mam teased. 'We'll never leave at this rate!'

That's the whole point, Aled thought.

The builders were arriving to start work on their house renovations today, so his mam had decided they'd move out for the summer. The cottage she'd rented for them was charming, according to her, or old and poky, according to Aled. It sat at the top of Bwgan Mountain, overlooking Nant y Bwgan – the tiny Welsh town where Aled had always lived.

Aside from the cottage, the only other property up there was the farm where Weird Mona from school lived with her parents.

'Don't look so glum, love. Think of it as an adventure! And your mates are only five minutes down the road,' Mam said breezily. Aled's mam was always breezy. It was like she felt she had to make up for the fact that Aled was *constantly* worrying about something. He worried over what his bedroom would end up looking like if he wasn't there to keep an eye on the builders. And whether his best mate Sanjeev would have so much fun working in the ice-cream van with his dad this summer that he'd find hanging out with Aled boring next term.

Aled wished he was spending the summer working in an ice-cream van. Anything would be better than being stuck on Bwgan Mountain with Weird Mona.

As Aled's mam drove them through town, he stared at the winding road that led up the mountain in the distance. It twisted sharply back and forth like an irritated snake.

'Won't be long now, love,' his mam said cheerfully. Aled said nothing. He couldn't shake the feeling of dread that had crept over him along with the shadow of the mountain.

PART TWO

Wind blasted over the mountaintop, making Aled huddle inside his hoodie even though it was the middle of summer. There wasn't much to see up here aside from the cottage, the farmhouse and a few sheep grazing beyond the rickety fences that seemed moments away from blowing over (the sheep *and* the fences). But then Aled spotted something odd.

'What's that?' he asked his mam, pointing. There was a heavy metal grid covering a dark hole in the ground next to the nearest fence. The grid was criss-crossed, like the bars of a cage.

'Oh, it's a safety cover for one of the old mineshafts. There's a whole network of them underneath the mountain,' Mam told him, busy unloading the car.

'Even under the cottage?' Aled asked, eyeing their new home even more warily. He didn't like the idea of a load of old tunnels running underneath where they'd be living. What if the ground caved in beneath them?

'It's nothing to worry about, love. The tunnels

are very old, and nobody's been down there in ages. And those mineshaft covers make sure no one falls down by mistake,' his mam insisted.

But Aled was now imagining himself plummeting down into the narrow mineshaft, getting wedged somewhere deep underground like a squirming beetle grub. He shuddered and tried to think about something else.

Like this grotty old cottage I'm stuck in all summer, with Weird Mona living next door.

He glanced over at the farmhouse, and sure enough Mona's pale face was peering out at him. As soon as she saw him looking, she gave a quick thumbs up, then disappeared.

So weird.

Aled hurried inside before she could reappear.

Last week, when Aled had been to look around the cottage with his mam, Mona had been standing in the yard between the big farmhouse and the cottage. She'd been holding a chicken under one arm and staring at him and his mam as they pulled up. Seeing her had distracted Aled enough that he'd barely paid attention to the place that was to be his home for the next six weeks. Now, though, he had plenty of time to take in the floorboards that creaked and whispered with every draught, and his lumpy single bed that smelled musty even with fresh sheets on it. Worst of all, there was a big crack above the fireplace in Aled's room – big enough to poke a finger in, had he not felt sick at the thought of it. He was certain the crack was full of spiders and he did *not* fancy losing a digit to a hungry horde of arachnids.

'I'm only down the hall if you need anything, love,' Aled's mam said later as she wished him goodnight. 'Sorry it's a bit more . . . basic here than at home.'

She smiled, but it wasn't her usual cheery one. Aled immediately felt bad. He'd been worrying all day about one thing or another, and he knew his mam hated it when she thought he was unhappy. He did his best to look cheerful. 'I'll be sorted once I've unpacked the Xbox. G'night, Mam.'

He lay in bed after she left, listening to the faint tapping sounds of his mam at her laptop – catching up on her work emails, even though she must be shattered.

I'm going to try to make the best of this, Aled decided. *It's only for a few weeks. And I'll just steer clear of Weird Mona.*

A fierce screech had him bolting upright in bed. It sounded like an angry pterodactyl, and it seemed to come from outside his window.

He crept across to it, heart pounding, and peeked through the curtains. It was dark out, no gentle glow of street lights to make the mountainside look any less bleak than it truly was. The faint silvery starlight told him where the noise was coming from: the gnarled tree outside his window, swaying and creaking as the wind buffeted it.

He tried to calm his still racing heart. Aled let the curtain fall back into place and was heading to bed when the floorboard underneath his foot shifted. He pressed down on it again, and again it moved.

Aled flicked on his lamp. The floorboard was loose, empty nail holes showing where it must've been prised up at some point. And even though Aled's head immediately filled with images of rats or bugs that might be living under the floor, he couldn't resist wiggling his fingers under the corner of the board and lifting it up to see what was down there.

A scurrying movement made Aled's breath catch in his throat, but the spider darted away, leaving him looking down at an old leather-bound notebook. There was no name on the dusty cover. The pages inside were yellowed with age, several of them filled with small, scratchy handwriting.

This is a tale of a time long ago, a tale almost as old as the mountain itself, and the boy who would become the bwgan – or ghost – and give the mountain and the town below their names . . .

Aled read on. The peculiar, scratchy handwriting told him of a boy named Drest who had lived in Nant y Bwgan many years ago, before the town was even called that. Before there even *was* a town. Drest was made to work in the copper mines under the mountain and spent so long in the dark tunnels that he grew afraid of the light, and the dust from mining copper turned his skin a sickly green. When the mine was finally abandoned, Drest got left behind, alone and forgotten.

And now he haunts the mine, longing for a friend to play with.

A shudder ran over Aled as he read that final sentence. He could picture it so clearly: a boy with dusty green skin, peering out from the darkness of one of those deep mineshafts. Alone, with nobody to talk to for years and years and years . . .

He tossed the notebook back under the floorboards and dived into bed, determined to forget all about it. But when he eventually slept, lulled by the wind howling over the mountain like a dying beast, Aled dreamed of a green-skinned ghost watching him from the shadows.

PART THREE

'Get the door, would you, love?'

Aled groaned at the sound of his mam's voice. He was still in bed and felt like he'd been tossing and turning most of the night.

'Aled! Door!'

He realized he could hear the shower going. Mam wouldn't be pleased if she had to get out to answer the door with her hair in a Turbie towel. Aled pushed himself upright in bed, and his hand landed on the smooth leather cover of the notebook he'd found last night. Blearily, he picked it up and took it with him as he stumbled to the front door.

Aled almost died as he found Weird Mona standing outside. She wore a massive woolly jumper that looked like one of her dad's cast-offs, and a red beanie pulled down over her orange hair.

She chewed her lip as Aled stared at her. Mona was always quiet, except when she was talking about weird things, like the time she camped out in a tent and found a tick in her armpit, or how she helped her parents pull lambs out of their mothers

249

during lambing season. *Then* she seemed to be in her element, like those things weren't entirely gross.

'Sorry if I woke you up,' Mona said. Then she added, 'I've got that onesie as well.'

Too late, Aled realized he'd opened the door wearing his Spider-Man onesie. It had been a jokey Christmas present from his mam, but it had somehow ended up being his favourite thing to sleep in. Not so much when he had to answer the blinking door, though.

'What are you doing here?' Aled knew he sounded rude, so he gave Mona a weak smile to make up for it.

'Mam and Dad sent me over with a cake,' Mona said as she held up a large Tupperware box. Aled peered through the side, wondering what kind of cake it was. Hopefully not fruitcake, which wasn't proper cake, in his opinion.

'What's that?' Mona said. She nodded at the notebook Aled had forgotten he was holding.

'This? I found it last night under the floorboards in my room.' At Mona's curious look, Aled realized she might know something about it – after all, her parents owned the cottage.

'Can I see it?' Mona said. Aled handed it over, and she immediately started flicking through the yellowed pages. 'This was Nain's,' she said at last, her eyes wide.

Then Aled remembered – of course, Mona's grandmother used to live in the cottage.

'I remember this story,' Mona continued, smiling fondly. 'Sometimes when I'd come over and visit Nain, I'd find her talking to herself, and she'd say she was telling Drest a story so he wouldn't get up to any mischief.'

'So it's just a story, right? I mean, there isn't really a green ghost haunting the old tunnels under this mountain, is there?' Aled gave a worried laugh, but stopped when Mona only chewed her lip again. 'Wait, you don't actually think ghosts are *real*, do you?'

'Of course they're real,' Mona said, like she was telling him that grass was green. 'My nain wasn't a liar, Aled.'

'No, I know . . . I didn't mean that . . . It's just . . .' But Aled wasn't sure how to finish that sentence.

Mona passed the notebook back to him.

'Don't you want to keep it, seeing as it was your nain's?' Aled asked.

'Put it back where you found it.' Mona nodded once, firmly. 'I think Drest should keep it.'

She turned and strode back towards the farmhouse without another word.

'Thanks for the cake!' Aled called after her. Then, a little more quietly, he added, 'Unless it's fruitcake.'

She really is weird, Aled thought to himself. *And I'm pretty sure I* did *put the notebook back where I found it last night . . . so how did it end up on my bed?*

 PART FOUR

led didn't mention the ghost to his mam,
worried she'd look at him like he was daft,
but he tried asking about the history of
Bwgan Mountain.

'I don't know much about it, love,' she said,
seeming distracted with work. 'Why don't you go
to the library and see if they have any books on it?'

So he did, riding his bike down into town and
checking the local history section of the library,
much to Mrs Evans the librarian's surprise.

'I thought you were more into comics, Aled,' she
said, but helped him find some books about the
Bwgan Mountain mines.

Aled learned that the mines were much older than
he'd ever imagined – over three thousand years old.
They had indeed been used to mine for copper, like
the notebook said. Back then, they hadn't had proper
tools to dig with, so they'd used sharpened animal
bones to find the copper deposits under the
mountain. They'd mined deep, deep underground,
with some of the tunnels so long and narrow that
only young children could fit inside them.

It all made Drest's story sound possible. But it couldn't actually be true . . . could it? Even if it was, how would Mona's nain have known about him? She'd been old, from what Aled gathered, but not *that* old.

Maybe Drest told her his story, Aled thought with a shiver. *Maybe he wanted someone to remember who he was*.

Aled kept reading and reading, searching for any mention of the green-skinned boy, but there was nothing.

That night, as the wind howled once more outside his bedroom window, Aled heard a strange scratching noise.

Probably something blowing in the wind, he thought, but then realized the sound wasn't coming from outside — it was coming from inside his room. He peeked out from under the covers and saw something move on the floor near the fireplace. Aled's heart thundered in his chest, but he didn't dare make a sound. As he peered into the shadows, a hand retreated back under the same floorboard where he'd found the notebook.

Was it the green ghost? It had to be . . . didn't it? But what would the ghost want with *him*?

Unless . . .

Was the ghost searching for his story – the one Aled had forgotten to put back?

Aled reached for the switch on his bedside lamp, his wide eyes still fixed on that creeping hand. The room flooded with the soft glow of his lamp, but before Aled could get a good look at the disappearing arm, the floorboard slid back into place with a *snap*.

His eyes flickered to where the notebook still lay on the table beside his bed. Mona had told him to put it back where he found it, but after his visit to the library his head had been so full of questions that he'd forgotten all about it.

Trembling, Aled slid out of bed and crept over to the loose floorboard, the notebook clutched in his hand. Images flashed through his mind of a green hand reaching up to snatch at his ankle, but he forced himself to lift the board until he could squeeze the notebook through the gap.

Aled flung himself back into bed, breathing hard. He knew that hiding under his duvet wouldn't do much to protect him from a ghost, but he huddled deeper under it anyway. He watched for any sign of the floorboard lifting again, but there was nothing. Aside from the howling wind making the tree creak outside his window, everything else was quiet.

Still, Aled couldn't imagine how he would possibly be able to sleep. But eventually his blinks grew longer, until he finally dozed off.

When Aled woke, the notebook was sitting on his pillow. It lay open, showing pages covered with a strange, scratchy symbol, repeated over and over again.

'Do you know what this is?' Aled asked, the moment Mona opened the farmhouse door. She blinked at him in surprise, then glanced down at the open notebook he was thrusting at her. No matter how long he'd stared at the weird symbol, Aled couldn't figure out what it meant. But it hadn't been in the notebook before, and it'd been drawn using some weird greyish scratches, as though someone had used soot and a twig to draw the symbols. And all over the page were smudges of some faint green residue.

Copper dust, Aled thought, his stomach churning. *Like the dust that turned Drest's skin green.*

Mona shook her head. 'It looks like lightning, but I don't know what it means. Why?'

'Last night, I saw a hand reaching out from under the floorboards, and I . . . I think it was Drest, looking for the notebook.' Aled paused, waiting for Mona to laugh and say he was being daft, but she didn't. 'So I put it back, like you said, but when I woke up it was on my pillow, with these weird symbols scribbled all over it. What do you think it means?'

257

Mona shook her head, looking a little paler than usual. 'It's very creepy, but I've no idea.' She must've caught the worried look on Aled's face because her expression softened. 'Look, I used to stay over at Nain's all the time, and nothing ever happened to me there. I'm sure Drest isn't a *bad* ghost. But if you see anything else, or hear any more weird noises, why don't you do what Nain used to do and tell him a story? She said it kept Drest out of mischief if she did that.'

Mischief? A ghost creeping around his room at night and leaving weird symbols for him to find felt like more than mischief to Aled. It felt like a threat. 'I'm worried it's gone past that. I think I've made Drest angry somehow.'

Mona stooped down and picked up a chicken that had wandered over to the front doorstep. She held it out to Aled.

'Here, hold this. I always find it helps me when I'm stressed out.'

'Holding . . . a chicken?'

Mona nodded, and he took the chicken, holding it like she did. He stroked the feathery crest on its head, and it made a happy little rumbling noise. It didn't really make Aled feel any better, but it was nice of Mona to try.

That night, Aled lay shivering in bed, jumping each time the wind bellowed outside. It made an eerie moaning sound as it forced its way in through the gaps around the warped windows. Sometimes he even thought it sounded like someone moaning his name, *Aleeeeed*.

He'd wanted to leave the lamp on, but his mam kept peeking in to see if he was OK. He felt too embarrassed to admit he was scared to sleep in the dark.

The notebook was back under the floorboards, just in case that might help keep Drest away. But somehow Aled knew it wouldn't. His eyes strayed to that crooked crack above the fireplace again, and he imagined he could see a sliver of a green face peering back at him.

There's nothing there, he told himself, but he didn't really believe it. And . . . had the crack grown?

Scriiiitch.

Aled froze, his eyes as wide as jam-jar lids. That

noise wasn't the wind outside. It had come from under the floorboards, he was sure of it.

Scriiiitch.

Aled's chest felt tight with fear.

'What do you want?' he called out, voice trembling even though he tried his best to sound like he wasn't scared. 'Leave me alone!'

SCRIIIITCH.

Aled had had enough. He jumped out of bed and landed with a thud on the bare boards. It sounded so loud and fierce, he did it again and again, thumping his foot down right on the loose floorboard.

'What . . .' *thump* 'do . . .' *thump* 'you . . .' *thump* 'want?!'

'Aled!'

He froze with his foot in the air as the lights blinked on. Aled's mam stared at him from the open doorway, a baffled look on her face.

'What on earth are you doing, love? I'm trying to make a work call in the other room and I can't hear over all this banging.'

Aled lowered his foot slowly to the floor. What was he supposed to tell her – that a three-thousand-year-old ghost was keeping him awake?

She'd think he was imagining things. Or, worse, making it up because he didn't like the house.

'Sorry, Mam,' he mumbled. 'I was . . . trying a new dance I saw online.'

'In the dark?'

'Yep,' he said, nodding like that was a totally normal thing to do.

'Well, OK . . . but maybe do it in the morning, yeah?'

Back in bed with the lights off and his door firmly closed, Aled finally started to drift off to sleep when another sound echoed through his room. It wasn't scratching this time but a low moan.

'What —?' He started to ask again what the ghost wanted from him, when he remembered what Mona had said about her nain telling Drest stories so he wouldn't get up to mischief. Could that be what the ghost wanted — for Aled to tell him a story? Maybe Drest had been missing hearing them since Mona's nain passed away.

Despite his fear, Aled felt a twinge of sympathy. Drest had been just a boy, same as Aled, when he got left behind in the mine. He'd been trapped in this mountain for years without his family or friends. Aled couldn't imagine being alone for that long, forgotten in the dark.

It must be very lonely being a ghost with nobody to haunt.

'OK, so, once upon a time, there was a boy called Drest who was sent to work in a mine . . .'

The moaning quietened down, so Aled kept going.

'Every day, he used sharpened bones to dig away at the earth, pulling out all the copper he could find, and his skin got greener and greener with the coppery dust . . .'

Aled's eyelids were getting awfully heavy. He hadn't slept much the night before, and he just needed to close his eyes for a second.

Within moments, he was asleep.

In his dream he was standing in the middle of his room, listening to the wind howling outside, his eyes fixed on the crack above the fireplace. As he watched, the crack grew bigger, streaking up the wall like a lightning bolt, and a thin green arm reached out from it to grab him.

Aled woke up with a gasp. He'd fallen asleep while telling the story, and he didn't know for how long. But he had the sense that he wasn't alone in the room. When he looked up, a figure loomed over his bed, eyes glittering darkly in a green-skinned face.

'*You*.' The ghost's voice was hard and grating, the sound like tumbling rocks. It was as if he hadn't spoken in years and years. 'Come with Drest now.'

Aled's blood filled with icy fear. He hadn't finished telling the story, and now Drest had come for him – and he looked *angry*.

'Wait, I –' Aled screamed in terror as the green ghost lunged for him, pulling the duvet over Aled's head and bundling him up so his shouts were muffled. He struggled and kicked, but couldn't seem to fight his way free as he was hauled up off the bed and dragged across the floor.

'MAM! *Help me!*'

But there was no way she could hear him. Aled felt himself being yanked over an edge of some kind . . .

And then he was tumbling in the dark.

PART SEVEN

Aled landed with a thud. He wasn't hurt, just a bit winded. Then he felt himself being dragged once more in the bundle of his duvet. Somewhere overhead he could hear thunder rumbling, but it was faint and far away.

'Drest? Where are you taking me?' Aled yelled, and his voice shook with fear now. But the ghost didn't answer. 'DREST!'

Aled gave a gigantic kick, and finally he felt the bedding loosen. He crawled out of the tangle he was in, eyes darting all around him, though he could barely see anything in the darkness.

Anything except the ghost boy standing beside him, his skin glowing an unearthly green.

'Where am I? Why did you drag me here?'

Hands trembling, Aled felt around him and found a jagged wall of rock at his back. There was another wall exactly the same an arm's length in front of him. But off to the sides, he felt nothing but cold, damp air.

Is this . . . a tunnel?

The moment the thought occurred to him, he

knew he was right. The dragging, then the drop —
he'd been dragged through the hole in his
bedroom floor and dumped into a tunnel below
the cottage. That *had* to be it.

'Warned you,' Drest said in his gritty, harsh
voice. 'You didn't listen.'

Drest studied Aled with his piercing dark gaze.
Aled had thought he seemed angry when he first
saw Drest looming over his bed, but now the
ghost's expression seemed more like . . . *worry*?

*But what on earth does a ghost have to worry
about?* Aled wondered.

As if in answer, a roll of thunder bellowed
somewhere in the distance, the sound muted and
faint, though it still made him jump.

'You warned me?' Aled repeated, his thoughts
churning. Drest hadn't said a word to him before
tonight, had he? He'd only left that strange symbol
inside the old notebook. Wait, was *that* what he
meant — the symbol was a warning?

But a warning about what?

'Please, just let me go! I don't want to get
trapped down here.' *Trapped like you*, Aled
thought, but he didn't say that part out loud. He
had a strange sense that Drest wasn't really trying

to frighten him at the moment, and he didn't want to say anything to change that.

At last, Drest seemed to sigh, then he took off along the tunnel. The ghostly green of his skin was the only thing Aled could see, so unless he wanted to be left alone in the dark, he had no choice but to follow and hope that Drest wasn't leading him deeper into the mines. Dragging his duvet behind him, Aled set off after the ghost.

They hadn't gone far when Drest stopped suddenly. He raised a slender hand and pointed directly up. There Aled saw a glimmer of light shining down on them.

'What's that?' Aled asked, but there was no answer. He looked at where Drest had just been standing and found nothing but empty darkness. Trying not to panic, Aled turned in a full circle, but there was no sign of him now – the ghost had vanished. Feeling very small and alone, Aled wondered what to do. *Well, I can either stand here worrying until I starve to death, or I can find a way out of here.*

He peered up at the light. It seemed to shine down through narrow slats, like . . . floorboards!

It was his room – it had to be. Drest had brought him back.

Feeling a million times better, Aled reached as high as he could, trying to touch the boards. He was a few inches too short.

Aled cursed silently. Then he had an idea. He wadded up the duvet into a tight ball and put it down on the tunnel floor. When he stood on top of the bunched-up bedding, Aled could just about reach high enough to push up, up against the boards. They fell away with a clatter, leaving a hole barely big enough for him to climb through. He grabbed on to the edge and used his feet to scramble up the rough stone walls. Finally, he managed to get his head and shoulders up through the gap.

A light flicked on. And then there came a skin-prickling scream.

'Mam?' Aled said, squinting against the bright light.

There came a gasp that really didn't sound like Mam. 'Aled, it's you! What the flip are you doing under my floor?'

As his eyes adjusted to the light, Aled saw Mona was in a Spider-Man onesie exactly like his. She was holding her school science folder over her head like a weapon. And she wasn't in his room.

He didn't even recognize this room, but it had to be Mona's.

'Are you going to hit me with that?' he asked, a little worried he was about to get smacked back down into the tunnel like in a game of Whac-A-Mole.

Mona shook her head and put the science folder down. 'What are you doing here?' she said, eyes still wide with fright as she helped him scramble out of the hole. 'You're lucky my parents are both out taking care of a sick sheep, otherwise we'd both be grounded for life.'

'Well . . .' Aled told Mona about the sounds he'd heard in his room, and about trying to keep Drest quiet by telling him a story and then falling asleep. 'Next thing I knew, I was being dragged out of bed and dumped into a pitch-black underground tunnel. I honestly thought I was going to be trapped down there forever, like Drest.'

Mona's frown grew deeper and deeper as she listened to his story. 'It's so strange, Aled. Nain said Drest could be mischievous, but she never said he was *really* bad. Are you sure it was him?'

'Yes!' Aled sputtered. 'He even spoke to me.

He said he'd warned me, but I didn't listen. I think he was talking about that symbol in the notebook.'

'Hmm,' Mona said, tapping a finger against her chin as she thought. 'If we can figure out what that symbol means –'

Her words were cut off as the wind gusted with hurricane force outside, followed by an ear-splitting screech. They rushed to Mona's bedroom window, peering out across the farmyard towards the cottage where Aled and his mam were staying.

'Oh no . . .' Aled said, voice trembling as he took in the now tilting tree outside his bedroom window. The fierce wind buffeted it back and forth, like an angry toddler shaking a rattle. 'Mam's inside the cottage!'

Before either of them could move, a great gust of wind surged over the mountaintop, the sound so monstrously loud that Aled and Mona both covered their ears. It was too much for the dead tree. With another screech, it smashed right through the roof of the cottage.

B y the time the sun came up, they could see that the cottage had survived pretty well, apart from Aled's room. The tree had landed right on his bed, where he *should* have been sleeping. His mam had been hysterical until he showed up safe and well.

Aled and his mam had stayed at Mona's while the fire brigade made sure there was no danger of it catching fire or falling on their heads, and now, in the bright light of the late-July morning, they went through the wreckage of his bedroom, picking out whatever they could save.

'Hey, Aled,' Mona whispered, nudging him. She was pointing at the old fireplace, where half of it had broken away along the jagged edge of the cracked wall above it. 'Look at that!'

A tree root, now long dead, had grown up through the wall. It must've been what caused the crack above the fireplace. Aled studied the remains of the crack that had worried him so much, his brain whirring.

Then his eyes fell on a familiar notebook lying

among the rubble. He picked it up, blew the dust from the cover, and opened it. And as he held it up, his eyes went from the drawings inside it to what was left of the cracked fireplace. He tapped Mona on the arm and showed her what he'd seen.

'The lightning symbol,' she said, nodding. 'It's the same shape as the crack in the wall! You realize what this means, Aled? *That's* what Drest was trying to warn you about! The tree, the cottage – it wasn't safe. He saved you!'

Mona didn't seem to notice that Aled was frowning. Because he wasn't sure the lightning symbol had been a warning so much as a threat: *don't ignore me, or I'll make you regret it!*

Aled didn't know whether a ghost could make an old tree come crashing down on purpose, but the shivery feeling running over him said he shouldn't trust a ghost to have good intentions. After all, Drest had basically kidnapped him.

He handed Mona the notebook. 'Mam and I are staying in a B&B while the renovations are finished at home, so you'd better keep hold of this in case you hear from Drest.'

She nodded, looking uncertain.

'I don't think he likes being ignored,' Aled

added. 'If you hear scratching sounds, make sure you tell him a story, like your nain did.'

Mona's face had grown paler, making her freckles stand out. 'I won't forget.'

Aled was relieved, because even though Mona was a bit weird, he liked her kind of weird. He hated the thought of anything bad happening to her or her parents.

'If I do hear anything ghost-y, I'll let you know at school,' Mona said.

'But that's weeks away,' Aled protested. 'I thought maybe we could hang out over the summer?'

'Won't your mates think it's weird if we start hanging out?'

Aled hated seeing Mona look so unsure of herself, but then he realized she'd probably heard people – even him – calling her *Weird Mona*.

'Nah, they'll be fine,' he said firmly. He was pretty sure Sanjeev would be on board when he got to know Mona better – and once he heard about their ghostly encounter on the mountain. After all, it was *way* more interesting than spending the summer serving vanilla Whippies in his dad's van.

Even if my other mates are *funny about it*, Aled

thought, *I'll deal with it when it happens. There's no use worrying over every little thing.*

'I s'ppose we could hang out sometimes, then.' Mona grinned, and Aled felt lighter than he had in quite a while.

THE GLASS HOUSE

Polly Ho-Yen

THE GLASS HOUSE

Polly Ho-Yen

It was your classic gnarly old tree. Twisty roots poked up through the ground beneath, which was bare as though the tree had killed off anything that had tried to survive there. A bulging trunk. Branches that reached out like arms, complete with clawing, bony fingers.

And, next to it, was the house.

'Well, what do you think?' Mum smiled over at me but her grin was painted on. She's never been good at hiding what she was thinking; she wanted me to like it, but she was worried that I wouldn't.

She was right to worry.

The house itself was like none other I'd ever seen. Glass and sharp corners, a roof that had

277

green bearded-looking plants growing out the top of it that spilled over the edges. There should have been a shack next to that old tree, not this glass box for a house.

'It looks kind of – glassy,' I said. I've never been very good at finding the right adjectives and I could almost hear Ms Siggins in my head telling me to think of another way to describe it.

Cold. Weird. Odd. Big – but small at the same time because it looked dwarfed by that big old tree. Behind were more trees that looked just as ancient, but there was just that one which was a little in front of the others and a touch larger, like it was their leader and had stepped forward. If trees could walk, which obviously they can't.

Come on, Maki, get with it.

'It's some kind of new design,' Mum mumbled. 'The owners had it built but then they had to move away quickly. Do you like it? It looks even more modern than I remember, like something you'd see on the telly.'

'How far is it from Bilton Road?' I asked, even though I knew the answer. I'd timed it exactly as we'd made the journey out that morning. One hour, forty-seven minutes and fifty-one seconds.

looked at the reflection of us in the glass house. A
boy and his mother – starting a new adventure, a
new chapter, the next step. These words had been
thrown around so often they'd lost all their
meaning.

There I was, a kid in a T-shirt that looked a bit
too small for him now, with his new home in front
of him.

Even back then, before anything had happened,
I looked scared.

We properly moved all our stuff in a week after
that first visit and started life in Box City, which is
what Mum and I called the piles of boxes that were
everywhere.

It felt like every conversation we had was
always, 'Where's my toothbrush/the television/the
chipped cup which belonged to Granny?' And the
answer was always, 'Er, somewhere in Box City.'

In all honesty, though, I liked the boxes. It made
me feel like we actually had proper walls. The
outside walls of the house were mostly glass. We
didn't have curtains up yet and so at night they
became sleek, glossy black rectangles that I felt I

might sink into. And in the morning the trees reared up all around us. But Dad came over as much as he could to help us unpack and he was full of enthusiasm for the place.

'Maki, the size of your room! It's about the same as my whole flat!' But then he realized what he'd said – that his flat was so very small – and he tried to cover it up. 'You could use this whole side for your robot. Mum said that Joy and Idris are coming over soon; you'll be able to get properly messy, get in the full creative zone.'

'It's not really like that, Dad,' I said. Dad always thinks that robotics is creative but it's actually pretty methodical. Joy, Idris and I were building a robot for a mini Robot Wars competition that was coming up with some local schools. Mum said that I didn't have to leave my old school and we'd make the journey work, though I knew it would only be a matter of time before I'd need to move to a school that was closer. For now, however, we could just kid ourselves that it was all OK and carry on like normal.

It was just as I was thinking about that when the ceiling light started to flicker and then went out.

'I'll grab a new bulb,' Dad said and ambled off

into the kitchen. I could hear Mum and Dad chatting and the up and down of their voices. I didn't really understand why they were divorcing; they kept telling me they were still good friends, and always would be.

The dead bulb suddenly burst with light again, flickering wildly a few times before dialling back to a normal glow.

Dad came in holding the new bulb. 'Ah, has it not quite gone? I'll put this new one in now, anyway. It must be just about to go.'

He left soon after that. I watched his car disappear down the drive, past the long shadows the trees made, and tried not to think about the tiny flat he now called home.

A few days later, Idris and Joy came for their first visit.

'Someone to see you,' trilled Mum as Joy raced into the room, her long black hair flying out behind her like a cloak. Idris stumbled in behind her.

'Where's my baby?' Joy said.

'Our baby,' grunted Idris.

'Through there.' I pointed.

Dad had been right about the size of the house. I had my massive bedroom and Mum had her room, as well as a large study. We had a bathroom each and there was a really huge area that was the sitting room, dining room and kitchen all together, but it was so big it didn't feel like it was all that stuff together. There was another room for our washing machine and another that was really tiny where Mum kept the cleaning stuff, and there was one more small bedroom as well.

As I showed Joy and Idris around I could see they were impressed. But maybe they were just feeling sorry for me because despite all the fancy space, it was just Mum and me. Our closest neighbour was so far away it didn't matter they were there. The closest thing I had for company were the trees that grew around the house and were all you could see when you looked out of the windows.

'Any developments?' Joy asked, patting the robot.

'No,' I admitted. 'I only just unpacked it.'

I thought I saw Joy and Idris exchange a look. I had the distinct feeling that the only reason they let me take our robot was because of what had happened with my parents splitting up. It would have made a lot more sense if they had kept it because then they could both work on it together. I'd even suggested that, but they insisted I take it. We weren't too far off from completing it and the competition was at the beginning of autumn and so we had a good month to work on it, as long as they made the trek over here to do it. Otherwise it would just be me by myself.

'We need to crack on,' Joy said, deftly taking off the motor's front panel. With its two huge wheels and bulky metal frame, the robot was large, much bigger than I'd imagined when we first had the idea. Idris had tried to spray the box containing the motor a sickly hot pink; the paint was left over from when his cousin had used it on their bike. Unfortunately, there wasn't quite enough, so the motor box was mostly grey with odd pink patches. We were in the process of adding the chains – the weaponry element to the robot.

Idris started rummaging through a box of what he calls gizmos. 'Let's add this light,' he said. 'It would look really sick.'

'We don't want it to look sick,' Joy retorted. 'All that matters is what it can do.'

'What do you think, Maki?' Idris asked.

'It would look good,' I said. 'But maybe we could add it once we've got the essentials down.'

They both gave me a little nod. I was the peacekeeper in our trio, and I wondered for a moment how they would get on when I wasn't around so much.

Just then, the room light started flickering, just like it had the other day.

'That's weird; it's a new bulb,' I murmured.

'Don't worry,' Joy said. 'We don't need the light on.' She jumped up and flicked the switch and we got back to work.

It went too quickly, that afternoon. Before I knew it, Joy's mum was pulling up to collect them and they left with instructions for what I should try and get done before I saw them next.

Mum found me while I was rummaging around for a bulb for my bedroom and helped me replace it.

'That was nice – having them round,' she said as she adjusted the new bulb. 'You three have always been such good friends.' She sounded a bit sad and I tried to ignore the fact that the house sounded so quiet without them – even more quiet than before.

'I was thinking that we could have pasta for dinner, but I need to find the colander,' Mum said.

'Box City,' I replied, and we started rummaging.

We never found the colander and Mum had to drain the pasta by holding the lid over the saucepan, but it slipped and most of the pasta fell into the sink.

I thought at first that Mum was laughing when it happened – her back and shoulders were doing that funny shaking thing, but then I heard the sound she was making. It wasn't laughter – she was crying.

'Mum? Are you OK?'

'I'm all right. I just need . . .' Then she straightened. 'Hey, I've got an idea – how about I take myself off to buy us a pizza from the Big Shop?'

There weren't many shops close by and so we nicknamed the little shop, which was the tiny village store that never seemed to be open the Little Shop, and the Big Shop was a slightly larger convenience store a bit further away that mostly sold crisps and sweets but did at least have a freezer with pizzas and stuff like that.

'I'll come with you,' I said quickly.

'It's OK, love. I think I need twenty minutes by

myself, actually. Would you mind?'

I didn't point out that the drive to the Big Shop was twenty minutes, so it would actually be forty minutes driving there and back, plus the time in the shop. More like an hour, in all likelihood.

'Will you be OK by yourself for a bit?' she asked.

'Yes,' I said, although there was a feeling brewing in my tummy that I couldn't quite identify. It was only as Mum was pulling out and setting off down the narrow drive that I realized what it was: I didn't want to left alone here.

There hadn't been a moment when I'd been here by myself. I looked out in the direction Mum's car had gone, wanting her to reappear. Instead my gaze fixed on the huge old tree. I know it sounds ridiculous but I had the oddest sensation it was watching me. I didn't think there was anyone out there, but I felt that the tree itself was studying me, taking in that I was all alone. I shook the thought from my head and turned away, busying myself with the robot. I looked at the to-do list, written in Idris's wobbly handwriting, and tried to focus on the words, although my eyes kept darting to the window and the silhouette of the big tree beyond.

We'd been working on a kind of a mechanism for the robot which, when it was working, would fling chains out to its side in a kind of random way. Our robot, was not meant to be direct in its attack, it was meant to be chaotic. But we hadn't got it working how we'd imagined yet, and as it sat in front of me, a grey and pink box, I wondered if we ever would.

I turned to reach for a screwdriver, but in that moment I thought I sensed something move in the corner, by the window. I swung round to see what it was. I don't know what I expected, a mouse perhaps, or something being blown across the garden . . . There was nothing there. The room was empty and there was nothing outside either. Only the big tree moving in the wind.

I looked back to the robot, and that's when I heard the small clicking sound it makes as it turns on: a definite *kerchunk*. Nothing strange about that, except I hadn't touched the button to switch it on – I'd been nowhere near it. But the robot whirred into life and started to bash around the room. Its once limp chains now flew out to its side, spinning wildly, and smashing into everything in its path. At first it charged in this direction and that, knocking over the teetering pile of boxes that were by the doorway and crashing into the walls.

But then it started moving in a way I'd never seen before. It charged right at me and I only just managed to leap out of the way before it crashed into my leg. Then it quickly spun around and once again rushed at me, as though it was full of a feeling – and that feeling was fury.

As it tore towards me, it began ejecting parts. Screws flew out from its organs.

Ping.

Ping.

Ping.

And they were all aimed right at me. I ducked, just managing to avoid the path of the screws and desperately reaching out for anything to cover my head, but all I was surrounded by was boxes. I dug around blindly inside one of the boxes and my fingers closed around something cold. I pulled out the colander that Mum and I had been searching for earlier and rammed it on to my head, darting away again from the robot's crashing wheels as it continued to chase after me.

There was a kind of crunching sound too, which made me think of grinding metal. Out flew another screw. I jumped out of the way just in time, and it hit the glass wall behind me with a deafening crack.

I looked towards that terrible sound and saw the glass window had a crack where the screw had hit it. Beyond, I saw the big tree was frozen again, its leaves fixed in motion, just like I'd seen on the first day I saw the house, but then the wind rushed around it and it started to shake and move back and forth with a kind of rhythm.

The robot was spinning round back to me and I knew it would charge again. I dug my hand into the box and this time I found another familiar object – Mum's marble rolling pin. I couldn't think about what I was about to do, I just did it: I dived towards the robot as once again it geared up to ram me, chains lashing. With all my might, I brought the heavy rolling pin down on to the motor box, smashing it over and over as hard as I could.

Destroy the motor – stop the motor – stop the robot.

The words ran through my mind with every blow and continued to, even after a trail of smoke grew from the smashed motor and a burning smell filled the air. The robot came to a silent halt, its chains falling to the floor.

Joy and Idris's faces filled my head: Idris mumbling something incoherent and Joy spouting with rage.

How on earth had it gone haywire by itself?

And then my next thought: it must have been all my fault.

I kept replaying again and again where I had been standing when the robot had turned on and the exact position of my hands, because I still couldn't believe that it had turned on by itself. Had my foot accidentally touched the switch? Had I inadvertently pushed a box towards it that had pressed the button? Even though I knew all that was unlikely, I didn't want to believe the alternative was true: that it had switched on by itself, or that something else, some kind of force, was controlling it.

When Mum came home, I was shaking, unable to pull apart my worry about what Joy and Idris would say from my shock over what had just happened.

'Maki, what is it?' Mum crooned as she rushed towards me. I was sitting in a rigid ball on the floor, tears silently trailing down my cheeks.

I felt her arms envelop me and for a moment I thought I might be able to let myself sink into them, but then I felt her stiffen.

'What happened to the glass?' she asked.

'I . . . I . . . it . . . it . . .' I couldn't speak, couldn't explain, couldn't make sense of it.

I looked towards the crack. The shape of it made me think of an exploding star; it didn't seem possible that it was done by just one little screw.

'It was the robot,' I managed to say.

Mum looked around at the room, taking in the damage and the fallen boxes. 'The robot?' she said.

'It went haywire and just started destroying everything.'

Mum picked up the colander, which had fallen to the floor, and hugged it to her before placing it the right way up on top of one of the boxes.

'I . . . I . . .' I tried to speak but the memory of the robot charging at me made me feel like I was choking. Finally, though, I found my words. 'I wish we'd never come here.' I'd not meant to say it, but doing so released a dam inside me and before I could stop myself, I was letting it all pour from me.

'I hate it here, I hate this house, I hate being far away from all my friends! And from Dad. I never wanted to come and you said it would be OK, but it's not. It's not OK. It's never going to be OK.'

My voice started to wobble and lose its vehemence, and I could feel tears pricking in my eyes. I'd been trying so hard to go along with Mum's plan, but I couldn't shake off the truth of it: I wish we'd never moved here.

Mum didn't speak at first. Her eyes looked glassy and her mouth made tiny movements in a pinched kind of way, as though she was trying to speak but was stopping herself. Then she carefully picked up her rolling pin that lay next to the smashed robot; I imagined she was thinking of me lifting it up and bringing it down on the robot with a crash, over and over again.

'I know you're upset about moving here,' she said very quietly. 'But you didn't have to do this.'

'I'm not upset about moving here; I hate it. I hate being here and I hate, I hate . . . you, for making me move,' I spat out.

Mum flinched, but when she spoke her voice was still calm. 'You didn't have to do this,' she repeated.

'It wasn't me; it was the robot,' I protested but I could see instantly she didn't believe me. Her whole face was quivering with emotion: upset, confusion and there was anger too.

'Stop, Maki, just stop.'

But I couldn't. I couldn't have her believing that I'd done this on purpose. I could see how well it fitted together – I was trying to get her to move back to Bilton Road. And that had made me start to get angry and make this mess. Because most of it was true: I wanted to leave; I didn't want to be here. But I hadn't done this. It was something else – faulty wiring in the robot, something switched it on. I didn't know the answer, but there had to be an explanation for it.

As I was thinking, I could see the trees outside becoming absorbed into the darkness that was falling around them.

'You have to listen to me, Mum,' I said. 'It wasn't me, I swear it. I swear on everything. I swear on Dad.'

Mum looked up at me sharply. Her face seemed to be twisted in a way I'd not seen before.

She didn't speak to me again that night.

She didn't speak to me for two full days. I mean, she said all the basic stuff like 'Breakfast is ready'

or 'I'll drop you at your dad's on Sunday' – all the business stuff – and if I asked her a direct question, she would answer me, but she didn't properly talk to me for two whole days.

It might not seem that long, only I didn't see anyone else at all – it was just Mum and me. We were meant to be decorating, but someone had come to look at the crack, and the cost of the replacement glass was so much that Mum said we couldn't afford to buy paint any more. The splintering screw crack looked back at me stubbornly, hour after hour.

I tried to fix the robot but each time I looked at it, I kept coming back to the same conclusion – there was so much that needed to be done and I didn't know where to begin. The wheels and the chain were the only things that were not broken – the motor box was so completely smashed in, it looked unrecognizable and the frame holding the box was broken and bent out of shape.

I hadn't told Joy and Idris yet. I kept hoping that by some miracle I might be able to work out how to fix it by myself, even though I knew it was impossible.

Some other things went wrong too – Mum's laptop got corrupted, so she couldn't work from home and had to go into the office.

The new light bulb in my bedroom blew again. This time I didn't bother replacing it and I just used lamps that I put in each corner instead. But then one of the lamp light bulbs went dead too and I wondered if it was something about my room.

I kept seeing that old tree and I asked Mum if I could get curtains because I was sick of looking at it all the time. I still had the strange feeling that it was watching me – like it was behaving differently when it thought I wasn't looking at it. But Mum broke her silence to say we didn't have the money for something as decadent as curtains and that was the end of that conversation.

'Dinner,' Mum said. I heard the sound of a plate chinking against the table.

She'd left a plate out for me and had taken hers into her study. I poked at the steaming macaroni a little and then pushed it to one side and decided to confront Mum.

She was trying to eat the too hot pasta and was blowing on a piece and then trying to eat it and then blowing on it again.

'Mum?'

I could see her react when I said her name —
even though she wanted to ignore me, she couldn't
help but look over when I spoke to her.

'Mum,' I said again. 'Please stop ignoring me.'

The evening was quiet, idyllic even. There was a
warm summer's glow which you only get at the
time of year where the days are long.

'I'll try and pay for the crack,' I said. 'I've looked
at my savings and what I could make if I sold some
of my stuff.'

I thought I saw her bend her neck a little to the
side like she really was listening to me.

'Please, Mum. I hate it here, but I hate it even
more now that you don't speak to me.'

'Hate's a strong word, Maki. You haven't given
this place a chance. This is our home now,' Mum
said, looking out of the window.

But as she said those words — *this is our home
now* — all the lights flickered in the house.

On off, on off, in time with how she spoke.

'What was that?' Mum said, her voice quick and
thick with fear.

I could feel it too. It was in the air, in my mouth,
in every one of my limbs. I looked up at the ceiling

lights. They weren't flickering any more. They looked just as they should.

'What was it that you said?' I asked. 'This is our ho—'

But I couldn't finish the sentence. Just as before, all the lights flickered on and off in time with my words, but before I got to 'home', they all went dark.

'Maki, come close.' Mum's hand was in mine, clenching me tightly.

Just then, the vacuum cleaner in the corner of Mum's study roared to life and rushed towards us with furious force. It slammed into Mum and she yelped in pain. As if it were in slow motion, I could see the vacuum reverse back so it could get ready to charge into her again.

'Mum, run,' I shouted, pulling her towards me just as the vacuum came bashing towards us. Mum wasn't quick enough and she cried out again as it ran into her once more. In the moments while it got ready to charge for a third time, Mum leaned heavily on me as we ran from the study into the kitchen; I knew from her breathing that she was in pain.

As soon as we got into the kitchen, a loud buzzing sound filled the air and I saw the blender whizzing away so fast that it was rattling in circles on the kitchen top, heading towards us.

I ran over to it and wrenched the plug from the socket, but it still went on spinning and the blades whipped around in a blur. It oscillated wildly towards us. Mum shouted as we tried to run away, but it ejected the cup part right at us. We just managed to dodge it, so it smashed into the glass window behind us. It made a bigger crack than the one in my bedroom. A kind of broken spider's web.

The house was silent for a moment until a clanking came from my bedroom . . . and then out it charged, our broken robot – so completely unfixable – but crashing towards us as though it were an escaped animal and we were the captors it hated.

And beyond it, through the window, there was the tree.

Only this time, it seemed like it was closer to the house. As though it were peering in, watching the robot dance. And that was when I knew it was the tree that was controlling it. The tree was somehow responsible for this. It wanted us out.

We had to get out. We had to leave. Those words drummed through my head with each desperate step.

The robot started to turn towards us and wheeled wildly in our direction. Mum seemed rooted to the spot, so I grabbed her hand and just managed to pull her away before it reached her. I ran to the front door, dragging Mum behind me.

Just as we reached it, I heard the sound of glass shattering, but I didn't turn back to see it fall.

We never went back to the house again.

Mum didn't want to go anywhere near it and neither did I. That night, we drove to Joy's house and stayed with them until we could find another flat we could rent close by.

We talked a lot about what had happened and I told Mum what I thought about the tree. I wasn't totally sure she believed me but I could tell that she wanted to. She bit her lip and said, 'We'll probably never be able to explain what happened but we both know it wasn't right because we were there, we saw it. And I'm sorry. Sorry I didn't believe you when it happened the first time.' Her eyes filled with tears even when I grunted that I understood.

We sent movers to get our stuff and life settled down again, although Joy, Idris and I couldn't enter the Robot Wars competition this year. Instead we started work on a new design for next year and it's already much better than the one we had before. I insisted that we keep it in Idris's dad's garage, though.

I worried about who would live in the glass house next and what might happen to them, but then one day I saw a news story that answered my question. It was about a freak accident that had happened while a family was away on holiday. They'd come back to their house and found it completely destroyed and no one could explain what had happened.

There was a photograph that went with the article. In it, the big old tree was standing victorious over the shattered remains of our old house, the glass house.

I knew it then, in my bones: the tree would always win.

THE ATTIC
ROOM

Phil Hickes

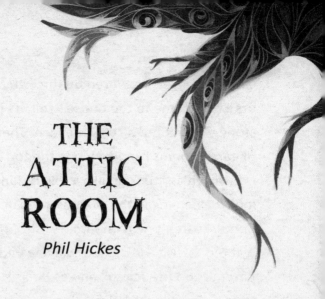

THE
ATTIC
ROOM

Phil Hickes

The school bus crunched into the car park to a chorus of cheers. It hadn't even drawn to a halt before the aisle was crowded with children, a bustle of bright waterproof jackets, beanies and baseball caps. Everyone was eager to get off and get started. Everyone except Jamie Duggan. On the back seat, Jamie sighed and stared at his reflection in the coach window, which looked as tired and bored as he felt. Then he pushed his face closer until his reflection disappeared and he could see exactly where they'd ended up. A large sign planted in the car park said:

Valcourt Manor House & Gardens

Jamie's eyes wandered up through the car park until they came to the house itself. Its blackened stone walls oozed a sulky menace. There was a row of garret rooms running along the top of the house, which stuck up like a row of fangs. It didn't look welcoming in the slightest. Besides, stately homes weren't high on Jamie's list of places he wanted to visit. He'd been to a few with both his parents and the school, and as far as he saw it, they were as dull as dishwater.

In castles, knights in armour fought pitched battles. There were great stone towers with arrow slits, where bowmen would have fired out at the besieging enemy below. There would be dripping dungeons with clanking chains on the wall. Castles were exciting. In stately homes, posh people drank cups of tea and that was about it.

Jamie peered up and saw large clouds billowing over the house, which were as black as his mood. Great, they were going to get rained on too. Just perfect.

Just then, Jamie noticed movement in one of the upstairs windows. A small, pale moon face peered out. Too far away to see clearly, but Jamie got the impression it was a boy. The face in the window moved slightly, as if whoever it was had suddenly shifted their gaze. Jamie had the uncomfortable feeling that he was now the subject of their attention and a chill snaked down his spine. *Somebody's walking on your grave*, his grandmother always said. The phrase gave him the creeps. He leaned back from the coach window, waited a second, and then peered up again. Whoever it was had gone. Probably just another bored boy on a school trip, Jamie thought.

Mr Varley, the history teacher, stood at the top of the coach with his iPad, checking names off the screen.

'Come on, Jamie, shake a leg,' Mr Varley called to him. 'Don't you want to go and see what's inside?'

No, I don't, Jamie thought. He knew what was going to happen, anyway. They'd be led through a succession of rooms filled with fancy furniture and paintings of snooty people wearing odd clothes. They'd walk past shiny wooden tables that were large enough to seat thirty people. There would be a library, of course. There was always a library, which might be interesting if they were ever allowed to have a look at the books, but you were never allowed to touch anything. If they were lucky there might be a maze in the garden to explore. They weren't too bad. Then they would all crowd into the gift shop and pick up everything and buy nothing. And that would be that.

Scowling, he heaved himself up from the back seat, before climbing off the bus and trudging over to the back of a pack of chattering classmates. Mrs Virani, the English teacher, was doing her best to get them in some kind of order, but it was like herding cats. Then the rain started to fall. They heard it first in the treetops, clattering down through the branches like a handful of pebbles. Then a cold drop landed on the back of Jamie's neck. Seconds later, and all they could see were great sheets of rain gusting towards them, like grey sails on an old ship. The children sprinted for the entrance and hurried up the steps, where they crammed into the hallway, their raincoats dripping on the elegantly tiled floor. Red-cheeked, Mrs Virani wiped a raindrop from her eyebrow and gestured for them to come closer. A low rumble of thunder from outside caused them all to stop and stare out of the windows for a moment.

'OK, class,' Mrs Virani said. 'Panic over. Now

please find your assigned partner. The quicker you find them, the sooner we can get going.'

This announcement caused a flurry of panic, like a game of musical chairs only without the music or the chairs. Jamie was the only one who didn't move. He hadn't been paired with anybody and didn't want to be. Normally, he and his mate Reza always hung out, but they'd had a fight yesterday and weren't speaking. Jamie wasn't about to try and make friends either. Reza could go wander around on his own. All Jamie wanted was to be left alone to get this stupid trip over with. It was at that moment he felt a tap on his shoulder.

Turning, he saw a boy he didn't recognize. He was smaller than Jamie, with eyes like pools of dark water. He was fragile-looking, as if he was made of bone china and might shatter at any moment. His thin dark hair was combed very severely to one side and he seemed to be wearing a black suit of some kind, more suited to an old man than a young boy, Jamie thought.

'Hello, Jamie,' the boy said in a quiet voice.

'Who are *you*?' Jamie snarled, feeling his own personal thundercloud rumble from somewhere deep within him. He had a feeling his day was about to go from bad to worse. Had he been given the booby prize for not wanting to pair up with anyone? And how did the boy know his name? He'd never seen him before and couldn't remember him being on the bus either.

'My name's William,' the boy replied. 'And you're exactly who I'm looking for.'

It was a strange turn of phrase.

'Are you new?' Jamie said gruffly. He certainly didn't want to be babysitting anyone.

'New?' the boy said with a thin chuckle. 'Not sure I'd quite describe myself that way, but yes, I suppose I'm new to you.'

Something about the way the boy put words together was very odd. And very annoying. Jamie was about to ask the boy who had paired them up, but he could hear Mr Varley calling to him.

'Come on, Jamie, find your buddy and keep up!'

Jamie gritted his teeth. This boy would never be his *buddy*. The group moved off into the house. Jamie could see Reza, right at the front, and tried to see who he'd been paired with. Not that he cared. He just hoped it was someone Reza didn't like.

Not waiting or caring to see if the weird new boy

followed, he set off in pursuit. Mrs Virani was calling back to them. Something about this house being built in the seventeenth century followed by the usual list of rules. Historic. Valuable. No touching. Stick together. Keep the noise down.

Jamie had heard it all before.

The children wandered down a wood-panelled corridor. Jamie turned, expecting to see the dark-eyed boy tagging along like a stray dog, but William wasn't there. Jamie stopped and peered around. Of course, *he* would be blamed if the new boy got separated from the rest of them. For a very brief moment, part of him regretted not being friendlier, though this feeling was immediately replaced by one of anger. What sort of new kid goes wandering off on his first school trip? Maybe he'd somehow got ahead and Jamie hadn't noticed. It was possible. William was small and they were packed into the corridor like a horde of shuffling zombies.

Anyway, what did he care? The teachers could go and find him – that's what they got paid for.

After passing through a rather grand reception room, they reached another huge hallway. To their left, two marble heads set on top of stone columns looked on disinterestedly, as if they were thoroughly bored of having yet more tourists disturbing their peace. Mrs Virani was busy telling them about how the house was a Grade I Listed property and had recently undergone a multi-million-pound restoration. Jamie was only half listening; he was too busy trying to see what Reza was up to. He could see him laughing with his other mate, Tom, near the front. They looked like they were having a good time and Jamie felt jealous. Well, Tom could go stuff himself too. Mrs Virani's voice cut into his thoughts.

'. . . and the house boasts an extensive art collection, including a painting by a very famous artist! We can go and have a look at some of them now.'

Mrs Virani gestured towards a grand staircase and the group followed her. Every inch of the walls was covered with paintings. Dotted in between pictures of horses and sunsets in Italy and the Cornish coastline, the stony faces of the house's previous inhabitants peered down at them. Jamie realized that these people, whoever they were, were literally looking down their noses at him.

He was still at the back of the group. Mrs Virani had, by now, handed the reins over to an elderly man with a handlebar moustache who was to be their tour guide from now on. While the group listened, he told them about the paintings, who they were, who had painted them and so on. Jamie found his attention drawn to one painting in particular. It showed two boys, maybe around the same age as him. They were standing on a lawn, one on the left, the other on the right. Between them, in the distance, he could see Valcourt Manor itself. A spaniel leaned up against one of the boy's knees.

Typical rich kids, Jamie thought. Bet they got everything they wanted with no questions asked. *And* they had a dog. When Jamie had asked for one, his dad had asked him who would look after it while Jamie was at school and he hadn't been able to think of a good answer.

'Their names are Austin and Edward,' said a voice at his elbow.

Jamie started. Turning, he saw William, the new boy. He was staring up at the painting with narrowed eyes.

'How do you know that?' Jamie asked. 'Have you been here before?'

'Yes,' William replied. 'I know this house well.'

'They look like spoilt brats to me,' Jamie

313

sneered. 'And look at their matching outfits, how embarrassing.'

'I expect their parents made them dress like that,' William said quietly.

'Yeah, what a tough life. Must have been awful.'

'It wasn't as easy as you may think, Jamie. Their parents were very strict. These boys were told what to wear, where to go, what to think.' William pointed further up the staircase. 'See, those are their parents further up on the wall, Lord and Lady Fitzsimon.'

Looking to where William was pointing, Jamie saw a portrait of a couple. A lady sat in a chair, wearing a billowing white dress. Her mouth was small and downturned, as if she'd just smelled something unpleasant, and her hair was fashioned into elaborate curls. Behind her, with one hand resting on her shoulder, a man with a thick moustache glared angrily out into the distance.

'They look like fun,' Jamie said sarcastically.

'As I say, they were very strict. I doubt you would enjoy living with them.'

Jamie turned back to the painting of the two brothers.

'So, did they inherit this place?'

William paused.

'No. They died. Not long after this was painted.'

The brothers in the painting didn't look like they were looking down on Jamie any longer. Instead, they appeared to stare accusingly, as if they could hear exactly what he'd said about them.

Jamie shivered. The hallway lit up. A second later, there was a growl of thunder. The house appeared to tremble slightly. Even though they were inside, they heard the harsh clack of heavy rain on the windows and roof.

'How did they die?' Jamie asked.

William cleared his throat with a gentle cough.

'Their parents went away for the weekend, to London. The servants had been left with strict instructions to watch over them, but the boys realized that this was finally their opportunity to have some fun, away from the watchful eyes of their parents.'

As Jamie listened to William's quiet, even voice, the noise of the rain, and the tour guide, and the impatient chatter of the other children faded into the background. As he stared at the painting, the trees seemed to sway in the wind. He could hear the excited barks of the dog. He could smell the sweet perfume of apple trees and spring blossom.

'They were put to bed at the usual time,' William continued. 'Afterwards, the servants assumed they were asleep and so went to their own beds. But the boys were only pretending. Once the house fell silent, they sneaked out and went into the grounds. It was midsummer. The day was still light. They were playing. It was all they ever wanted, to run around in the fresh air and climb trees. But then the boys spied a ditch. They jumped into it, not knowing there was a large bee's nest inside it. The bees swarmed. Realizing what had happened, the boys tried to run, but they were stung, again and again. They were stung hundreds of times. Their bodies were recovered by the servants the next day. They were both quite dead.'

Jamie didn't know what to say. Part of him didn't want to think that these boys were anything other than he imagined them to be – a couple of spoilt brats. But to think that even as they stood for this portrait, they didn't have long to live, well, the thought made his blood run cold. For a moment he heard a low, growling buzz, imagining the sky growing dark with an angry swarm. Lost in gloomy thoughts, he realized that he and William were standing on an empty staircase. Everyone else had disappeared.

'I suppose we should go and catch up,' Jamie said. 'Don't want you getting into trouble, not when you're all dressed up in your smart suit.'

'As you wish,' William said, seeming to ignore Jamie's subtle insult.

Their footsteps echoed on the varnished staircase. Jamie peered out of the landing window as they walked upstairs, catching a quick glimpse of swaying trees and grey rain outside. He glanced over his shoulder. William was following behind him, head bowed, hands clasped together, taking each step very carefully as if afraid to trip. He didn't just speak and dress like an old man, Jamie thought, he walked like one too.

Once they reached the top of the staircase, they could see their group, standing half in and half out of a room a little further down the corridor. The tour guide was saying something, though they couldn't hear exactly what. They shuffled closer.

'. . . the library has a number of valuable first editions, though, of course, they're kept under lock and key. However, many of the other books you see here are also very rare, with many no longer in print. We can go and have a closer look but please don't touch any of them and make sure to stay behind the guide rope.'

Jamie rolled his eyes. As expected, you weren't allowed to touch one of the few things that might be worth having a closer look at. He felt a soft nudge on his elbow.

'Would you like to see a more interesting part of this house?' William said, as if sensing Jamie's frustration. A lopsided smile crept on to William's thin, pale lips and his midnight eyes seemed to shine. He pointed back over his shoulder. 'It's just two flights upstairs. We can be there and back before they notice we're gone.'

'What is it?' Jamie whispered. Despite William's rather disconcerting manner, he was intrigued.

'It's the other boy's bedroom. The one who isn't in the paintings.'

'What boy?'

'The younger brother of Austin and Edward.'

'There was another son?' Jamie said.

'Oh yes, he was born just after the two brothers died. But he didn't have a happy life. I can tell you more if you come with me. The tourists never go up there so his room hasn't been interfered with.

It's just as he left it.'

'Hmm, I don't know,' Jamie said, casting a look in the direction of the rest of the group, who were wandering on ahead. 'Mr Varley always keeps a close eye on me; he'll notice if I'm gone.'

'He won't,' William insisted. 'It'll only take a minute, I promise.' Pausing, his lips curled once again into a sly grin. 'You can touch anything you want in there too. All the boy's toys are just as he left them.'

Jamie glanced around once more. The group hadn't quite left the library yet. William was right; he could be up and back down again before anyone noticed. And he might actually get the chance to salvage something interesting from the trip. He imagined Reza and Tom stuck back down here looking at teapots. What a pair of mugs. Besides, this whole family drama was beginning to intrigue him. If the two older boys had died, what had happened to the younger one?

'Go on, then,' Jamie said. 'If anyone says anything when we get back, I'll tell them you had to go the toilet and I was helping you find one.'

'I don't think anyone will miss one lost boy, Jamie, do you?'

Once again, Jamie found himself a little irked by William's curious phrasing. He sounded older than his years, and Jamie felt like he was being talked down to by an adult. William moved on ahead before pausing to see if Jamie was following. He beckoned Jamie forward with a rather theatrical curl of his finger.

William led them to another staircase, which wound its way up on to the next floor. But instead of continuing down the hallway, William ascended again. This time, the staircase wasn't wide and grand, but narrow and rickety, the sort of staircase that might lead to the servants' quarters. It was cold up here. Cobwebs clustered in the corners of the banisters. Quiet too, Jamie noticed. It was as if they were the only ones in the entire house.

Jamie had a sudden feeling that he should turn back. Something wasn't right. This place felt private and forgotten. As if he had intruded into something he shouldn't.

Yet William was waiting for him at the top of the stairs, in front of a small wooden door. Jamie realized that this must be one of the upper rooms that he'd seen from outside. The ones with small, spiky roofs. The attic rooms.

The door creaked as William pushed it open.

'Are you coming?' he said. 'You're not . . . afraid, are you?'

'Don't be stupid,' Jamie said. He stepped up and roughly barged William aside.

The room was small. A strange smell wafted out. A chemical aroma that suggested either cleaning products or medicine of some kind.

'This is his bedroom,' William said, closing the door gently behind them.

There was a large, iron-framed bed in the centre of the room, which made the already small room seem even more cramped. It was hard to believe they had rooms this small in such a large house. A lone strand of cobwebs hung from the sloped ceiling, swaying gently in the draught like hair from an old man's head.

There was a wooden table beside the bed, on which were placed a series of small brown bottles containing murky liquids of some kind. Over to one side was a wooden chest. Noticing Jamie's gaze stray in that direction, William gestured to it.

'You can open it if you like.'

Jamie walked over and knelt beside it. As he opened the creaking lid, he smelled dust and that strange medicinal aroma again. The first thing he pulled out was a small wooden box. A second later, the lid flew open, and something leaped out. Jamie recoiled and instinctively squeezed his eyes shut. When he opened them, he was staring at a carved doll. It rocked on its springs, as if silently laughing. It had been painted to look like a clown of some kind. It wore a blue-and-white-striped cap and had what Jamie thought was a creepy smirk on its face.

'Made you jump,' William said, chuckling, his dark eyes unnaturally bright.

Annoyed at himself, and at William for laughing at him, Jamie placed the creepy jack-in-the-box to one side and continued rummaging through the chest's contents. There was a set of tin soldiers clad in bright red uniforms. A ball attached to a piece of string, which in turn was attached to a wooden cup. There was a threadbare teddy missing an eye and a paw. A drum with a pair of sticks. Jamie gave it an experimental tap, but it sounded dull and flat.

'So, this other son, he lived in here?'

'Yes, as I said, he came along shortly after his older brothers died.'

There was one thing Jamie couldn't quite make

sense of. 'But why did he live in this tiny attic room? It's not as if they were short of decent-sized bedrooms, is it?'

William wandered to the window. Jamie noticed it had bars on it.

'No, his parents could certainly have given him a much lovelier room. But after what had happened to their first two sons, Lord and Lady Fitzsimon were determined that their newborn son would never be exposed to any kind of risk. And so they kept him in here. He wasn't allowed to ever leave the room. His meals would be brought up by the servants. He had to take medicine every day, even though there was nothing wrong with him. But after a while, he did become ill. The muscles in his body *atrophied* – do you know what that means, Jamie?'

For a moment, Jamie felt like he was back in class, but his annoyance was overcome by his curiosity.

'No, I don't.'

'The muscles begin to shrivel and waste away from lack of exercise or movement. Can you imagine, Jamie? Day after day, just lying in bed, staring at the ceiling, until you're barely able to pull yourself up. The bitter taste of medicine always on your lips. Nobody to talk to, no one to play with, just boredom and nightmares, day after day after day.'

William steepled his fingers together and bent his head to one side, as if he'd just finished a lecture.

'What an idiot,' Jamie scoffed. 'If it was me I would have escaped. Screamed out of the window or something.'

'Come and look,' William said, gesturing to the barred window. 'You could have the loudest scream in the whole world, but nobody would ever hear you. And what if they did?' William laughed. 'Would you bend the bars with your bare hands?'

Jamie walked to the window, gripped the cold bars and glared out, over the car park and the gardens beyond. William was right. The house was miles from anywhere.

'I'd still get out of here somehow. There must be a way to escape.'

He heard William's cold whisper in his ear and resisted the urge to shiver.

'There was a way, yes. One that required a lot of patience. You see, William eventually realized that a replacement must be found. Someone to swap places with, so that his parents wouldn't notice he was gone. Somebody who would willingly come into the bedroom and then stay here, in his stead. A decoy.'

'Who'd be stupid enough to do that?' Jamie said. He heard the door open and spun around just in time to see it being slammed shut.

Running to the door, Jamie tried to open it, but it was locked.

'William?' he yelled. 'Let me out!'

The only answer was the sound of steps, fading away as they descended the staircase. Jamie yanked on the handle as hard as he could, but the door refused to budge an inch. He ran back to the window, a cold panic beginning to spread from his chest to his fingertips. He tugged on the bars but despite their rust they felt solid. Was this William's idea of a joke? It wasn't funny in the slightest. When the strange boy reappeared, Jamie would soon wipe that smirk off his face. Peering down, Jamie could see their school bus. It calmed him a little. Even if he was locked in, Mr Varley would notice he was missing soon enough. They wouldn't leave without him.

Then he noticed his clothes. He'd been wearing jeans, sweatshirt and trainers. Somehow, his clothing had changed. Now he wore a burgundy suit of some kind. There was lace at the wrists. His trousers ended at the knee and were tied to his leg with ribbons. His socks were long. On his feet were black shoes with silver buckles. His legs seemed unnaturally thin. What was happening?

He ran to the chest. He'd seen a drum in there. Maybe he could bang it to get attention? He pulled it out and closed the lid. On top of the chest, he noticed a brass nameplate. Jamie bent closer, reading it again and again until he was sure he'd read it correctly.

Property of Viscount William Fitzsimon.

William.

How could it be? The William he'd met couldn't possibly be the same one. This boy had lived hundreds of years ago. And yet his insides curdled with fear.

The boy had known all about the home and its inhabitants. He knew the layout. Knew all about the family history and the death of the older sons. Plus, Jamie had never seen him before. And what had Mr Varley said?

Find your buddy.

Mr Varley thought Jamie was alone because he couldn't see William! The boy's chilling words echoed in his head.

A *replacement must be found. A decoy.*

Grabbing the drum, Jamie ran to the window again. Now, down in the car park, there was movement. The children from his school were beginning to emerge.

'Hey!' Jamie shouted. 'Up here, I'm locked in!'

But the children continued to file towards the bus. He spied Reza and Tom. They were with another boy, their arms around his shoulders, one who seemed strangely familiar and was wearing the same clothes Jamie had come in. They were all laughing together as if they were having the best time ever.

'Hey!' Jamie yelled, so loud it made his throat hurt. He banged the drum. 'Reza, mate, I'm up here!'

Relief flooded through him as he saw the boy in the middle of Reza and Tom stop, turn and look up. Jamie found himself staring right into William's dark, brooding eyes. Even from up high, Jamie could see the smirk on his face. William raised his hand and waved, before following Reza, Tom and the other children towards the bus.

'Hey!' Jamie yelled again. 'Hey, hey!'

He heard a voice behind him, from the stairwell. A woman's voice.

'William, whatever is all this racket about?'

Jamie heard the lock click.

'I think we'll need to double your medicine today.'

Then the handle on the door began to turn.

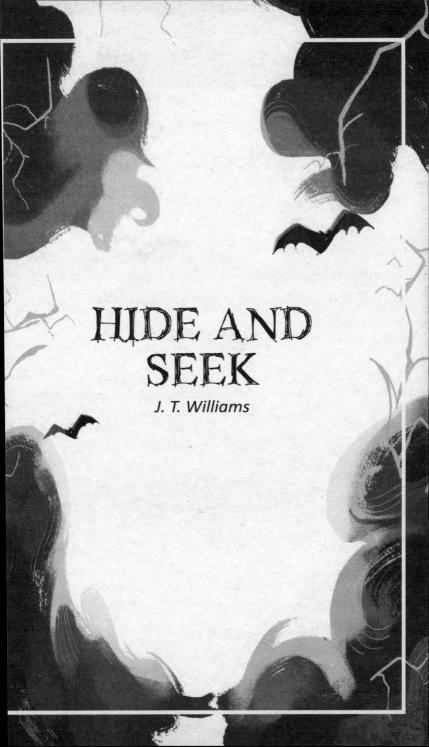

HIDE AND SEEK

J. T. Williams

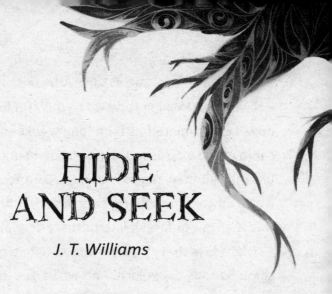

HIDE
AND SEEK

J. T. Williams

PART ONE

'It's a rite of passage!' Mum says, as if to reassure herself.

She watches from my bedroom doorway as I stuff another T-shirt into my rucksack. I've already packed five T-shirts for a three-day trip but I have this habit of over-preparing. I'm a 'what if . . .' kind of person. I like to plan for every eventuality.

'You probably won't even miss me!' she goes on breezily, side-eyeing the crumpled clothing now mushrooming out of the top of my bag.

I grab a notebook and two pens from my bedside table and slide them into the rucksack's front pocket. It's unlikely that I'll have time to write, but — well, you never know.

The four of us – Lexie, Sam, Ade and myself – have been looking forward to this trip for weeks now. Lexie's invited us for a long weekend in a cabin in the woods at the height of a blindingly blazing summer. Year 6 is done, SATs are done, and we're all going to different secondary schools, so this is a kind of farewell to primary-school life.

Lexie says there's a river to swim in, trees to climb, woods to explore. And we've got the cabin to ourselves – no grown-ups! Lexie's grandparents live in another cabin a few minutes' walk away. They've offered to make us dinner in the evenings if we want, but apparently we've got our own kitchen in our cabin. We're planning to spend as much time as possible out of the company of adults.

Lexie's given us each a list of foods to bring. I'm in charge of the essentials: crisps and popcorn.

'Of course you can always call, love,' says Mum, inspecting her scarlet nails. 'Any time you want.'

'Apparently the reception's not great out there,' I say, zipping up the rucksack with a decisive sound. I shoulder it on to my back and straighten up. 'But yeah, I'll call if I need to.'

Mum's biting her lip as if to stop herself from

crying. Wow. I didn't realize it was that big a deal. Now I feel kind of responsible for my mum, even though she keeps telling me I'm not to feel like that and that she's the adult and I'm the kid and that I need to 'cut loose' from her and enjoy myself more.

'You know, hang out more with your friends.'

She worries because I spend a lot of time writing in my notebook. But I'm going to be a writer. The way I see it, writing a diary, writing stories, that's me preparing for the future.

So you'd think she'd be glad that I'm 'cutting loose', even if it's just for three days. But no, she's on the verge of tears.

'Don't worry, Mum!' I throw my arms open for a hug. She draws me in close. I breathe deep. The scent of the coconut oil in her hair hits me; something catches in my throat. A sense that I really will miss her, I guess.

The sweet smoky smell of coconut oil is the essence of my mum. When I was about five, I lost her once in one of those massive hair supermarkets. You know, with the mad colourful aisles packed with shampoo, conditioner, relaxers, curl moisturizer. I was staring wide-eyed at a vast wall of garish boxes covered in pictures of girls who looked like me but with straightened hair, smiling bright smiles, when I was engulfed by the scent of coconut oil. I turned and instinctively followed the woman walking away from me towards the counter, believing she was my mum. I was standing next to her, humming to myself, as she heaved her basket on to the counter to pay for her things, when suddenly she looked down at me and – she had someone else's face! I mean, like, it wasn't my mum at all! I was convinced that this total stranger had pretended to be my mum, so I started screaming, 'What have you done with my mum! What have you done with my mum!' and suddenly my mum – my actual mum, that is – came running over and wrapped me in her arms and I was so relieved I cried for an hour straight, no joke.

Now, over my shoulder, Mum sniffs back tears and I take comfort from the burnt, sweet coconut 'mum-ness' smell of her hair. *It's only three days*, I tell myself.

The four of us – that's Lexie, Sam, Ade and me – have arranged to meet at the train station and I've even managed to persuade Mum not to come with me there on the bus. It's not far and I've convinced her that the 'independence' she was so keen to encourage should begin as soon I leave the house.

'It's all good, Mum,' I say, drawing myself up as I open the front door on to the noisy street. 'I'll be back before you know it.'

It's funny now, looking back. At the time of telling her that, I believed it.

PART TWO

'Awesome!' whispers Ade as Lexie unlocks the door to the cabin and throws it open.

The cabin is small, functional. A living room with a battered sofa pushed against one wall. On the opposite side of the room, an old-fashioned gas cooker, a small counter and a sink. A little window ushering in a bright shaft of sunlight.

'So, yeah, my grandparents built this place,' says Lexie sheepishly, his hair falling over his face in a straight black curtain. 'We'll drop by and say hello to them tomorrow. They love having guests.' He dips his head down and flicks the hair out of his eyes. 'They're super old, but they're pretty cool.'

That figures. Lexie is one of the coolest people I know. He joined us in Year 3, straight from New York. He has this amazing accent. Ade says it's a transatlantic drawl. But being considered cool makes no difference to Lexie, which, in my book, makes him genuinely cool. He asks the questions in class that teachers can't answer, not because he's trying to come across as smarter than them or anything, but because he has electric levels of curiosity.

We all traipse up the stairs after Lexie and follow him into a bedroom, largely empty except for two bunk beds and a painting on one wall.

'So, we're all in the same room – two bunk beds . . .' Lexie slaps the beds as if to prove that they are real. 'I usually sleep in this one.' Pointing to the top bunk on the left.

'Then I'll take the bottom one, thank you!' says Sam, throwing his bag on to the bed underneath. Ade and I exchange glances. Who actually chooses the bottom bunk?

That leaves me and Ade.

Our eyes flick to the top bunk of the remaining bed.

'Play for it, TJ?' Ade offers.

We drop our rucksacks to the floor and each raise our right fist into the ring for rock, paper, scissors. Since Year 4 most of our choices are decided by the classic win-lose game.

Ade throws scissors in the same moment that I push a rock. Yes!

I sling my rucksack on to the top bunk and haul myself up after it. The bed is dangerously close to the ceiling and I have to lie low so as not to crack my head on it.

Ade and I have been hanging out for most of our lives. Ade is serious on the surface, with a dry sense of humour. Bespectacled, serious-minded, and strong, she rocks in a big way. When we started school, our mums bonded through a chance argument over whether the best jollof is Sierra Leonean or Nigerian – Sierra Leonean, obviously – and since then, Ade and I have considered ourselves honorary siblings, or cousins at the very least. We just get each other.

'No offence, Lexie, but there's something really weird about this room.'

Sam, lying on his ill-chosen bottom bunk, hands behind his head, frowns at the wall opposite. 'Can't work out what, though.'

'No window,' affirms Ade with confidence, laying out her pyjamas on the bed. Ade likes order. 'There's a painting where the window should be.'

It's true. There's no window in the room. The light comes in through the door from the window in the bathroom opposite.

Sam swings his legs off the bed and sits up, staring at the painting on the wall.

'My grandparents did the place up since I was last here,' Lexie says, emptying his rucksack on to the bed. Out tumbles a torch, a compass, matches. 'The picture's new.'

I haven't paid it much attention until this moment, but now I approach the painting for a closer look. Sam and Ade are right. Set dead centre on the wall opposite the door, the painting gives the room an odd feeling.

A landscape: a woodland scene, in summer. Dense thickets of trees cluster around a clearing by the edge of a river. In one corner of the canvas, a purple plume of smoke snakes up into the sunlit sky. Beyond the woods, open fields of yellow and gold stretch away into the distance. The foreground of the painting seethes with people. I lean in closer to see their faces. Not just people. Children, teens. Dozens of kids, everywhere you look. It's like a world of kids caught in endless play. They dangle dangerously from the branches of trees. They splash in the silver-white water of the river. They peep from the bushes that cluster at its edge. And they are all laughing and waving at the viewer. At me.

I am transfixed. The canvas hums with a restless energy; as though while you are staring at a figure in one corner, someone is moving in another.

'It gives me the creeps.' Ade, her chin on my shoulder.

'Don't sweat it,' says Lexie, tipping a mountain of sweets out of his bag on to the floor. 'We're only sleeping in here. The rest of the time we'll be in the woods. You're gonna love it!'

The following morning, we breakfast early on a combination of multicoloured cereals and popcorn – toffee, sweet and salted, like I said, essentials – throw our clothes on over our swimming things and set off to spend the day in the woods.

Outside, the sun dazzles through the trees, splashing the ground with golden-green light.

Lexie, fired up, marches ahead, calling over his shoulder, 'Come on! Stick together! You don't want to get lost in these woods!'

'Why not?' Sam shoots back nervously, running to catch Lexie up.

'You don't wanna know!' returns Lexie with an impish smile.

Ade throws me a sidelong glance. I grimace. What have we let ourselves in for? We are total city kids.

Lexie stops suddenly and nods towards a dirt track running off to the left of us. In the distance, between the trees, I can just make out a large wooden cabin. Smoke rises and drifts from the chimney on the roof. 'That's the cabin where Mops and Pops live,' explains Lexie.

Sam snorts with laughter. 'Sorry!' he says, shaking his head. 'But Mops and Pops!'

'Little respect, Sam?' says Ade. She turns to Lexie. 'Should we go over now, to say "hi" maybe?'

Lexie pauses, considers it. 'No, I don't wanna disturb them before they've had their lunch. Mops can get seriously hangry if she hasn't eaten.' He continues up the path. 'We'll drop by on the way back.'

We follow without question. While we're out here, Lexie's in charge.

'Wait till you see the river!' he shouts from up ahead.

Truth be told, I'm not wild about swimming in the river. I can swim, but I prefer a pool. I like to know what's in the water. And as far as I'm concerned, that should be, well, just water.

'We'll be fine here,' says Lexie, stopping in a small glade at the river's edge and throwing down the tent bag.

'Is it deep?' I ask, as coolly as I can manage, as I peer in.

'Ha!' shouts Sam. 'What's the matter, TJ? Can't you swim?'

Thanks, Sam.

'Not particularly,' says Lexie. 'It gets much deeper further downriver – that's where the rapids are.'

I nod nonchalantly, like I'm completely familiar and comfortable with 'rapids'.

'This will be our base camp for the day. We can make a fire over there,' says Lexie, pointing to a clearing a few metres away. 'We can cook, swim when we want to, chill here, and then drop in on Mops and Pops on the way back to the cabin.'

Ade shoulders off her bag, takes in the scene, nods slowly, approvingly. 'That sounds cool.'

Lexie gives us our instructions to set up camp on the riverbank. I'm to clear the ground of stones and rocks so we can pitch the tent on flat ground. Sam and Ade are tasked with deciphering the tent's instructions and organizing its parts, while Lexie goes off to fetch firewood. 'Because I know where to find it,' he says, sauntering off towards the trees, leaving the three of us standing in a bemused triangle. 'See you back here in ten!'

Who first came up with the idea of hiding from Lexie?

Was it Ade? Unlikely, knowing Ade.

Was it Sam? Possibly. Wouldn't surprise me.

Was it me?

Not gonna lie here: I really can't remember.

That's the trouble with groups. If you're not careful, what you want and what you think and even what you do can get all mixed up, all blurred together with everyone else's ideas and plans.

So, no, I honestly don't remember who suggested hiding from Lexie while he was off fetching firewood. But suddenly we were running, scattering off in different directions.

I do remember climbing a tree. It was beautiful. A great, graceful deep green conifer, with low, spreading branches as thick as trunks themselves, just perfect for climbing, as though that was what nature had intended for it.

I pull myself up with ease, enjoying the feeling of climbing higher and higher, my limbs springy and strong. I stop about halfway up. The view is breathtaking. The feather-light tops of trees sway gently towards and away from one another in the breeze. Beyond them, a patchwork of fields. Hills hunch like sleeping beasts, their backs ridged with lines of dark hedges: ribs, spines.

I'm casting my eyes over the scene in front of me, wondering where Sam and Ade have decided to hide, when it hits me. Where we are is the scene of the painting on the wall at the cabin. That hill, the river, the way the trees huddle in groups at its edge. And there, Lexie's grandparents' cabin, sending curls of blue smoke into the sky.

'Hey, guys!' Lexie, appearing below me in the clearing, his arms full of firewood. 'I've found the –'

He stops, looks around, realizes none of us are in sight.

I pull my legs in towards my body, press myself closer to the branch I am clinging to.

I watch from above as Lexie carefully places the logs down in the centre of the clearing.

'Guys?' He sweeps a casual gaze around him.

It is an odd feeling, seeing him, remaining unseen.

I feel powerful, there's no denying it.

But the power has an undercurrent. A darker edge I do not like.

'Guys?' Lexie wanders over to the river now, looking both ways up it. He turns a slow circle, scrutinizing the woods. Then he races over to one of the bushes, pushes aside the foliage.

'Gotcha!'

There is no one there.

A small frown knits Lexie's brows and a guilty

feeling flickers through me.

Something about the expression on his face? A glimmer of fear, perhaps? Or the note of hope in his voice as he rushes to each possible hiding place, only to be disappointed.

'TJ?' He spins around. 'Ade? Sam?'

Guilt tightens its grip on me. Why did he call my name first?

'Okaaay, guys!' says Lexie, running his hand through his hair and looking anxiously about him now. 'Not funny any more!'

An impulse to call out to him, to shout down and wave, to reassure him, rises up in me but it is instantly quashed by the realization that if I reveal myself to him now, he will know that I have seen him from up here, seen his fear, and done nothing to allay it.

Worse than that, I have been watching him.

I'm not proud to admit it, but in that moment the desire to conceal myself, to conceal what I have done seems more important than offering Lexie the comfort of company.

So I say nothing. I simply cling to my branch and continue to watch as Lexie ventures back into the woods in search of his friends.

After about half a minute, I unpeel myself from my branch and clamber back down the tree, leaping from the lowest branch, thudding into a deep crouch on the grass below.

In the same moment, Ade emerges from the wood, brushing leaves from her shoulder.

'TJ!' She casts her gaze up to the top of the tree. 'Were you up there all along?'

I nod, feeling nauseous. 'Where were you?'

Ade nods towards the dense thicket behind us. 'I found a hollow tree and climbed inside the trunk.' She flicks a woodlouse from her sleeve. 'Where's Sam?'

'No idea. Maybe he's with Lexie?' I offer hopefully.

As if on cue, Sam steps into the clearing alone. 'Where's Lexie?'

I dart my eyes back to the woods. 'Not sure.'

'So he didn't find any of us?'

'Did anyone see him?'

I take a breath. 'I saw him. He went back into the woods.'

Ade rounds on me. 'You let him go back into the

woods? You didn't say anything?'

I spin to face Sam. 'I thought he had gone back to find you.'

Sam catches the note of accusation in my voice. 'Why?' He throws his hands up. 'I was hiding just like you were!'

Silence sits between us for a moment.

'It doesn't feel cool that he's wandering about by himself, guys,' says Ade. 'We're his guests, man.'

'Well, he went that way,' I say, pointing to the trees off to the right. 'Come on.'

'Maybe someone should stay here?' says Sam. 'In case he comes back?'

'Wouldn't it be better to stick together?' Ade flicks a nervous glance from me to Sam. 'We don't want to lose someone else.'

She's right. We all know the importance of 'sticking together'. We've seen enough movies. So we agree to search the woods as a group.

We tramp around in the tangled undergrowth, shouting for Lexie until we are hoarse: nothing. We return to the riverbank. There's no sign of Lexie there either, and the tent bag and our things are still spread out on the ground where we left them.

'He's hiding from us,' concludes Sam bitterly. 'It's revenge.'

Lexie doesn't strike me as the vengeful sort, but it's true that he's nowhere to be seen.

'Let's head back to the cabin,' I suggest. 'I reckon that's where we'll find him.'

We stay close to one another as we make our way back up the path towards the cabin, calling Lexie's name and scanning the trees as we go. My stomach is tightening with every step and I'm really wishing I had just called out to him from the tree I was in when I had the chance . . .

As we approach the path that leads to Lexie's grandparents' place, we stop. A plume of smoke drifts from the trees where their cabin must be.

'Maybe we should check there first?' suggests Ade.

'And risk meeting hangry grandma? No way!' returns Sam fiercely. 'I reckon Lexie's back at our cabin, probably polishing off all the sweets and popcorn. And laughing at us.' There's a savage note in his voice.

I imagine 'hangry grandma' must have eaten by now, but we've never met Lexie's grandparents. The idea of turning up and confessing that we've lost their grandchild because we played a trick on him does not appeal.

'I reckon we keep heading to our own cabin,' I say, sounding more authoritative than I feel. 'If Lexie's there, job done. If he's not, he has to be at his grandparents' place.'

'And if he's not there either?' proposes Ade quietly.

My worst fears start to take shape in my mind. My voice, when it comes, is dark and low.

'If he's not there, then we need to tell Lexie's grandparents that he's missing.'

PART FOUR

When we arrive back at the cabin, we find the door wide open. We take this as a good sign: surely it means Lexie's here?

'Lexie! We're back!' Ade calls into the empty living room. Everything looks just as we left it this morning.

'Lexie?' I pass through the living room and creep up the stairs, eyes flitting between the bathroom door at the top on the right and the bedroom door on the left. If Lexie is hiding from us out of revenge, it's fair enough.

So, if I were going to hide in this cabin, I would choose . . .

The shower!

I brace myself, turn the handle of the bathroom door and open it slowly. My heart kicks in my chest. In the mirrored cabinet above the sink, I can see that no one is hiding behind the door. But what about the shower? The curtain is pulled across the bath, obscuring any potential hider from view.

Keeping one hand on the doorknob, I reach my other hand, trembling, towards the curtain.

351

My mouth is dry. I yank the curtain aside in one violent action. Nothing. Just an empty space of bath and wall. I breathe again and step back, closing the bathroom door behind me.

Sam and Ade are listening at the bedroom door.

'Can you hear anything?' I whisper.

Ade puts her finger to her lips and shakes her head.

Sam twists the door handle and throws open the door. The room appears empty. The duvets lie in twisted heaps on our beds. Ade pats them all down in turn. Sam drops to his knees and looks under the lowest bunks. He stands, runs his hands through his hair and holds them there, eyes widening now with panic.

'He's not here!'

But my attention has been caught. I sense something.

Sense it, hear it? It's hard to say. I turn slowly to look at the painting on the far wall. There it is, just where a window should be. I move towards it, almost against my will. The silence in the room amplifies to a ringing in my ears.

My eyes are drawn into the woodland scene once more. I was right – we were just there.

There's the glade, that bend in the river, the hills beyond.

And I know this sounds crazy, believe me, but it really is as though the painting is . . . alive! A whisper moves through me when I look at it. The distant sound of water trickling over stones. Of leaves whistling and shushing in the treetops. A shout, even?

I look at the figures. All those kids. Waving from the trees, waving from the river.

And then I see it.

A tiny figure in the foreground of the painting. One that wasn't there before. He rests one arm on the riverbank, the other is stretched above his head as though he is waving. A curtain of jet-black hair hides half his face, but there's no mistaking him.

It's Lexie.

'I've . . . I've found him.' My voice is a strangled whisper.

'What!' snorts Sam.

Without turning from the wall, I reach back and beckon Ade and Sam towards me.

'Oh. My. Days.' Ade, beside me.

'What the . . .?' Sam, on my other side.

Ade peers in closer. 'That really does look like Lexie.'

We all three stare in silence for a moment.

'So Lexie's in the creepy painting his grandparents hung on the wall,' sneers Sam suddenly, turning away. 'So what?'

'No, you don't get it.' I shake my head, not taking my eyes off the painting. 'He wasn't there before.'

'What d'you mean, he wasn't there before?' says Sam. 'You mean you just didn't notice him before!'

I spin around to face Sam. 'I'm telling you, I looked at this painting, I really scrutinized it, every inch of it, and that person –' I point to the tiny version of Lexie, waving from the water – 'was NOT there earlier!'

'It really does look like him,' murmurs Ade, peering closer. 'Maybe it's a joke? Maybe Lexie came back here and drew himself on to the canvas before we got back.'

All three of us stare at the tiny figure, weighing up this explanation. I so want Ade's idea to be true: after all, it is easier to swallow than my initial idea that Lexie is somehow trapped in the painting. But the figure is painted in meticulous, photographic detail. How exactly is Lexie supposed to have managed that?

The colour has drained from Sam's face as he's been studying the picture and his forehead glimmers with sweat. 'If it is a joke, it's not very funny,' he says miserably.

'Maybe that's what Lexie thought when we were hiding from him,' concedes Ade.

This thought hangs in the air for a moment.

'Come on!' I say briskly, trying to bring the energy up. 'He's playing a joke on us, for sure. Let's go to his grandparents' cabin. Betcha anything that's where he is.'

Outside, darkness has fallen.

The moon is out but the thin slice of silver casts a dim light and Lexie, wherever he is, has the only torch. The silhouetted trees cast strange shapes between them that shimmer and shift in the faltering light.

Sam thumps off ahead, doggedly. I throw Ade a glance of solidarity and we push on behind him.

'Sam, wait!' I hiss after him, afraid of throwing my voice too far. 'Lexie said to stick together, remember?' The irony of this does not escape me.

We take cautious steps through the darkness, searching for the path that should lead to Lexie's grandparents' cabin.

'Look for the smoke, maybe?' Ade suggests.

But all we can see are trees looming in the darkness. With every step we take, all I can think of is, how are we going to find our way back?

Somewhere above our heads, a great rustling of leaves. A giant, wide-winged bird lifts off into the sky.

Sam stumbles wildly on.

'Where is it?' he says suddenly, rounding on us, his face wretched with confusion. 'Where is the cabin?'

Ade stops dead. 'We need to go back.'

Something twists inside me. Ade's right. We're just walking further and further into the darkness of the wood now. Why didn't we stay where we were?

'You're right,' I say, my breath quickening. 'But which way?'

'That way, for sure.' She points a finger towards the trees.

An odd moment of quiet.

Then Ade's voice again. 'Where is Sam?'

I turn in a slow circle, but all I see are trees, endless trees.

I spin around. How on earth . . .?

'Sam!' I call into the darkness up ahead.

No sound but the breeze sweeping through the treetops above our heads, whispering, shushing.

Ade cups her hands to her mouth and yells, 'Sam!'

Her voice drifts off into the night sky.

My chest floods with ice water. Instinctively, Ade and I move towards each other, reaching for each other in the darkness. Pressed back to back, we turn in a slow circle. I can feel her trembling violently. Or is it me?

She is whispering quickly to herself now. I think she's praying.

'Do you . . .?' My voice is so thick in my throat, I can hardly get the words out. 'Do you know the way back?'

'I think so,' Ade breathes, barely audibly.

'Step by step,' I whisper, trying to keep a hold on my voice, on my nerves. 'And we do not separate for one second.'

'Agreed,' says Ade gravely. 'This way.'

She takes my arm firmly and we walk, side by

side, as quickly as we can, up the path, heads switching around us in every direction.

Thinking back now, I don't think I've ever been as scared as I was in that moment.

The leaves crackle underfoot and the dark shapes in front of us seem to grow, to sway, to shapeshift in the moving darkness. The trees reach their branches over our heads, shielding the moon from view.

'There!' cries Ade, out of the blue. 'The cabin!'

We race up to the front door, throw ourselves into the living room and slam the door shut behind us. I glance nervously from the stairs to Ade. There's no way I'm going back up to the bedroom! I don't want to see that painting again. As if reading my thoughts, Ade scans the room and nods towards the sofa.

'We'll sleep on that – help me move it against the door!'

Together we drag the sofa across the room and shove it hard up against the door. We grab blankets from the cupboard in the kitchen, scramble into our makeshift bed, and clasp each other's hands. Whatever we do, we must not separate.

Tomorrow, we're out of here. We can fetch help for Lexie and Sam.

A small shaft of dim moonlight spotlights the floor, casting a shadow moon there. In the darkness, Ade and I comfort each other with talk of home, stories of our families, hands joined in a death-tight grip, before sleep carries me off into another world.

That night, I dream.

The scent of coconut oil envelops me. I see Mum, in our flat, going from room to room, as though looking for something.

I yell and I shout at the top of my voice and I wave my hand frantically above my head.

'Mum! Mum!'

I shout until my throat feels like it will crack open.

But she continues to move back and forth in front of me, unseeing, searching, searching, as though she cannot hear me.

 PART FIVE

I awake to the gentle sound of birdsong and running water. A moment of bliss before the memory of the night before kicks in my head.

My hand is empty.

I turn towards Ade. She is just a hump under the blankets.

Sunlight pours into the room. It's comforting. Now, in the safe light of day, I think to myself that Lexie has probably been at his grandparents' cabin since yesterday afternoon and that Sam has joined him there. That must be what has happened.

Ade and I will be able to find the other cabin in daylight. Funny, I think to myself, how the night plays such tricks on the mind. How it can conjure terror out of nothing. I decide in that moment that I'm definitely going to write a story about it.

I reach over to shake Ade awake, but when my hand presses on the blankets it sinks down. I throw back the blankets – there is no one there!

'Ade?' I whisper, eyes darting around the room.

Silence, but for the trilling of birds outside.

Trembling all over, I stand up on wobbly legs and

call up the stairs. 'Ade?'

The singing of birds grows louder. The sound of rushing water fills my ears. I am drawn to the source of the sounds outside.

I open the front door on to a blazing-hot day in the woods. The trees, a ferocious shade of green, seem to pulse around me. The daylight dazzles. The path down to the glade stretches out before me and I follow it, unquestioningly, all the way to the river's edge.

My tree. My perfect climbing tree. I feel a compulsion to reach up into its branches and begin to climb. Up and up through the twisted branches, up and up to my vantage point near the top.

Now, from here, I see it all.

The silver-white river bending through the smooth green glade. The gold-splashed fields rolling away beyond the lowering hills. And in the trees around me, girls, boys, sitting motionless in the branches, arms suspended over their heads as though waving. The riverbank is lined with stilled people: everywhere I look, figures are frozen mid-movement.

There's Ade, crouching, half hidden, inside the trunk of a great oak. I open my mouth to call to her, but no sound comes out. Smoke rises and drifts from the chimney of a log cabin. At an upstairs window stands Sam, statue-still, one palm flattened on the glass. And in the sparkling river, Lexie, jet-black hair falling heavy over one side of his face, mouth open mid-shout, one hand clutching the grassy bank at the river's edge, the other, thrust into the sky, fingers splayed, reaching out towards me.

A CRY FROM
THE GRAVEYARD

Jasbinder Bilan

A CRY
FROM THE
GRAVEYARD

Jasbinder Bilan

It was late one chill autumn day, weak sunshine
spun through the trees outside and I was
distracted. It felt like something was about to
happen. One of those ordinary days when
everything seems normal but for some reason your
heart won't stop hammering against your ribs.

I told myself to stop being dramatic, after all I
was only sitting in class next to my best friend
Jamaal, listening to Miss Grail our history teacher.
And all she was doing was dictating our homework
for the weekend.

'So, Year seven,' she began. The wide leaves on
the trees outside cast a sudden shadow across her
face. 'I – I want you to focus on local history for

your project.' For a second she paused as if she'd lost her thread. 'By that I mean you must research either an event or a person – something that has a connection with the area's roots.'

I guess even teachers are human. It had been a warm day and just like us she was most likely wishing for the weekend.

The class bent their heads over their new diaries and scratched away with their pens, obediently jotting down the task. We'd only started at secondary school a few weeks earlier and everyone was still keen to make a good impression.

Miss Grail pushed a few stray hairs back from her face and began gathering her things together. 'Pick something you really want to find out about, something unexpected.'

At that exact moment I looked up and we locked eyes. I'm sure it was only my imagination but it was as if she was speaking directly to me, her dark eyes delving into mine for a brief second. Again, I tried to shake off the feeling that something was a bit off.

'I want you all to do a presentation,' Miss Grail continued, 'so make sure it's compelling, with lots of exciting facts.'

As the bell rang we streamed out of class,

everyone desperate to get some fresh air.

Jamaal elbowed me. 'Hey, Alta, looks like teacher's got a new pet!'

I felt my cheeks flush and elbowed him back.

'The way she looked at you.'

'I think she just wants us all to do our best, Jamaal.'

'Yeah, maybe.'

We walked quickly away from school, the cool afternoon blowing away the strangeness of the last few hours, until we reached the high street. My uniform was still stiff and itchy. I wasn't used to the blazer or the tie that was firmly knotted at my neck. I tugged it loose even though we'd been told to stay smart, especially on our way home.

'See you over the weekend?' said Jamaal as we approached the crossroads where we usually parted ways.

'Text me.'

I waited at the corner and watched him run for his bus. He pulled a funny face that made me giggle and the knots loosened, knots I didn't know were tightening my stomach.

I didn't much feel like going home to an empty house. Both Mum and Dad worked late, and now I was at secondary school, I was allowed to let myself in. A lonely feeling snagged my insides and I wish I'd gone home with Jamaal like I did sometimes.

But it was too late now, so I walked slowly past the takeaways with their enticing smell of fried chicken, past the toppling displays of fresh yellow mangoes at the greengrocer's and past the neat little nail bars with their red flashing lights that bled into the gathering afternoon gloom.

I still don't know why I did it, but I turned off the main road. And when I reached the graveyard, instead of hurrying past like I usually would, I stood before the black-railinged gates that stretched towards the darkening sky, and paused.

Chains of twisted ivy bound the gates together and I pressed my face between the dark leaves, peering at the graveyard beyond. It felt like Miss Grail had picked me out, as if she was compelling me to find a particular story: there between the headstones and the patches of fading light.

So I guess that's why, even though I felt the prickle of fear creep slowly up my spine, I took hold of the thick strands of ivy and tugged with all my strength. They were wrapped firmly around the gates and it took some determination to loosen their hold enough for me to squeeze through.

Part of me wanted to run so hard I could barely keep my legs still, but I ignored the leaping heart in my chest and forced myself forward.

The graveyard was vast, stretching before me like a forgotten world. I'd walked past lots of times. My grandma had always told me to shield my eyes in case you saw wandering spirits and they tried to overpower you. And I always told her that ghosts were made-up things that didn't exist. They were stories to scare children and to make them behave.

I tried to remember that as I walked along paths that meandered between the headstones. Craggy trees swept their shadow-branches towards me like accusing arms as daylight slipped away like it does when you stop paying attention.

My hands trembled as I took out my notebook and peered at the name and date on the lichen-swirled headstone to my right. I bent my head closer and scribbled some details down. All the while, a strange, jittery feeling was tugging at my belly and I tried to push it away, but it stayed there, twisting into anxious knots. I looked instinctively towards the gates. I couldn't see them – it was like darkened ivy had grown over, obscuring the gates from view. I felt a lurch in my stomach; maybe this wasn't such a good idea after all.

A sudden movement beyond the headstone sent my heart racing. My notebook dropped to the ground and I began to sprint away.

'Over here.' A small voice pulsed mournfully against the wind. 'Don't run away,' it pleaded. 'Don't leave me.'

I stopped in my tracks, fear and confusion clawing at me. Who was hiding out there? What should I do? As I searched the growing darkness, faces of the worst monsters and murderers leaped from the shadows. They were big and bad, wielding all sorts of weapons, and they wanted me.

Springing on to the balls of my feet, I made to run away once more, but a tugging on my sleeve yanked me back.

'Let go,' I screamed. 'Get off me!'

A firm hand caught the edge of my blazer with a strength that could only belong to someone who wanted to do me harm. But I didn't dare look down. My breath came fast and heavy as I realized that I couldn't move forward and no matter how hard I screamed I doubt whether anyone would hear me.

'You have to help me,' said the soft voice between sobs. 'They're after me and they won't give up until they catch me.'

As the sun burst through the trees, in the early evening shadow-light, I realized the hand didn't belong to a monster or a murderer but to a small, dirty boy.

'Who are you?' My voice was croaky and shaky. 'What are you doing in the graveyard?'

'I'm John,' he whispered. 'John Dean.'

The boy had roughly chopped blond hair which sat in unbrushed clumps against his head, and his face had dirty smears across it where tears had dried across his pale cheeks. He looked scared, really scared. And though he was small, there was a look in his blue eyes that made him seem older, as if he'd seen things he shouldn't have.

I wondered how long he had been hiding out in the graveyard. By the look of him it could have been days.

'Come on,' I said, squeezing his hand gently. I pulled him towards the church in the middle of the graveyard. 'We'll hide in there until they go.'

But who were they? What sort of losers would hunt down a little boy like John? My anger flared. Then the trees behind us began to shake, as if heavy limbs were thrashing through the leaves.

'Quick,' I whispered. 'I'll give you a piggyback.' I slipped my phone into my blazer pocket and threw the rucksack to the ground.

Snapping branches echoed in the darkening graveyard. Whoever was chasing John was getting closer. I swooped him on to my back. He was feather-light, it was like carrying nothing, and I had to glance back to check he hadn't fallen off. But he was still there, clinging to my neck with his slender fingers.

'I won't let them get you, I promise.'

Darkness spread behind us like flapping crows' wings – they – whoever they were – were hard on our heels, chasing us along twisting paths, up and down the overgrown graves. It sounded like a whole gang. We tried to lose them by hiding behind the gravestones but still the pounding feet were loud and urgent.

The church appeared in the distance, a large, semi-derelict building with a spire that reached up towards the yellow half-moon that had appeared from behind a grey cloud.

It took all my energy to make the final laboured steps up to the church doors.

John leaped to the ground and again took my hand in his. Breathless and exhausted I leaned against the wall of the church.

He rattled the heavy church door. 'Come on,' he cried. 'We have to get inside.'

I heaved open the doors and tumbled into the building, John following close behind. It was dark but the moon shone through the stained-glass windows spreading rainbow light across the floor.

'Behind here,' I said, leading him towards one of the pews, thick with years of dust.

I allowed myself a beat of satisfaction. Incredibly we had outrun them, but whoever wanted John so badly would soon be inside too and the thought made my throat tighten.

John gave me a small, frightened smile. Panic tore through my chest. My heart beat so loudly it felt like it would fly into the room. Whatever was going on here was too big for me to deal with by myself. I pulled out my phone and with shaking fingers pressed 999.

Nothing! The battery was flat. I stuffed the phone back into my pocket in frustration.

The footsteps were here, outside the church, pounding the ground.

'What's going on, John? Who are they and why are they chasing you?'

John began to bawl. 'I didn't do it. They said I did it but I didn't.'

'Shhh . . . we have to be quiet.' I pressed my hand gently over his mouth. 'What didn't you do?' I whispered. 'I can't help you if you don't tell me.'

'They said I set fire to the barns.'

'Which barns?'

'Down along the river by old Windsor town. They belonged to the lord of the manor and were full to the brim with wheat.'

'What are you talking about? Is the Lord of the Manor a pub?'

John looked as confused as me. 'I was stood by, close like. I saw the ones that done it. I just wanted to watch the fire . . . and *they* ran away but I couldn't follow them cos my legs are too short.' He trailed off and began quietly sobbing again.

'It's OK – look, don't worry. We'll deal with that later.'

The pounding of feet outside grew louder, hands hammered at the windows, voices boomed loudly. 'Out, out, out,' they roared.

I clutched John tightly as the whole building began to shake. Bits of broken furniture flew across the room, the windows blazed orange as if there was a fire outside.

I couldn't believe what was happening; it was like being at the centre of an earthquake.

John grabbed my hand. 'This way.'

We slid along the marble floor towards an archway, which turned into a narrow passageway. We could hear frantic footsteps behind us. The sound was ear-splitting, feet thumping the ground and haunting voices chasing behind us.

The dark passageway curled ahead and I flipped out my small pocket torch, shining it into the dusty gloom ahead of us. John flinched at the sudden burst of light.

'It's only a torch,' I said soothingly.

It was no wonder John was so jittery. I was exhausted too, fear filling every small corner of my body. It felt like everything was caving in on itself. Images of what might happen next spun through my brain – none of it was good. Even if John hadn't set light to the barns, I don't think they were going to listen to sense. All they wanted was John, and how was I going to stop them? I grabbed hold of his hand and together we ran as fast as we could.

The floor began to grow steeper and ended in a flight of stairs.

'Yes,' said John, between shallow breaths. 'Down here.'

I swallowed – were we going even further under the church? John seemed confident now; as if he knew exactly where we were heading.

The stairs opened out into a circular room. The footsteps were still behind us, reaching us in waves of hollow noise. As I shone my torch around the room, it dropped from my hand and clattered to the hard floor.

Where had John brought me? I heard a loud scream filled with horror. After a heartbeat, I realized the sound was coming from me, a raw cry tearing through my lungs. The smell of death was everywhere.

I scrabbled along the ground for my torch and with trembling hands pointed it again at the walls. It was lined with row upon row of human skulls. 'John,' I cried. 'Where are we?' Was this the place

I was going to die? The feeling I had in class today, that something was about to happen, returned. There must have been a reason why I felt compelled to enter the abandoned graveyard.

I fell to my knees and buried my head in my lap. It was my turn to sob now.

I felt a gentle hand on my back. 'Thank you, Alta,' whispered John.

Lifting my eyes fearfully, I watched as John took a roughly made bag from his shoulder. He opened the drawstring and dipped his hand in, bringing out a small, paper-pale skull.

My hands clutched my chest and I opened my mouth to say something, but no words came out. John continued as if he knew exactly what he had to do. He took the skull and, carefully placing it under his arm, he began to scale the wall of skulls, which I now saw were surrounded by other human bones.

John climbed nimbly, skilfully, using footholds in the wall to ease himself up. Shining the torch at the wall I could see a shadowy gap just above John's head. He took the skull he'd carried in his bag and slotted it into the hole. The skull was much, much smaller than any of the other skulls, but it fitted perfectly. Then John went back into the bag and started to pull out more bones; so small and fragile-looking.

When he had finally finished and the tiny body was complete, John looked down at me; his face was beaming and had lost its look of fear. 'Thank you.'

'I don't understand,' I replied. The sound of the footsteps, I realized, had stopped.

John jumped down from the wall and landed beside me. 'They've gone now,' he said. 'You made them go away.'

'Me?' I asked. I suddenly felt so tired. What time was it?

John stood back and gazed up at the wall again, a look of peace softening his features. 'I had to be up there, see, with my family. My ma and pa.'

I had to use all my strength to stop myself from crying out again. 'I-is that you? Is that you up there?'

John nodded. 'After it happened, they threw me in the ground, but I needed to be here, in the family crypt. Now I can finally rest in peace.'

I felt as if I was dreaming.

'Shall we go?' said John.

I nodded. He slotted his little cold hand in mine and led me back up the stone stairs. We didn't need the torch because pale moonlight was washing through the passageway, leading us into the church. Everything was still and quiet.

We pushed the thick oak doors open and walked into the graveyard, the moon shivering through the lacy trees. Walking silently together back along the still dark paths, the events of this strange time raced through my mind. I was trying hard to make sense of it but I couldn't explain any of it.

'I have to go home now,' John said suddenly.

'A-are your parents there?' I blurted. 'You're a bit young to be out alone, you know.'

'I can look after myself,' he said, giving me a hug. 'I'll be nine on my next birthing day.'

I ruffled his hair. 'You don't look nine! You need to eat more.'

'We won't meet again,' he said seriously. 'But thank you, Alta. I'll never forget you.'

I watched his small frame race away beyond the trees and when I raised my hand to wave I couldn't see him any more. He had disappeared into the darkness.

I realized I was back at the spot where I'd first

heard John's desperate voice. When I looked down, my notebook was still on the ground. I yawned and picked it up in a daze. It was curled from lying on the damp ground.

Here was the gravestone obscured by lichen that I was about to look at. A shaft of moonlight lit up the writing that was carved there. But before I could see it properly, my phone came to life and pinged with a hundred frantic messages from Mum and Dad.

This meant serious trouble. I turned my back on the headstone, but just like the moment when I felt compelled to break into the graveyard, something told me to turn round.

I swivelled back to the headstone and that's when I saw the writing clear in the brightening light.

John Dean
Died April 1626
Hanged

The graveyard spun like in a dream.

A sound in the air startled me.

'Who's there?' I cried, fear pinning me to the spot. But it was only an owl screeching through the trees.

I glanced back towards the church, at the doors strung heavy with chains and firmly locked with a dozen rusting padlocks.

From the corner of my eye I thought I saw John again, hand tucked firmly inside a smiling woman's hand. They seemed to float in happiness along the path lit by the shimmery moon, her long skirts trailing behind.

A shiver crept from the tips of my fingers, slowly along my arms, through my body and rippled down to my toes.

'John Dean,' I murmured, wiping a tear from my cheek. 'Hanged for a crime you didn't commit – now you can rest in peace.'

Like a ray of sparkling moonlight, I now knew exactly what I had to do – I had to tell John's story for my history project. That's why he'd appeared to me. It was up to me to finally put the record straight.

JENNIFER KILLICK

Jennifer Killick is the author of the *Dread Wood* series, *Crater Lake*, *Crater Lake, Evolution* and the *Alex Sparrow* series. Jennifer regularly visits schools and festivals, and her books have been selected four times for the Reading Agency's Summer Reading Challenge. She lives in Uxbridge, in a house full of children, animals and books. When she isn't busy mothering or step-mothering (which isn't often) she loves to watch scary movies and run as fast as she can, so she is fully prepared for witches, demons, and the zombie apocalypse.

IF YOU LOVED *READ, SCREAM, REPEAT*, YOU'LL LOVE THE DREAD WOOD SERIES, OUT NOW!

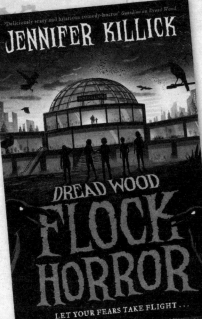

'Deliciously scary and hilarious comedy-horror' *Guardian* on *Dread Wood*

JENNIFER KILLICK

DREAD WOOD
FLOCK
HORROR

LET YOUR FEARS TAKE FLIGHT . . .

... scary and hilarious comedy-horror' *Guardian* on *Dread Wood*

JENNIFER KILLICK

DREAD WOOD
DEADLY
DEEP

IT WAITS FOR YOU IN THE WATER . . .